THE POLYVERSE
Being Beneath the Pleasure Zones II

PAUL GREEN

© Paul A. Green 2016

First Edition

All rights reserved. No part of this work may be reproduced, stored in a retrieval system. or transmitted in any form or any means, electronic, mechanical, photocopying, recording or otherwise without the prior permission of the publisher. Paul Andrew Green asserts all legal rights of paternity, integrity and intellectual property under the 1988 Copyright Act.

Published by
Mandrake of Oxford
PO Box 250 Oxford OX1 1AP (UK)

Also by Paul Green
Beneath the Pleasure Zones : The Rupture

Contents

PRELUDE:
An Update from the Quantum Brothers — 5

Book 3
Problems across the Whole Lobe Infrastructure — 11
An Expanded Portal — 20
Possessed by the Talking Heads — 30
Warriors of the Waste — 45
Last Rites — 56
Fissile Existences — 88
Each star has a number — 107
Enlightenment — 110

Book 4
Coming Forth by Day — 138
Eschatonics — 150
Dreadlock — 155
The True Tale — 198
Survivors — 218

For Cathy - and for Jez Welsh who first evoked the Quantum Brothers...

PRELUDE:
An Update from the Quantum Brothers

Greetings! We are the Quantum Brothers. Our name is legion. If you haven't heard of us, we're disappointed, because we're living legends. And if you've already encountered us, closely or otherwise, let us remind you once again of our status in the Polyverse.

We are the ipsissimi, polymorph pervoids of the Chaosphere, post-modern, pre-historic, we're the spawn of yesterday's alternate tomorrows postponed and cloned into infinity... We stream everywhere, all at once, like demented quarks, under rigorous laboratory conditions. Or consider us as astral egregores, ultra-intelligent entities from the Intervoid, if you're more comfortable with that. A few centuries ago you would have needed an expensive grimoire to chat with us. Now we're open-source.

Whenever you have seen us, as pop-up interventionists in this very human story so far, we've taken great pains to assume reassuring personae. We're confident you would be quite comfortable with our two identical grey faces, our Caucasian virtual flesh. We're manifesting especially for you as clean-shaven, forty-plus, solid of jowl, sombre-faced. Sober square-headed men in suits and ties, anyway. Sensible no-nonsense men, with shiny well-parted hair. You might like to call us iconic. Like old 1950s publicity photos of bandleaders, movie gangsters, radio announcers, black-and-white TV hosts — or ghosts. Or maybe today's multi-national Chief Executives. We're the acceptable faces of the Men in Black, anyway. Two Grey Men in a flying saucer. Now you see us/now you don't. Some dubious characters will call us Qliphothic, but ignore their hysteria.

For we've been keeping an eye on things for you, in your best interests as consumers and stake-holders in the gravity-pits of your dark Earth. This story is always top news, at the top of the hour from our towers of power. Even since young Lucas Beardsley blundered into the Polyverse and released the so-called Qliphothic forces, creating the Rupture and the localised breakdown of your everyday causality, we've been on your case. We've been logged into all those personalised case-histories, as well as giving you a unique overview of the alternative history that has overtaken your septic isle. And what a tangle of time-lines it's turned out to be!

For your poor little Britain has been totally subverted by the Rupture. Even years later anomalies keep erupting from the Polyverse to undermine the reality consensus. Yes, the Undermind keeps niggling in the inner ear like tinnitus, while you just can't trust an electron to behave any more. And you can't talk about the Interweb either. Nor Farcebook, nor Witter. Everything's gone all Lobe-shaped. Except the economy, which has gone turd-shaped. A dysfunctional dystopia. But Pleasure Centres plc has been trying to ramp up its virtual reality ops to keep their various demographics happy. We have been consulted throughout the management of this process, which promises some exciting outcomes. Fear not, we'll explain later.

In this scenario, it's hardly surprising that your unfortunate urban citizens have tried to immerse themselves in the virtual techno-delights of Pleasure Centres while the rurals and ex-urb bohos at outposts like Leynebridge in the Anglo-Welsh Borderland have embraced the Lore, their homebrew of wicca and earth-magick, with a few psychedelphic fungi tossed in the cauldron for luck.

As far as we can see (and our divination skills are well-honed) the only real active players in the great game of Albion are the Fundamentalist militias, the Heavy Shepherds and the Mo-Boys who've been battling to establish their rival monotheisms across the nation by various asymmetric strategies. We've been keeping score but it's too early to predict the outcome.

We admit we were surprised when Lucas first surfaced in Leynebridge, given the chaos he'd caused all those years ago by opening that Qliphothic Rupture in the Polyverse. He was such an outsider there, barely scraping a pittance, doing bits of tutoring to bored kids and babbling away on the community radio to nobody, except us. He kept his little pointed head down for a while, fighting the mental static of the Undermind and nurturing his obsessions with magick and all those ex-lovers like Carla Leppard, Leila and Robyn. Especially naughty Carla, far away now playing Lobe-mistress in the pleasure-dromes of the wicked capital. He also had a little yen on the side for local girl Vivienne, grand-daughter of village Elder Elaine. Which was doomed because the entire community regarded him as an Incomer – and because brawny Aran had already had his horny way with Viv and now wanted her as his betrothed wifelet, according to Leynebridge Lore.

The Lore - so quaint and picturesque! - still runs everything in Leynebridge - its rites and feasts and fights. So the town is low-tech and there's no Lobe, as far as they're concerned. Their Serpent Path is supposed to protect them from the evil emanations and intrusions of the cities. The Feast of Smoke is the climax of the year, when there's much marching with blazing torches as well as random shagging in funny hats and mock sacrifices.

So when they learned that Pleasure Centres plc was planning a virtual-reality 'heritage' facility at their sacred site, Leyston Burrough, the Village Elders – Elaine , old Noah Dodd, Bookman Gavin Wharton, Forgan the Arch-Fool – furiously opposed it. Trader Price, of course, thought it was a good business plan, good for the winter economy – so there were gatherings and arguments and speechifying and ritual cursings. Meanwhile Viv, wearying of Leynebridge – wouldn't you? - consulted her oracles and decided to try her luck in London, the City of Dreadful Light...

...where Elaine's ex-husband William Crowe, an old burnt-out computer boffin, was brooding on a career in nuclear weapons research which had ended in amnesia and redundancy. He'd loved his equations and his vintage warheads and the Establishment had hunted his head for a major project, but now there was a black hole in his fat head. He'd even blown his marriage – Elaine was long-gone to the Borderlands decades ago with long-lost infant Dawn.

Now he was stuck now in Mrs Kalyoubi's bedsit empire out in the suburban danger-zones, preparing for a long-shot last-ditch job interview with Pleasure Centres. To empower him, we decided to appear unto him, on his Lobe-screen, but he didn't get the message at first. Nevertheless he braved the trip into the centre of the city – and was given the post of supporting Pleasure Centres artistic director – yes, Carla Leppard, no less - in recreating old adult movies and action games as multisensory cyber-experiences.

Trouble-shooting the glitches in porno-kitsch was quite a gig for an old geezer – too old, thought Carla - but William was one of the few humans left who could do hard science in the melt-down of the Post-Qliphothic Rupture. He even told Pleasure Centres director Dominic Pullman how Pleasure Centres might steal a march over Korean rivals Fast Fun Electrics. We were quite impressed. It could even help in our personal development.

We're also pleased to inform you that Viv found employment at Pleasure Centres, although it was more menial work, assisting portly Korean salary-men to suit up for their virtual pleasure-zoning in the red-lit cubicles. And Viv's magickal arts were fading in the hostile environment of the City.

Our agents informed us that while Lucas brooded on his lost magickal arts back in Leynebridge and wrote curious poetry, William was tasked to fix a mystery bug in an old action-game scenario, Dub Demons, at London's flagship Pleasure Centre. Time for some cyber-poltergeist fun, we thought. The fuddled customer assistant (your friend Viv) couldn't even find the Dub Demons game, leading William to suspect that he'd been set up to fail by that hostile Carla. So William decided to test the cubicle hardware with another old feature. Yes, he decided to relive the guilty pleasures of his urban wilderness years. The senior citizen got zipped up for

Porno Madness, a lesbo-punk orgy in torn fishnets and leather collars. Imagine, dear readers, his deep shock and awe when those latex corsets dissolved – and We appeared in all our solemn splendour. He fled in terror, the system flaw uncorrected...

Carla has always had many lovers (as well as poor old chump Lucas) but her latest stud, young Omar Majid, couldn't comprehend her wild transgressions, or his own. Even his kind old Uncle Abdul wouldn't understand his dalliance with a kaffir woman. He dared not tell his acquaintances in the Mo-Boy units. Not wise for him to seek distraction in Pleasure Centres, either, playing the dangerous doggy-style Dub Demons. The neural overload, which we authorised, was just too much, my friends. Omar died in his headset, to become a pin-up boy for the Mo Boys. Their martyrdom poster-boy.

Of course, Carla couldn't reveal her verboten passion but blamed senile William for a Pleasure Centres PR disaster. To save his tired old ass he made a rash promise to upgrade the software. Struggling to recall the coding lost in his breakdown, he visited the derelict Weapons Establishment.

Meanwhile we haunted Viv, so Mark Rinehart was able to initiate her as a Pleasure Centres 'artiste.' But Carla was sick all over the porno-celebs at Keith Lombard's party, lost her job and her corporate flat, and was reduced to dossing in a Heavy Shepherds shelter and packing Bibles. Lucas withdrew into a trance state, yet again burrowing into his astral safety-zone.

Pleasure Centres CEO Lombard bribed William into exhuming his secrets by giving the old boffin a virtual frolic with some Lobemistresses – and then shooting him in the hip just to remind him that Keith Lombard was a serious man to do business with. That's real leadership for you. And forcing William to revive his aborted Cold War project - the British Reconstructive Application Network. For BRAN was designed to cope with apocalypses. Mr Lombard's plan was to power it with astral energies generated during the Feast of Smoke in Leynebridge. That way our cunning Lombard plotted to rationalise the reality-flux and bring back business confidence. You would all be in debt to its heritage.

While Viv was groomed as rapper Quantum Slut, Carla was forced to join a Heavy Shepherd mission to the Borderlands, which was ambushed by the Omar Majid Martyr brigade. She fled the carnage and, guided by the Harvesters and their psychetronic probes, she discovered a bunker where Lucas lay entranced. Her hot slippery sex-magick revived him and they briefly entered the hidden depths of the Polyverse, where, frankly, we struggled to keep up with them. We believe the Harvesters were destroyed but we're not very reliable narrators...

Mo-Boy Brigade member Hisham forced Omar's uncle Abdul to join him on a special operation in the Borderlands. Stolid chump Aran begged Elderwoman Elaine to locate his betrothed through clairvoyance but when her visions revealed Viv apparently in sexual congress with both Lucas and Carla, he lashed out, inadvertently slaughtering her, a move he immediately regretted.

Hisham arrived at the Feast with a suitcase nuke, 'mislaid' when the Weapons Establishment was closed. We were quite shocked at the orgiastic pagan pageantry of this Feast, climaxing in a mock sacrifice. Especially when Carla appeared on the scene and Lombard seized her for actual immolation. As William initiated Lombard's project, the Polyverse underwent further fission, instead of integration. We disclaim all responsibility.

Aran heroically intervened to save Carla while Abdul sabotaged his nephew's nuclear suicide mission. It was all ending too happily. Then Carla got primaeval on Lombard's arse, with remarkable results; and we found it necessary to have a little talk with William, to discuss various post-human agendas...

Problems across the Whole Lobe Infrastructure

Dawn

A raw dawn: mist drifting across the mound, the grey video screen over the stony Burrough collapsed, fires still glimmering among the roofs of Leynebridge. Crows circled over bodies scattered across the slopes. Ritual games of death and desire had been enacted all around the mound and throughout the town. Arms and legs were still entangled in passion or combat. Forgan, wandering at random, could no longer distinguish which. He couldn't read the shape of the smoke signals any more, there were no omens scribbled across the morning sky, and the drums were silent, as were the edgelands of his mind. Was he a shaman or a mere juggling fire-breather? His inner voices were confused, the alignments were all skewed. Perhaps Elderseer Noah or Wharton, Scribe of the Great Book, could divine what had happened. No sign of either. But Forgan could already see the Scribe's gilded chair overturned in a mudbath lower down the hill, its splintered arm-rests poking through the shattered rim of the great Time-Wheel lying on the bank. Mrs Nixon was no longer bound to it. He hoped that she'd at least escaped torture and had gone pleasuring among the multitudes.

Forgan's people were layered deep around the entrance to the Burrough chamber, where they'd poured in, impelled by the current of the Feast - only to stampede out again. He'd evoked a rout of Pan, a Panic attack - but after that the re-enactment in his mind was scrambled, dissolving fragments of overlapping dream clips, conflicting narratives. He shook his head, to shake out the devils.

He had to find the village children.

He slithered down the hillside, picking his footholds between the catatonic bodies, as he scanned the trampled grass for the tiny purple hoods that marked out the Children of the Lore, some of who were almost certainly his - Alys, Loki, Poppy… Surely one of his consorts, maybe the steadfast Willow, would have gathered them before the Rites went rampant. All he wanted now was to get home and tell them a long story.

A few yards below the wreckage of the great Time Wheel, he heard a faint cry emanating from under a pile of torn banners. Scrabbling at the heap he uncovered the bloodied head of Noah. The old man was mumbling, eyes closed. Forgan extricated him with some difficulty, for a heavy palsy had seized his mentor's limbs.

'Where are they? Where…?' Noah slurred and dribbled. 'Where are they hiding? They may come to us…'

'I don't know where the children are. You must rest. I'll get help.'

'Where are *they*? They're not children. Not your children?' He was hoarse with indignation. As Forgan shrugged he opened one bloodshot eye and fixed him with it.

'Where are the Dead, Fool? After the ordeals you've put us through, the Dead must come through.'

Forgan was alarmed at the old man's agitation. He tried hoisting him across his shoulders, to carry him down to the village, but Noah's struggles made it impossible.

'Put me down, Forgan… I'm waiting… waiting for the Dead. Where are they?'

Forgan propped the old seer against the Scribe's chair and tried to make him comfortable. Understanding was dawning. Of course,

Noah awaited the Dead. After the cataclysm up at the Burrough, all the bioplasmic power crackling down the nervous channels of the earth, the ley of the land, the ancestors would surely manifest, according to his Lore. But at this moment all Forgan could see were jumbled bodies under a grey sky. In the distance, one of them - a man - stirred, slowly stretched and stared in bewilderment, before staggering off towards the village.

Noah was trying to raise an arm and point towards the Burrough. 'Coming now - coming down the mountain…' His throat rattled, a mucus laugh. Forgan stared at the earthwork. 'They come out, even at dawn. Carrying the blue flame… Look!' Forgan surveyed the smouldering fires that dotted the hillside, yet couldn't persuade himself to see any flickers of afterlife. He could hear distant voices as other survivors of the night began to surface. Noah had half-raised himself and was still pointing.

'They're coming from the dark groves… from the shadow realms … the warriors and the priests… we've freed them to roam…"

Amoebic shapes swam at the edge of Forgan's vision. His eyes must have been sore from the smoke and the morning chill. There was a wedge of cloud over the weak November sun — and then over the top of the Burrough, a kind of fracture in the light, a crooked slit in his viewpoint. Later he told himself that a coagulated darkening mass had briefly expanded over the bodies, the hillside, the grey roofs and the dark tower, then vanished. In any case Noah had smiled; and ceased breathing.

Tithe Ye as Ye shall be Tithed

In the smoky depths of Leyston Burrough Lombard crawled through the debris of his hub, the overturned work stations daubed with sigils. He slouched on all fours, sobbing and choking on the fumes of burnt-out transistors and processing units.

'I need help! So help me Lord God. The Scarlet Woman has possessed me. By my holy rectal vessel. With her Shaft of Gomorrah. An anal seizure of righteousness. The abominable vessel itself... I'm so humbled - yet in my shame I am exalted in the dark places and am reborn in a new Faith. Find Jehovah for me, Liggett, find my Jehovah in this bloody smoke-hole, where is Jehovah my Mighty Lord? Get me a Heavy Shepherd, Liggett!'

Human Resources Officer Liggett was crouching in a foetal position on the far side of the Burrough cave, his torn suit drenched in blood. The obligatory response to his Chief Executive was not forthcoming. He could only whimper wordlessly. The semi-naked Lombard crawled over to him and whispered urgently in his ear, one hand thumping Liggett's skull against the ground for added emphasis.

'I want to feel the full weight of a Shepherd's cross-cut club splintering on my shoulders, I want to offer my blood to the Lord God, as my tithe. Tithe ye as ye shall be tithed, for He has spoken, I heard His voice in my long night of shame, and I am born again, again, please bear me all over again, for He hath slain my Serpent and called me unto righteousness via the Sacrifice of Sodom. I don't understand, Liggett, I don't know where His voice is coming from, but it's coming through... You gotta help me.' But Liggett had shut his eyes tight and could only gasp and moan. Lombard lost interest and wandered back to the wrecked virtual-reality console, sniffing the wisps of smoke still fuming from the cabinets as if they marked his mammalian territory.

Technical Director Rinehart lay on the ground staring up at the earthworks, trying to ignore Lombard. The Chief was always creating scenes – although this recent one would be unlikely to feature on the Pleasure Centres data base. Rinehart wondered, abstractly, if any keystones reinforcing the structure of the Burrough had been dislodged in the uproar of the Feast of Smoke. Any one of these boulders would crush him to death. This had been built as a paleolithic death-structure. A giant stone igloo, once brimming with crushed skulls. Perhaps that threat of collapse could be a feature of a new VR game, a revised Iconoclasm, with a Leynebridge setting, even a torch-lit procession option. Until now, he'd been a complete skeptic about these Borderland cults. They must be getting under his skin. Like insect burrowings…

He scratched, shook himself hard and rose, very cautiously. The batteries for the emergency lights were going to fail soon. He was shivering and found it hard to move his neck. He thought of trying to arouse Liggett from his post-traumatic shock but there seemed little point. As an ally the ingratiating soft-skills flunkey would be more of a hindrance than a help

He watched the bare-assed Lombard padding around like a wounded bear. The Chief snuffled and muttered, paying Rinehart no attention, for which the technician was grateful. To be buggered by a witch and converted to the Heavy Shepherd creed was an unexpected development but then the Chief had always been full of surprises. There was nothing to be done here, the connection to the Lobe was terminally blown – and there would be problems spreading across the whole Lobe infrastructure…

He began moving cautiously towards the Burrough exit, stepping around the massive stone pillars and the incinerated workstations. Normally he would have been desperate to probe the debris in an attempt to locate the bug that had caused such a massive malfunction, but now retreat seemed the best strategy. Rinehart didn't want to know happened to the aged Dr William Crowe in his Virtual Reality Pleasure Zoner pod, with the very latest enhancements, although it was a probably a replay of the Dub Demons scenario. Old fraud had it coming to him. Dr Crowe had cocked up yet again. Connecting the Lobe to his old-time post-nuke software was doomed.

Lombard would just have to cope with the evolving situation. Liggett would revive somehow, he'd always be ready to grovel and help out. Time to make a low-profile exit and get back to London, back to work, to work this hallucination out of his system. Best to be at the centre of things, especially if he had to take over as Acting Chief Exec. Very carefully he ducked under the half-collapsed lintel over the exit, breathing the cold air with relief.

A Very Special Effect
Quantum Slut really existed in studio time. The industrialization of the Babalon Effect began there and then at the epicentre of the Pleasure Zones. That was proved by audience research. Studio time was reality-time. Time was the square root of money. That was London prices for you. So she had to get on with getting it on for her mystery demographic. She was now taking private directions from top producer Jack Cusimano. He was directing all aspects of the audio-visual recording process. So she was entering a completely arbitrary arrangement of limbs. She felt she was being slotted into

the private part of an elaborate display unit. They used to call her Vivienne. Or Vanessa? She was weighed down by soft bodies, by the interleaving of tawny breasts and creamy thighs. The recorded body of the pale-breasted redhead they labeled Carla was patterned by a leather harness. Carla was a Valkyrie momma, an all-dancing star. That sinuous neck was collared in silver spikes, as specially ordered. Hands, real or virtual, hard to tell which, were exploring all the women. There must have been a kink in their genomes. Pleasure was the side-effect of a complex bio-mechanical process. It was a very special effect. It had to be transmitted for public consumption and recycling. You could wrap it around you on the Lobe. But the Zones had to elide nicely. Directions kept coming through via her inner ear. So she filled the nearest mouth with her nipple. She wondered if she tasted bitter or sweet. She was certainly a mass, almost a mess of bits. The naughty bittiness was all part of this unscrolling event. She was going all over the Feelies, all over again. A thigh slowly rolled across her vision. She was probably just a blur of hair. They were all in some kind of sexual hypercube. Perhaps it was a steel cage, with bunks. Carla or some simulacra of her sprawled above her, splaying her pubis against the silvery bars. Their celebrated lives paraded before them to the sound of synth-flutes.

The Electronic Tulpas

Lucas was in deep shock. The half-light drizzled around him. He couldn't quite remember how he'd escaped the Burrough. His overriding compulsion was to get away from those thrashing bodies, the noise and smoke and screaming. Now he was lying on a bench by the Leyne looking up through the overhanging willows at the disused railway bridge. He couldn't stop seeing Carla tied to the sacrificial pillar so close to death. He almost convinced himself that he'd seen a mist of blood spraying from her butchered neck, a corona of red hair tumbling to the ground. But another shutter in his memory clicked open and he could recall the glistening arc of Aran's sword cutting her free, his own cry of relief. And he kept re-running that sinister image, grotesque and inexplicable – Carla, still 'his' Carla, strapping on a polished stone-coloured phallus and plunging it into the writhing rump of that creature they called Lombard. After that, it was all chaos. How, why could she commit this…

And all the time this cataclysm had been brewing he had lain entranced in his hillside bunker, floating through the hazy shells of the astral realms. Meanwhile the techno-culture of the despised Carbonites had generated its own magickal phenomena.

For he couldn't stop recycling another image : Vivienne as Quantum Slut drifting over Leyston Burrough, a dancing priestess of lust, like a shimmering clone of Carla. It must have been a collective psychic projection taking physical form, what the Tibetans called a tulpa.

Earlier electronic tulpas had manifested in different ways. Maybe in deceptive ways. *Solid no-nonsense men, with shiny well-parted hair. Like old 1950s publicity photos of bandleaders, movie gangsters, radio announcers.* But the Quantum Brothers were also mistaken for pre-Rupture celebrity look-alikes or front-men for obscure tribute bands. The astral pollution of TV and radio broadcasts, still swirling through the aether before the Rupture must have created a kind of plasma soup in which hybrids of the media landscape emerged as living entities and dictated the lives of their audience.

These were the nocturnal emissions he had dreaded for so long. Now these Quantum Brothers had coagulated into coherent entities, ready for show-time. And they were going to show him, in some shape or form. He was probably on show to them, even now.

He realised that he was freezing, and that he'd lost full control of his lower limbs. He couldn't stop shaking and twitching. Although there was no wind the bare twisted bushes along the opposite bank of the Leyne were shivering too *tangled hair of the earthbeast its jelly eye on you...* He had to move and find sanctuary somewhere. Find food and drink. Find a safe house. Mute the hissy Underminding in his head *witchfinders keepers burn out his peepers.* With an enormous effort he rose to his feet, fell over in the tangled grass, and got up all over again. This time he could stand and move one foot in front of another.

His skull felt top-heavy, as if he was about to trip over the tangle of tree-roots as he trod very warily along the narrow winding path beside the river bank. He tried to focus on the existential moment, one footprint at a time. He struggled through the gloom, trying to envision a protective sphere of white light around him, but it flickered, only partially blanking out Undermind ramblings *Beelzebub's babe bonked the big boss* and the feeling at the nape of his neck that those Quantum Brothers were documenting his every awkward move.

Eventually he reached the bridge and turned up the path towards High Town. He would blag some sustenance. Sebastian Hackett owed him many drinks. Gavin Wharton was a civilized person. They'd know he had done Leynebridge some service. And somewhere, in the Red Hag or the Unicorn he would find Carla and confront her *tosspot totty who went to pee in a sieve.* A futile gesture, irrelevant almost in the social collapse that would probably end his life in a few days, but he needed some closure. He needed to understand, too, how Vivienne, of all people, had become part of Pleasure Centres' machinations.

An Expanded Portal
The Spirits in her Headphones

cyber-tribe gotta buy more fibre
buy fat city on a slimline chip
this way you get the key to the highway
my way - interface my lips!

Against a backdrop of smoking pyramids pale-faced Vivienne/Quantum Slut, chained to a granite pillar, mouthed the vocal around the silver microphone, as her twirling backup singers, two Nubian nubiles with bare pointed breasts, converged on her, to run their gold-ringed fingers down her belly towards her sex...

information 'cross the global nation
multiplies faces like copulation
Rolling Clones on the MTV
look at me look at me look at me look at me

The love-cry of Quantum Slut reverberated through the time-strata as the dancers knelt to lick her nipples, caressing their own breasts, flexing the elegance of their buttocks...

I'm a roadrunner riding your overload
gonna keep my media stud on hold
I put the byte on your tower of power
go-go guerilla girl going for gold!
cyber-tribe gotta buy more fibre

buy fat city on a slimline chip
this way you get the key to the highway -

Then silence. Dead air, dead ears.

The Pleasure Centres studios had lost power. Perhaps the whole of London had blacked out. A terminal surge in what was left of the grid. For the Lobecam had suddenly died, killing off the music as the studio light bulbs tinkled and fractured and the VR screencams sporting her dancers failed. Quantum Slut paused, mouth half open in mid syllable, and opened her eyes in real time.

The silver grill of the microphone glinted in the shadows but the spirits in her headphones had expired, the digital ghosts caressing her had evaporated and the sonic mummification that preserved her ID had peeled away. She was alone with the drift of her thoughts. She felt post-operative and scared. The synaesthesia was wearing off and the awkward latex clothes bit into her thighs. She was waking up in the wrong rite, somebody else's compulsive enactment. A mass of diffused lust had been recycling through her, confusing her. Her voyage through the Pleasure Zones had compelled her to re-script her body language, her delinquent pout positioned exactly to offset the discrete brand on her flanks, this year's new model ass - all this to appease the ghost-men, the salary-men, whose reality had been diluted at source? Or, ultimately, to empower her?

So where was roguish old Jack with his absurd expectation of fellatio on the control room couch? Before the session she'd spurned his unfeasibly large penis, to his obvious irritation. Had he blown the whole system out of spite? In the faint glow of the back-up lights she wandered through - and tripped. At first she thought she'd stumbled, quite literally, across one of his perverse jokes. A rubber suit, with a mask in the exact likeness of Jack, moulded by an expert, flopped across his chair, like a discarded costume from a carnival. It looked tacky in every sense, extruding skeins of translucent spittle, like the salivations of vampires, which extended from its fingertips to the faders on the console. Perhaps this was the only way his strings of sticky molecules could anchor themselves in the material world. She had to look away, quickly. The smell was unbearable.

She ran out of the control cubicle, still averting her eyes from Jack's rubbery pseudo-suit, draped over the faders and the chair like a sloughed snakeskin. Or a used condom. He was her user and wannabe abuser, now apparently disembodied. So he'd been ghosted somehow. Serve him right.

The external world seemed busy. Even through the padded walls of the studio she could hear shouts and screams in the outer Complex, breaking glass, the rattle of gunfire. The usual dystopian sound-bed was cranking up. They were crying from deep throats out there. Whatever was happening on the streets she daren't let it in.

She stumbled down a spiral emergency stairwell to the basement, an executive zone normally restricted to senior management. The door at the bottom swung open - the yellow-painted tunnels with their dim emergency lights must have already been evacuated. No sign of that vicious Rinehart man or creepy Pullman. They were probably safely secured in Mr Lombard's penthouse, high above the ructions of the street and its fake carnival of the repressed. It was a bad case of demonic repossession all round.

A carnival. A carnal feast of fun boys in the dark. She had this nagging false memory syndrome of doing a midnight gig on the top of a grassy mound. She'd projected herself there. Her space was in two places at once. She was Vivienne playing at Quantum Slut; or Quantum Slut playing with Vivienne. She couldn't help it, maybe she was beyond help but she had to find something or someone, an Other to give herself some grounding.

She ran at random for a while along the labyrinth of empty tunnels, her shouts echoing down the curved ochre walls. Eventually she found herself at her starting point at the foot of the stairs, staring at the emergency warning notices and the signage. A few yards away a refreshment area led off the main tunnel. Laboriously, like a defective robot, she levered open the door of a vending machine with one of Jack's screwdrivers and snatched a green carbonated lifestyle drink.

Channeling Quantum Slut (if that was what she'd done) had burned her out. She needed food. So she couldn't stay in the depths of Pleasure Centres HQ indefinitely, despite the menace of the mobs on the streets. It wouldn't be too long before some faction forced their way down. The Mo-Boys and the Shepherds would fight over who had more right to wreck the technology that enslaved the cities, while the urban kids would be in there to nick it. She needed to find her own centre, as Vivienne, to align herself with the four Angels, the co-ordinates of her old spiritual compass.

She stood in the empty tunnel and began tracing the pentagrams, as Elaine had taught her. She tried focusing on Elaine as she recalled the invocations; but she felt a worrying blankness, an absence/presence like a phantom limb.

Struck Down by the Devils

When they finally dragged William Crowe out of the Lobe control pod, Lombard was twitching with anxiety, swearing at Liggett as the PR man, still shaking, bungled the zips as he attempted to unpeel the tactile immersion suit. Lombard, now wrapped in an improvised kilt, clasped his new Plain Folks Bible and sank to his knees beside the sprawling body. 'Supposing Dr. Crowe's dead, Liggett, our best asset dead to this world and he never made his peace with the Lord. Hurry, man, hurry…'

The pallor of William's ageing flesh alarmed Liggett. The arms hung limp, the pot belly protruded, a discoloured gourd. His eyelids were closed, his mouth had twisted into a rictus of frozen bewilderment and he drooled, mumbling incoherently.

'He's had a massive stroke,' said Liggett, 'like the boy in the Dub Demons incident. Major neural damage…'

'He's been struck down by the devils we've evoked. I should never have let my technology be compromised by witchery. All those crazy people. Yet it seemed so logical at the time - new product, new audience, expansion outside the cities. Why Leynebridge, Liggett? Something the Centre's database threw up to fit that profile. Rinehart told me you could still trust the Lobe. And Pullman should never have brought us here. I was betrayed, Tom Liggett, betrayed! But we must revive our best brain.'

'I think Pullman's already taken a car back to London. Mark Rinehart, too. To try and sort things out for you.'

'They have no faith, Liggett. We have to stay here now and fight evil in its dwelling place, restore the order of this land we have so sorely breached.'

'But Dr Crowe needs our private clinic in London. There's

nothing we can do for him here.'

'We can pray, Tom Liggett. And I will find strategies. I always do. The Lord was always with me even though I didn't know it. Book us rooms at that public house…'

'The Red Hag?'

'Do it now. And get bearers to take him down the hill.'

A New Pitch

Dominic Pullman was trying to pull something together in the grand debacle that Pleasure Centres now faced, with its Chief Executive apparently abdicated and its Centre under siege. Getting back to London had been a lucid nightmare, lit by rivulets of flame coursing down the central reservation of the M4 near Reading where a chain of petrol tankers had been torched. His own precious fuel was low. The shapes of ghost cars in interweaving formations, often head-on, had materialised and then vanished in front of him as he drove over the Chiswick flyover, towards the fortified corporate towers, into the ever-changing topography of the city.

The retro-pagans had queered everything. The geography of the metropolis was in melt-down. Road signs flickered and morphed in the glare of your headlights, even as you squinted at them. In his terror and confusion he might have hit at least one dark form rolling in the road outside a roofless church, but he couldn't stop, he had to maintain velocity. He felt that if he stopped some long flexible entity would flow out of a side turning and engulf him in sweetish black sludge. Only an intensity of concentration that left him with bleeding lips enabled him to grip the wheel and steer for Lombard's tower apartment overlooking the Pleasure Centres site, scraping the car through narrow lanes and alleys, new jagged lines of sight, that ended, quite unexpectedly in the right underground car park.

He couldn't see Lombard's minders, usually lurking at the entrance, and most of the lights were off. The emergency generators were supposed to run for weeks. At least the lifts still worked. In the lounge of the top floor suite he found Rinehart calmly checking the contents of a drinks cabinet. The technician had changed into a smart monogrammed shell-suit as if that would normalise events and disconnect him from everything that had transpired in Leynebridge, that accelerating blur of improbability. He ignored Pullman as the latter slumped into an ornate chair, custom-made as a replica of the Papal Throne in St Peter's. Lombard sometimes liked to conduct his orgies from it; and Pullman admitted it gave one a certain status.

He sat there for a few minutes, trying to control his adrenaline flow and fight his migraine – and this nagging sense that a voice was mumbling at the back of his skull. *Neurons are rotting old man rotten show.* He was waiting for Rinehart to congratulate him on his escape from Leynebridge and ask him about the heroics of the journey, but his colleague simply pulled the tab off a beer and switched on a large monitor on the wall. With his back turned to Pullman, he knelt on the carpet and stared up into the screen.

As the digits flickered across animated spread-sheets, Pullman suspected that yet another Great Crash was underway. Not only Pleasure Centres assets but millions of accounts across the globe were fluctuating wildly, out of control, without any logical relation to trading or agreements. Rinehart spoke, at last.

'Are you watching this, Dom? Fifteen per cent of Pleasure Centres UK shares are transferred to Fast Fun Electrics in Seoul.

Lombard's going to go even madder.'

Pullman squinted at the big data. 'Who the fuck is Mrs. Iqbal Kalyoubi ?' She's just had a chunk of Krasco Inc (Personal Defence Systems) transferred to her Post Office Savings account. I thought there weren't any Post Offices left.'

'The demon bugs are scoffing the fat of the land. We're just got to surf the wave, Dom. Get down under the Zones, ride the riot...'

Rinehart turned towards him. He picked up an old storyboard from the table, as if he was about to launch into a Monday-morning presentation.

'OK, try this for a strap-line, Dom. "The dream that we have designed for you will bring you a multitude of life-chances…" We got to try something fast. Before the whole bamboozle collapses. A new pitch for an expanded Portal. This will blow Fast Fun Electrics out of the water, the Pacific Rim will go down the plughole.'

'What new Portal?' All Pullman could recall was a brief vortex of confusion in that cave of unknowing, the claustrophobic stonework, the smoking circuitry. And all those hooting people with torches and bare chests. 'We have the Venusberg VR stuff to finish, somehow, without Carla, but we've only got a beta-test of Iconoclasm, which old Crowe sabotaged in that bloody Burrough. He's still holed up with Lombard and Liggett up there in the sticks.'

Rinehart laughed. 'I know Lombard's freaked out right now but eventually we'll be able to run new stuff past him. His Heavy Shepherd craze will run its course pretty damn quick. If it doesn't, the whole fucking circus is up for grabs...'

Pullman recollected the shock of beholding the buggered Boss lumbering through the smoky cave bellowing his testimony of faith and wasn't so certain he'd recant his sudden conversion. But this new project might be their only bargaining chip in whatever new Pleasure Centres regime emerged. He might as well run with it.

'Where does your new Portal idea fit in, where does it take the punter? Hopefully it will take them off the streets.' He pointed to another jerky monitor, depicting young Korean men in bowler hats torching a PC facility in the gated suburb of Raynes Park.

'It could take them into their alternate selves. Even if only for a brief flash. The quivering things they might have been. That you might have been, Dominic. And me. The lost life chances we all regret – or dread in retrospect. If only I had... Thank fuck I didn't... If my father had never... If only my mother...'

Pullman tried to review his life-chances which had somehow collapsed into this dark farce. 'How can you process an infinity of lost lives?

'Until now we've only accessed this in dream-time. With no clear fixture or focus on any one alternate form of your being. Dreams are fluid, all fluxed up. They're all morphed and muddled, where faces fall apart and the backdrops change as soon as you look at them. What is this magick but an attempt to release the potentials of the Polyverse by focused concentration? I'm a convert, Dom, I tell you. It just needs some cyber-tweaking. The Lobe, revisionist occultism plus new technology, could offer a magick that works!'

'Even if you can make it work, what of the side-effects? It could take years off your one-track life! The old idiot Crowe probably got his brain fried. Mad and blind. Your post-Portal condition could become infectious, a contagion – random manifestations of the alt.self.'

'OK, with so many people arriving back in post-Lobe mode, it's going to be more difficult to keep up with a single-track model of a collective history. But look how we've coped with the first Rupture. We performed a valuable social service, Dominic. When common sense was collapsing around their ears, we offered people relief and escape.'

' But the whole tapestry of the past could unravel. With so much subjective multi-tracking, it's going to be impossible to have any coherent sense of history. It's going to be constantly re-drafted in retrospect.'

'It's just Lobe Therapy, Dom! People will take the alt-selves trip as a way of confronting -'

'Or evading -'

'The consequences of their choices...'

'Or more retrogression as trips towards guru-hood, shamans, alt.life coaches?'

'Or as attempts to gain knowledge that could re-write the root-world!'

They felt possessed with a sudden burst of energy. Two minds had merged, almost telepathically, against all the odds. A collective entity had budded forth. Pullman had always been an arts man, not a scientist, but already symbols were dancing across his field of vision, as if back-projected from nowhere into his optic nerve. He scribbled on the back of the story-board. 'Here come the probability-wave equations that open up the Polyverse!' Rinehart grinned and opened the command-line interface on his work station. Without any conscious effort he tapped out a line of code, which generated a rapidly expanding tree of commands. He was in the zone. Programming had never been so easy. He almost felt he was being written by some external Entity. Fortified by a case of Lombard's prize vintage Budweisers they got on with summoning It.

Possessed by the Talking Heads
An Industrial Haunting

Even as he trod the alleys of Leynebridge Lucas was still locked into semi-trance mode. A burning hole crawled across the sky. Was it the sun or the moon? They always burnt the moon in the Feast of Smoke. It was only a paper moon. Now and then the time-windows were dirtied over. But the Quantum Brothers were inlaid into the woodwork of reality, in the red-lit Quantum Brothels of Pleasure Centres. He realised he was becoming obsessed but the obsession at least drove out the Undermind *wandering through high town with his pants down the outsider couldn't get inside her...* At least partially.

So Lucas was looking for patterns in the language that might help to decrypt the Quantum Brothers. He'd make them crawl out of their black holes. They had created themselves from millions of faxes and hexes. They must have always existed in the glow of keywords on keyboards. He imagined them stored in great tanks of ice-cold sperm, vapour steaming around the valves and dials. Perhaps they had lost their hearts which teetered off into the night like lumps of old meat on spindly legs. Perhaps they were huge bricked-up clumps of neural tissue. Carla obviously thought they were sexy big spenders and had decided to play their game plan as a power undresser, it was the way of the worlds. The Quantum Brothers over-ruled. That was why his shoes were leaking, his bowels curdling, that was why in a world of altered states he was a stateless person.

He stopped outside Elaine's cottage, hoping to centre himself, as the townspeople had been taught, by recalling the rites she'd taught. He couldn't believe the rumours that Aran, hero of the Burrough, had slaughtered her. A staunch warrior of the Lore would never kill an Elderseer. But her door hung crooked on torn hinges, and the diamond panes were cracked. Flat-heads were looting already. A torn Tarot card lay on the door mat. He recognized the upper portion of the Queen of Swords, a martial figure holding the severed head of a man. He could only interpret this as another signal from the gods. Lucas Beardsley was headless as well as stateless, a babbler in the Undermind – or he was eternally re-possessed by the talking heads of the Quantum Brothers.

The QBs were a post-industrial haunting. Had he once in distant pre-Rupture times glimpsed their vague faces in broken wing mirrors, faulty cash-point displays, rainy hotel windows? Their jowls could be embossed in plastic tokens. Their lines were always open, while their hungry brains acted at a distance. Their sub-selves were bonded paying high rates of public interest. They were highly charged with deliberately creating a weird atmosphere with the use of overlapping in-store beats. It was a multi-phase they were going through. They pumped old electrons all around the world. There goes another economy, another ecology. Meanwhile he had to dream up a magick against hunger.

On the deserted High Street he pondered the feasibility of stealing something edible from Trader Price's boot-shop but decided against it. Even in better times the Trader's rusty cans had been suspect. For a moment he was tempted to take the long walk up to the Burrough, to see if he could scavenge any scattered offerings from the Feast of Smoke – bruised fruit, morsels of smoked meat, stale bread, anything... Then he recognised that he was only postponing this last decisive encounter with Carla. He'd find her in a saloon bar, as ever.

Old Scroll

Gavin Wharton felt like a blank papyrus. He'd become an old soul, poring over the ancient scroll of memory, its glyphs already half-erased. Days - how many? - had elapsed since the events on/in the Burrough but he was still exhausted from the ciphering, the flash of those speeding digits, a code that had almost broken him. What had become of the Great Book of Leynebridge? It had been wrested from his grip during the Feast of Smoke by some fat boy and torn apart in an hysterical tussle between the youth and two village mushroom-girls who were trying to protect it. Now its scattered fragments had been ground into the soil of Leyston Hill. What did it mean? He could only pose rhetorical questions.

He adjusted the cardboard protecting the shattered bay windows of his shop and sank into his chair, huddled against the chill. He would be expected to write an address, maybe even a invocation, for Noah's funeral, but the infrastructure of the Elderseers, already shaken by Elaine Crowe's murder, had fallen apart since the death of its founding patriarch. No one was willing to take responsibility for organising the ceremony. The coffin still lay in a temporary mortuary behind the Unicorn. Forgan had wanted to float the corpse down the Leyne on a blazing barge, but Trader Price had objected, citing the danger and disruption to business caused by recent processions and events at the Burrough.

For the first time locals had listened, forgetting how Noah's elemental Lore had created a more-or-less sustainable community in times of chaos. Wharton hoped that his old friend would at least get a peaceful burial under the stones of the Serpent Path by the river.

He needed a resolution to all this. Surely this universe was finite, a closed system with boundaries. It couldn't just bud off into infinite recursions, despite the evidence of his most recent hallucinations. Had that red-haired woman been decapitated by Aran at the climax of the Feast? He tried to tell himself it wasn't so but he couldn't be certain. If so, he'd somehow been complicit. Linear causality was degenerating still further. The Lore of the Elderseers had tried to accommodate the first after-effects of the Rupture. Yet this new development - in which they as a community were now enfolded - twisted the old magicks into new terrifying paradigms.

The door rattled and a large heavy-jawed man in a stained business suit strode towards Wharton's desk. He stretched out a hand, flaunting a massive gold ring embossed with a cross and a shepherd's crook.

'I know you probably don't think much of me, Gavin. And we've hardly met. I'm Keith, Keith Lombard, and I want you to know that I'm with you in Jehovah.'

'We have very few religious tracts for sale, Mr Lombard. Moreover, I have no plans to buy any more. There's not much demand in the Borderlands.' He rose from his seat to show this reformed Great Satan the door.

'Gavin, I understand you're angry and confused, like so many people in this idyllic community. But I haven't come to convert you from heathen ways, no! I'm here to apologise and explain. And I am a former customer.'

Wharton sat down and lit the last of his illicit Algerian cigarettes. It might mask Lombard's peculiar odour. He wished he could lay hands on his old staff and at least make a show of psychic resistance but he'd lost it in the melee on Leyston Hill. Lombard was pacing up and down, gesticulating forcefully.

'I have a proposition for you. We both desire the same outcome - the restoration of stability, optimum trading conditions and so forth. Now we've had a taste of the latest perversion of the Polyverse. But it really was my intention to end all this polyversity. I hired the best scientific minds. And I'm sorry, I truly repent of making it worse, of creating more chronoclasms, Satan's peepholes in the fabric of time wherein ourselves are depicted acting out of character - or doing a disappearing act. I'm so sorry about old Mr. Dodd and Elaine Crowe, by the way. Such stalwarts of village life. But you know on my way here today I had a little chronoclasm just by the Clock-Tower and somebody's shop had a crackly wireless on, which was announcing your death by trampling at the Burrough and then it faded into solemn music. It was awful, Gavin, this level of diabolical distraction. I wouldn't want you to think -'

'Your proposition?' Wharton inhaled deeply and tried to keep his voice steady. Despite recent events Lombard could still be bluffing, luring him into some dubious coalition by playing on his unease, this increasing sensation of not quite being in the same world from minute to minute. He stared at his worn Axminster carpet and the floorboards, anywhere to look away from Lombard's staring blue eyes and vast craggy jaw. Something was eagerly squirming beneath those surfaces of flesh and fabric.

'I shall soon be able to supply you with unlimited numbers of Plain Folks Bibles at a very favourable discount. There's going to be an enormous demand as the plague of chronoclasms increases, heralding the approach of the End-Times. The poor people of this benighted heathen community will seek solace in the plain truth of the Word and the simple linear narrative of the Holy Book. Their witcheries have been suffered to live for the Lord has given them this final opportunity for repentance. You can be part of the spiritual regeneration of Leynebridge and make a substantial profit from the fruits of your labours. There may even be time to taste the sweetness of said fruits, for none knoweth the hour of the Lord's return to take us to His Kingdom…'

Lombard ran a finger along dusty shelves of paperbacks. 'I have a vision - these shelves cleansed, bright with the gold lettered spine of the Plain Folks Bible, constantly emptying and refilling.' He squinted down a shelf and whispered. 'I can see it, Gavin, a good kind of chronoclasm, you seated at the desk, wrapping the books and taking in the coin. Writing the numbers in your ledger. Do you share my vision?'

Wharton closed his eyes and briefly saw himself thus in a tiny bubble of sepia light. Then he grunted and shook his head hard, imploding the vision.

Lombard sighed. 'Such a pity. A nice little business you have here, Gavin. We wouldn't like anything to happen to it.' As he swung towards the door he ran his huge hand along the first editions shelf, scattering dozens of volumes across the floor. Scraping his heels over a flattened grimoire, he lumbered into the street.

Nothing Personal

The Unicorn was almost empty and Carla was sitting opposite him, smiling over her glass of mead. She'd clearly charmed Fat Albert the landlord into extending credit. Now she was dressed in the Leynebridge fashion, in a flowing black gown with a silver pentagram chained around her throat, ordering bread, cheese and beer for her grubby companion. She was as elegant and fragrant as he was squalid. Her eyes glowed. Despite their astral ordeals, she'd never looked better or more desirable. But Lucas wasn't going to succumb. This had to be their end-game. He sat in silence, arms folded, waiting for her to speak.

'Listen, Luke, we've been there and back and inside-out, I know. I know what you're thinking. But you have to understand the force that's driving me. It's nothing personal. In fact, it's impersonal, a current of pure energy. When we look back on everything -'

'I don't want a post-mortem.' Yet it was his post-mortem. He felt like an assemblage of body parts. His vamp had virtually resurrected him, back in the hillside bunker, his home-made mausoleum.

'It could have been my post-mortem, Lucas. In another selection of worlds I'm a headless chick...' Her laughter grated. She was all wrong, too loud, too dangerous. He should have known all along.

'I have to go, Carla... At least in this edition of the time-slot.' Her slotted throat. Perhaps he'd actually willed that possibility, back in the anarchy of the Burrough. He didn't know where he was going, as there was nowhere to go. But he got up quickly, bumping the table and spilling her drink.

'You're such a clumsy hypocrite, Lucas. If one of your precious Leynebridge maidens had done what I've done, you'd be talking about a sex-magickal act of subversion that reversed aethyric modalities.' Yet Vivienne had submerged herself in Lombard's techno-sex empire. It was becoming increasingly hard to distinguish it from magick. Carla must have been aware of Vivienne's transformation, but wouldn't admit it. Another fracture in whatever trust remained between them.

'What compelled you to do that to Lombard? Did you know what you were releasing?'

'It was an experiment. A grand transgression.' She began swaying back and forth with implausibly girlish laughter. 'The expression on his face was so wonderful...'

'Lombard's more dangerous than ever, crawling around town trying to ingratiate himself as a reformed Shepherd of Souls. He's planted his arch-Carbonite techno-wizard here, recuperating in a room at the Red Hag. Gavin Wharton saw one of his minions dragging the old bastard in. I think you're just addicted to sexual dominance, by whatever route. We're just vessels for amplifying your power.'

'Well, I dragged you back out of the astral junkyard, didn't I? I've rescued you from the mud huts of Middle Earth, haven't I? All those hobbits banging on with their little drums. You enjoyed the trip, you loved every fucking moment of it. I've never seen you so hot...'

It seemed so remote, already. His body had lost the memory of her probing touch, her soft fissures and sudden paroxysms of lust. He'd been another person altogether. He had a flash of tiny nude figures coupling in a translucent sphere, a shrinking bubble that imploded into nothingness. They'd participated in a kind of black alchemy. He paced back and forth in front of the bar, gulping his drink, determined to keep silent again for a few moments while he plotted an exit strategy.

'Aren't you going to sit down again and eat something?' She pushed the plate of bread and sheep-cheese in his direction. 'Simple pleasures. At least we've got those left.' He slumped into the chair and bit into the stale slices.

'Food of the Goddess, that is,' shouted Fat Albert, appearing from the kitchen. 'You won't get that at the Red Hag. Not after all the trouble at the Feast. Your lady's really looking after you.'

' Listen, Lucas! We still have to work together, just to survive. You have to accept that I'm polymorphous, polyamorous and perverse. And so are you, once you strip off a few levels…'

She was already tuning into the wandering frequencies of the community's psychic chatter, the mutter of the Undermind *off with her old head and she stuffed it right back lost it in the rampage* - and his own intermittent pulses of lost lust: *Leila/ Robyn/ Carla/ Vivienne/ Carla/ Carla/ Carla…* But he had to resist his black-robed succubus.

'Your "polyamory" damaged a few people, didn't it? I'm not your only victim.'

'What do you mean?' She raised her defences. He was trying to penetrate certain painful strata.

'The Moslem boy. The posthumously celebrated Omar Majid.'

'How do you know?'

'I'm simply following my intuitions. You took him to bed, didn't you?'

She nodded.

'If he hadn't slept with you, he'd still be alive. You encouraged him to sample the software, as well as taste the flesh. So he died in the embrace of Pleasure Centres.'

Her under-lip was trembling but her voice went into corporate mode.

'Poor Omar died in a freak accident. A kind of cerebral haemorrhage, induced by a magnetic resonance overload, caused by failure to upgrade the software.' She reprised the spokesperson statement briskly but she was starting to relive her shock, the terse mail from Rinehart, the evasive blustering of that senile technician Crowe, all the tears she'd suppressed.

' You really are a bit of bastard to exhume all this...'

'How can you even talk about working together? Working for what? A complete Pleasure Centres take-over, the whole country locked down into the next pseudo-reality upgrade? You're in bed with the Quantum Brothers, Carla, admit it…'

'So how do you know about the Quantum Brothers?'

'I've had flashes, pre-cogs, whatever. When we were lost in the Tunnels of Set. Embodied in the God of Confusion. Following your Left hand Path...'

She grinned. 'You liked it, Lucas. You're addicted to those magick hand-jobs. Eighth-degree workings, you used to call them. And don't get all proper and proprietorial. I can handle the Quantum Brothers...'

He couldn't cope any more with her word-play, the way she played him like a glove puppet. The Undermind was seeping louder in his ear, too, with its incessant verbal dribble: *can't fangle the bitchcraft forgot his big booby bangeroo now we're smoked out of our own witch huts his fumbly fault the dod-man died in a mudbath blood of elders all over the field couldn't even stop it with a fire-fuck the serpent all tangled up High Town in the rage of Aran don't know where it's going to stop*

'Listen, Carla. It's over. It's over between us, and the whole stupid universe is running into overtime. I'm burned out, the worlds are going to burn themselves out, one way or another. Human beings have been a brief flare-up in the long night of time. Your new friends the Quantum Brothers are the final symptom of the process. For all your alleged clairvoyance you can't see it.'

'Lucas, you're being absurd -'

'Probably. We live in an absurdist cosmos. *Credo quia absurdum* - Tertullian, a grumpy father of the Church. But the Gnostics knew it all, better than the Catholics. The Heavy Shepherds and the Mo-Boys just repress the knowledge, hence their panic mode.'

She leaned across the table and gripped his palm, gazing into his cloudy eyes. 'You're in panic mode, Lucas. Trust me, we can work something out...'

He withdrew his hand. 'Who can I trust? I can't even trust myself. The QBs are the Archons, they're in control, push our fleshy buttons, pull the sinewy strings. You know, I'm beginning to hate all bodies, everybody, even yours...'

'Please hear me out, Lucas. You won't believe me, but I'm changing. After what happened in your bunker and in the tunnels and in whatever realms we penetrated beneath the Pleasure Zones, I have to acknowledge your magick.'

So the techie girl had a little taste of gnosis. The bitter knowledge. The Moebius stripperama of good and evil, matter and spirit. He found it hard to believe her. It was almost easier when her world-view was in total opposition to hers, when she simply acted out the materialist Lobe-strumpet and took no prisoners.

'And if we can work as comrades, brother and sister, we can help to change things. If we made the Quantum Brothers, surely we can un-make them.'

'Their infra-structure runs too deep. Do you really think anyone can turn off the Lobe, now that it's reinforced by bioplasmic energies and generating random personalised chronoclasms and time-slits? Lombard tried to play techno demi-god and got the exact opposite of what he intended. A classic magickal misfiring. The consensus was fragged enough already after the Rupture and he pushed it into fast-forward. It's only a matter of time before the Rupture goes exponential. We don't have the scientific knowledge to penetrate their network. I doubt if even Lombard's pet boffin understands it. And the magicks of Leynebridge are feeble and confused.'

'But if we could create an alliance, a sharing of forces - you and I, Forgan, Gavin Wharton - '

'You still don't get it. The QBs were created through our psychic weakness, our acceptance of the multiple-drafts model of consciousness, our de-centred selves. They're our cultural archetypes come alive and kicking. The ancients had spirits, demons, gnomes, salamanders, nymphs and sylphs reflecting and empowering their engagement with the elemental forces.'

'Isn't that what the Lore of Leynebridge tried to do? Re-engage with those forces?'

'The Elders were on the margins. Lore-abiding idiots. A little lost tribe of panto wizards. The mainstream culture - putrifying in its glass dish – could only relate to corporate logos, validation through brands, celebrating the power of a plutocracy that creates the targets we've used to destroy ourselves and the planet. All that was fuelled in the random forces of the Rupture. In the cities we created managerial demiurges to orchestrate our production and thereby define our identity through the funfair mirrors of consumption. '

'Who's we?'

'Beautiful people just like you, Carla. This was happening even before the original Rupture and now it's escalating madly. The ancients envisioned angels in chariots of fire, flying ships of stone. In the QBs we have created entities who are totally appropriate to the era of quantum physics, who are random but discretely quantifiable, who act at a distance, just as we've distanced ourselves from each other. They jump in and out, back and forth in sub-atomised isolation, as remote from each other as an electron from a proton in the emptiness of the atom. You spent your years at Jouissance and Pleasure Centres manipulating little icons of desire for an atomized demographic; and now the screen's going kaleidoscopic, the headset's shrinking us into a terminal blip and we're going into final count-down under the glare of our imploding iconography...'

'That's great radio rhetoric, Lucas, but where's your notorious True Will? Isn't it supposed to be the core of your magick? To act, not react. You could invoke your gods, maybe your god of scribes and hidden knowledge, Thoth. Perhaps he can show us the path through all this.'

Lucas was silent. She was testing him, even taunting him, as ever. He wasn't ready to envision Thoth, entity of ancient Egypt, Lord of Wisdom and Utterance. Best keep Him veiled. During that terrifying initiation years ago, in a darkened room in the spectral suburbs, under the guidance of Leila and the Order of the Brazen Head, he'd sworn an oath to the ibis-headed apparition, Guardian of the Books who wielded the Wand of Double Power, who knew his life-script and had defined his role as scribe. Yet all he'd done since was scribble in the ruins of the Rupture. He couldn't face Thoth's judgement.

'I don't think He exists any more. If He ever did.'

'You're in denial. As you say, it's a bad joke. You've half-convinced me of your magick but now you're scared of it.'

He tried to suppress the sub-text: *you're scared of me...* 'Are you surprised? After the Rupture and what we found in those Tunnels and what was released at the Burrough? I'm doing a Prospero and breaking my wand.'

'Breaking wind in the cosmic darkness, more likely. If we don't act, you're going to break up even more.'

He needed to act – with nowhere to live, no resources, his identity on the blink. But he also had the absurd notion that the saloon bar of the Unicorn, charged with the presence of the Elders and the practice of their Lore , might even offer a kind of sanctuary, a safe haven. Perhaps action could be postponed and he could sit here for ever gazing at Carla's tumbling red hair. 'Have you got any money left? I need another drink. '

'There'll be no more drink in Leynebridge by this time next week. It's rather inhospitable out there.' They looked up to see Sebastian Hackett lurching through the doorway. His tweed jacket was covered in plaster dust. The aged dandy's arm was suspended in a sling and he sported a plum-coloured bruise around his left eye. 'We're under siege. The bloody Mamelukes again, clustering at the gates. Or Mo-Boys, whatever they call them. The Crusades in reverse. Arrived an hour ago. A whole brigade in motor cars with rockets. Fired a grenade at the alms-houses as a warning shot, so this venerable scholar trips up over the remains of his front porch. They mean business.'

'You mean - they're going to trash the town? They'll kill us all!' Carla was abruptly hit by flashbacks of an ambush, the blazing caravans, those hideous screams. She barely managed to control her voice.

'What sort of business?' Lucas was almost detached now. He'd been expecting a final reckoning for a long time now, if not in this form. Thoth might be the mediator of the gods but this would be a sore test of His divine diplomacy.

'They want to do some kind of business with Lombard. He's the only person they'll negotiate with. They sent Mr. Wharton away with that very message. Said if he came back again by himself they'd cut his throat. Fatty Lombard is their preferred channel. An unspeakably vulgar envoy, if you ask me, but they seem to be rather bloody-minded people.'

'Lombard's nothing to do with Leynebridge. And he's become a Shepherd, their arch-enemy!' Carla couldn't stop shaking. She thought the astral travels had blotted out a replay of earlier traumas, but not so.

'My enemy's enemy is my friend. If Lombard hands over the pagan population of the town, they'll grudgingly allow him to redevelop it as a Heavy Shepherd outpost. I think that's the idea. Meanwhile, they'll starve us out, I suppose. Probably aren't enough of them to do a mass cull. Who knows…?' Hackett shrugged and limped to the bar. 'Time for a dry sherry, I think…'

'You have a local militia, haven't you?' Carla sounded incredulous, as if she couldn't believe the incompetence of these country folk.

'Maybe a shambolic bunch of Flat-Heads with shot-guns and

pick-axes.' Lucas laughed, bitterly.

'Flat-Heads?'

'A few local youths who've never bought into the Way of the Lore. They like a ruck on Saturday nights.' He recalled some close encounters and shivered.

'But some one could organise them - that man with the sword, who nearly killed me...'

'Aran, who killed the Seer Elaine, as the saviour of Leynebridge? Forget it. He's disappeared anyway.' Lucas rose from the bench and began walking towards the door, very slowly.

'Are you going to leave me, then?' Carla was quietly challenging him; and every muscle in his body wanted to stop and turn back. The sudden vulnerability in her voice triggered reflexes of nostalgia, desire, guilt. No one had ever shared so much with him, given and taken so much. But he had to escape her zone of influence, her contracting magick circle. He let the inn door swing in the wind behind him.

Warriors of the Waste

Seeking Vengeance and Knowledge

Night, it was always going to be night. Darkness and the faint scarred face of the moon. Despite his heavy backpack Aran had to keep running. He had cast himself out by raising his sword against that wretched city harlot and then striking down an Elder, most sacrilegious murder. What malformed troll-spirit had infected him?

For the tree-creatures were whispering against him. He was certain of it as he plunged through thickets and bushes, their wet branches lashing against his cheeks. The warped pillars of their trunks concealed watchers, who would pool their fleeting impressions with the demon-doggerel of the Undermind: *he did in her head the wise woman bled left her for dead buried in the depths of the earth...* He was a warrior of the waste now, heading out from Leynebridge towards the citadels of darkness, seeking vengeance and knowledge.

He craved simple certainties. That deflowering of his bride-woman, debauched in a sinister triad - was that Carbonite craftworking, a techno-phantasm to provoke his wrath? Or was it the raw animal truth? Or - unthinkably - a deception by the Elderseer herself, to goad him into action against the demons in the depths of the Earth? Only a confrontation with the Pleasure Centre would satisfy him. They said its Chief Elder, King Lombard, was still in Leynebridge, that after the red-haired whore had serviced him he'd gone mad and become a raving Heavy Shepherd. But that was surely yet another ruse. Aran knew he would only learn the bitter truth, whatever it was, on the shop-floor of the dream factory where the artisans of fabulated desire forged their machineries of deception. He had to march on London and its turrets of Babalon. Maybe he could still redeem himself even after slaying a wise woman.

Meanwhile, he was stumbling on the boulders of a stream, then striding thigh-deep through ferns and bracken towards a gap in the tree-canopy, where the woods gave way to farmland. He'd bypassed the road to Old Hallows and emerged near Tothman's Bluff. On the rising slope of the fields ahead he could sense a dim shape wandering in the gloom. For a moment he paused, suspecting Harvesters on the prowl, creeping about on their obsessive missions. Yet he couldn't sense any muted mental chatter, only intermittent indistinct sounds, which he eventually recognised as the bleat of a solitary sheep.

He walked to the top of the ridge; and found himself looking down on a small farmyard - a cottage adjoining a barn and stables. A light flickered in a window. He sensed a high thin emanation of anxiety filtering in and felt uneasy about what he had to do. This deed wasn't according to Lore. Nevertheless, he made his way carefully down the bank and across the rutted mud of the darkened yard. He shoved open the cottage door.

In the candle-lit kitchen a ragged boy of about eleven was crouching behind an oak settle, rigid with fear. He gripped a wooden pole with rusty nails embedded in its tip.

'Go away, fucking Leynebridger, get out! My dad's going to get you…' Aran glanced around the room, at the dusty chairs, the single dirty plate on the table. The fire-grate was choked with cold ash. He sniffed the stale air.

'So where is he, kid? Are you going to give him a shout?'

The boy hurled the pole at Aran's head. The warrior caught it with his left hand and drew his sword.

'I hope your dad's got the same spirit as you. I could use a good fight.'

The boy tried to screw his face into a mask of indifference. 'He'll be back. And he'll flatten you. He'll stick that sword up your arse. I'd be going if I were you.'

Aran took a step forward.

'Don't you touch me! Borderlanders, Harvesters, you're all the same, out every night to steal children.'

'You really think I'd want to steal a scrap like you?'

'The Harvesters use private parts of boys. For their secret experiments. The Leynebridgers catch girls, to dance in their dirty feasts. That's what my Dad said. He could cut them to bits.'

'What's he saying now, kid? Is he sharpening his knife out there in the barn? Or is he stabling his horse? I could use a horse.'

'You're not using anything. You're useless,' shouted the boy, edging around the table towards the door. Aran grabbed him by the scruff of the neck.

'I need that horse, understand? I need to get to London. I just don't want to kill you yet.'

'Nobody takes Fairfoot.'

'I'll make it worth your while. I can give you something in exchange.'

'So you're a charity-man. A booter. Big deal. Show us then.' The boy made a grab for the pack. Aran thrust him against the wall.

"Tell me, how much food have you got left in that larder? You're not going to get through the winter, are you, out here fending for yourself. How long have you been like this?'

The boy shrugged. Then his face suddenly crumpled and he began crying. 'The Shepherds came. They wanted Dad and Mum to…' He couldn't go on, but just sobbed uncontrollably.

Aran waited until the sobs subsided; and put a hand on the boy's shoulder. 'Don't worry, lad. You don't have to tell me if you don't want to. Just show me the horse, and I'll make sure you get help.'

The boy shook his head.

'Go on then. Kill me, Mister Big Hero… I don't care any more.'

Aran laid down his sword and opened the back-pack. Slowly he withdrew a package wrapped in silk and undid it. It was time to let go. With a heavy heart he placed the Mating Cup on the table. The boy's eyes widened.

'Yes, it's worth a lot. Take this to Leynebridge and ask for Forgan and Gil Norwood. Tell them Aran sent you. I'll write a note to make sure they see you right. Go ahead, pick it up. Just give me the horse and it's yours. It's probably no good to me now.'

The boy didn't speak for a while. He ran a finger cautiously around the base of the cup, as if testing its materiality. Then he lit a storm lantern and led Aran through a small kitchen-garden behind the cottage. In the lamplight Aran could see a crude wooden cross over a mound of earth. Pinned to the cross was a faded framed photo of a smiling man with a moustache and his meek-looking wife. The boy paused.

'One morning three Heavy Shepherds came from across the border in a Land Rover. They told Dad we had to convert to the true faith or some rubbish. He said he didn't need any conversion, he'd been a true churchman all his life, baptised and confirmed and married at St Michael's, no happy clappy nonsense for him. He threw their fake Bible back at them. They said he was possessed, they were going to beat the devil out of him. With baseball bats…' The lamplight flickered as the boy shook with anguish. 'Then they took Mum into the barn. She was screaming. After a bit I heard them drive off. I never saw her again.'

Aran sat with the boy by the makeshift grave, head in his hands. The Way of the Lore gave no protection. The random viciousness of the universe was too much. He was complicit in it, too.

'What's your name?'

'Adam. Adam Butterworth.'

'I'm sorry I can't do more, Adam. The Cup will bring you some money. I'm sure Forgan will take you in. Leynebridge has to be better than this.'

Adam looked uneasy. 'They believe in weird spirits.'

'Maybe. But they wouldn't have done that to your mum and dad.' He tugged a pencil and a scrap of paper from his pack, wincing inwardly as he realised it was one of Viv's sketches for a serpent brooch, one he'd never made. On the back he wrote *FORGAN THIS IS ADAM BUTTERWORTH I CHARGE YOU TO PROTECT THIS BOY SELL THE CUP BACK TO GIL AND GIVE ADAM THE MONEY PLUS ALL MONEY FROM MY CRAFTWORK FOR HIS KEEP SIGNED X WITH THE RUNE OF GEBO ARAN.*

Adam scanned Aran's angular script suspiciously.

'What's X The Rune of Gebo?'

'The sign for all matters in relation to exchanges, including contracts and partnerships.'

Adam mused and nodded. He took a deep breath. 'I'll saddle up Fairfoot for you. Just look after him.'

Sub Vox Networking

Lucas walked to the edge of town, trying to erase all memory. He wanted to flat-line his emotions, blank out the tiny burning icons of Carla, wipe out the smiles of the Quantum Brothers. He couldn't handle any more charms, omens and dreams, he'd burnt his magick fingers. Perhaps he was having a chronoclasm. Very cautiously he recalled a dead acoustic, an airless room, the hum of computers. It was so long ago he couldn't quite believe it had happened.

Pullman spoke awkwardly on that occasion as if finding the activity of using his voice unfamiliar and slightly repellent. Their dialogue had played out at a low key, no histrionics. Its banality was almost comforting:

PULLMAN: I don't like telling you this, Lucas.

LUCAS: You don't really like talking, do you, Dominic?

PULLMAN: Frankly, Lucas, in a twenty-first century communications environment I find it clumsy and anachronistic -

LUCAS: Like me, I suppose. You're letting me go.

PULLMAN: Listen –

LUCAS: Can anyone listen, any more? After the static of the Rupture. Snap, crackle, pop at fifty thousand watts...

PULLMAN: Thank you. My point exactly. Broadcasting as you understood it is dying. Sub-vox networking will be the way to go. My problem – our challenge - is transforming a fragmenting radio network into a peer-to-peer digital media hub. It's an audio equivalent to our visual/tactile immersion projects. Consumers don't need to hear some mouthy presenter acting out intimacy in a studio when they can network sub- vocally head-to-head, share all their music and their personal data direct. Our mission now at Pleasure Centres is to create a sub-vox digital infrastructure and create marketing content and promotional slots for our clients.

LUCAS: So the audience becomes the programme?

PULLMAN: We can't afford a man at a microphone talking to no-one in particular playing any old music. You're dead air, Lucas. It's over. There's always the non-profit sector, of course. Places like Leynebridge. Some funny stories coming out of there. They're all away with the fairies and hearing mystery voices. You could serve their community, Lucas. They'll need volunteers. It should suit you well.

But sleight-of-mind couldn't block the mystery voices: *fairy castles burning bright in the dumpsters of the night.* He was still walking the Serpent Path.

Night of the Quantum Sisters

'Look what I've found…' Rinehart dragged Viv across the penthouse living room and hurled her across one of Lombard's bulging sofas. 'Our Quantum Slut herself, wandering about on the lower levels, trying to steal from a vending machine. A dismissable offence if Mr Lombard were around.'

'You can let me go. I'll take my chances.'

'Do you really want to go out there, Vivienne?' Pullman, retaining a vestige of his Etonian manner, gently took her elbow and escorted her through the glass doors on to the balcony. 'This is the Night of the Quantum Brothers. And their Sisters. Behold…'

He gestured at the skyline, the black towers backlit by an orange glare. Whole blocks of the city were blacked out but in the direction of Westminster, fires were raging. From the streets, many storeys below, Viv could hear faint high-pitched screeching, either human or electronic, it was hard to tell. She had to keep her mouth shut against the mass of dark particles floating in the air.

'The latest cognitive dissonance has just got too much for the urb-masses. They're erupting again. We've probably lost a few Centres. But in the long run it's good for us. And you're quite safe here.'

'It's all over for Pleasure Centres, isn't it?' She wasn't going to be stitched up any more in their parody of reality.

'It's only just begun,' smiled Pullman. 'We're drilling down to new levels of quantum granularity. Watch this space.'

'Where's Lombard, where's your pet mad scientist?'

'They're no longer in executive roles,' interjected Rinehart.

'And you can be part of a new post-Lombard strategy that might just save the cities from more of this. Once people have sampled our new Portal - have sampled and remixed themselves, you might say - they'll be distracted from mindless ruckus on the streets.' Pullman drew her back from the balcony rail and steered her inside.

'It's only a beta-test, of course,' added Rinehart, 'and we can't be certain -'

'We can't be certain of anything - but that's the humanoid condition, isn't it? Let's descend to the new Portal.'

Rinehart had set up the Portal on the floor below, in what had been Lombard's master bedroom. The Persian carpets were rolled back and the retro gilded four-poster had been shoved aside to make room for a lash-up of PC towers, circuit boards and control panels.

'There's still a link to Leyston Burrough, of course. Old Crowe's BRAN system is very resilient.'

The interior of the capsule had changed. The suit was now vestigial, a semi-transparent harness with a silver helmet but the umbilicals connecting it to the servers were even more complex, a glistening rainbow entanglement of cables and translucent membranes that formed an intricate webbing - to entrap the subject like a glistening fly, thought Vivienne.

'We think you'll be an ideal volunteer,' Pullman informed her. 'We value your previous VR experience with us, plus the skills in dissociation and controlled disorientation you learned from your Borderland heritage.'

'You won't be in there long. Just enough to give us some feedback.' Rinehart was frantically keying in code. 'This will be the first authentic alt.life. inter-action. No more cheap porno or game-shows. An upscale life-changing experience.'

Suddenly she was going to do it. To show them up. To show off herself in all her crazed biographies. Curiosity was overcoming terror. The expanding multi-track of her lives. Too much already for Jack Cusimano to equalise. But she could hear it all.

Everything would be true, so everything would be permitted. So she let them bind her to this trickster net of their Techcraft. She'd twist it to her own ends, to trawl the high astral.

They placed the helmet over her face. For a few seconds she could only sense two vertical slots of darkness in the grey void in front of her.

Then a sharp pain began, at her forehead above the bridge of her nose - the anja chakra. Her third eye was virtually blinded by an overflow of radiance, a plane of light running vertically through her spine, bisecting her - and rising from the earth to meet it, another beam of light drilled upwards, penetrating her almost sexually, bifurcating her muladahra chakra, forcing her apart, tearing her comfort zone into tiny parallel strips, as her energy field, whatever that was, was forced, irresistibly through the vertical slits.

'Slut's going through the light-slits. She's well alight!' cried some creature with a rich port-wine braying voice. It was no good, she was a particle waving desperately to her alt. selves as her spirals of DNA unzipped and splurged. She was split into bands of light, which unscrolled into pictures and she was moving in and out of the moving pictures:

...it's the BA Show at Goldsmith's and everybody's waving their goblets of white wine and talking about Veronica's metal sculptures based on Tarot

motifs, her tutor Gilbert Norwood is so pleased and she's the glitter in her grandfather's eye, old Sir William is delighted, not that the ancient grand-dad understands these arty tangles of silver...

...Vicky doesn't understand why she changed her name to Electric Chick, her new boyfriend Aran the roadie told her that's the new name of the band they're all Electric Chicks, but now she's on stage at this grotty festival in a field somewhere in Wales and it's raining and they're starting to throw beercans before she's sung a note, another cover of a Close-Fitting Girls tune, it's madness, the whole thing seems pointless...

....no point in going out in the rain for movies or even a takeaway, Vanessa feels so cosy snuggling up on the sofa with Georgia, her big domme personnel officer, a perfect partner, they're happy to watch reality TV on a Saturday night and drink mushroom soup and Vanessa's really looking forward to her new customer service job on Monday...

...except it's Sunday morning and she segues into a new life in Jesus right here at the Tabernacle of the Holy Nazarene, a tented church on Clapham Common. Vandella is proud of her mixed race parentage, her mum Dawn has had happy years with Delbert, so she gives thanks and praises, riding a high altissimo over the rest of the choir, opening the heavens...

Vivienne/Veronica/Vanessa/Vandella flip past like a hand of bright cards, their tiny face(s) shimmering with quantum jitters. She/They have multiplex vision, eyes like the fly, tracking a spiral of mirrors as they freeze and melt into new torsions of time. There are infinite permutations in the cosmic dust, smoke of dead stars...

Then the worlds collapsed around her, crashing her back into that tight harness, crushing her tits; and everything hurt horribly.

Last Rites

God-Form

Lucas walked the Serpent Path once more in the November mist. He'd been walking it every afternoon for a week as he had nowhere else to go during the daylight hours. It was important to keep moving and engage with the raw world in front of his senses. If he paused to introspect , even for a short time, his obsessions with the Quantum Brothers and Carla would start flooding back. And all the time, like a phantom ear-ache, the jabberworkings of the Undermind:

all feasted out and fucked over our dread bodies the dod-man dead no meats for his wakey-wakey...

After his last encounter with Carla in the Unicorn he avoided the inns and now that the village was encircled by Wahibist militia, there was no safe route back to his wrecked bunker in the hillside. Gavin Wharton had given him some rations and had permitted him to sleep 'for the duration' in the bookshop attic where Vivienne had once crafted and sketched. He had offered to assist the bookseller in his frantic efforts to fortify the shop against an alleged threat from Lombard but his attempt to help Wharton fit a metal grill over the shopfront had ended in a twisted cradle of metalwork. Wharton had reverted to painting protective sigils over the doorway, which, given the increasing complexity of phenomena they now faced, seemed a better option.

Lombard remained holed up on the upper floor of the Red Hag. It was rumoured that he was in negotiations with the Islamist militia, but if so there was no sign of action on either side of the roadblock that they had set up by the bus stop on the Old Hallows Road, where, it was said, you could see a pair of militia men asleep at their machine-gun post.

He followed the familiar route yet again. Despite memories of all his astral forays in the Intervoid, which at this moment seemed as faint as worn incisions in an ancient stone tablet, he was still slowly orbiting Leynebridge which was now encircled.

Unicorn Street was almost empty. A few people hurried past clutching boxes of groceries, the fag-end of supplies from Trader Price. A field-hippy from Old Hallows, who'd come in last week to sell his crop of organic veggies and was now trapped in the village, stood on the corner playing a tuneless tin whistle, the lament of a puzzled rodent.

Lucas kept on course. But he felt it was incumbent on him today to divert and visit his old studio in the Tower, even though Noah had effectively sabotaged it by ordering the removal of the antenna. If Wharton grew more paranoid it might offer an alternative shelter.

The street door had been forced, so he was expecting the worst as he climbed the stairs. Drunken Flatheads would have taken the opportunity offered by the chaos of the Feast to steal the equipment, even if they didn't know how to use it.

He lit a match and gazed round the chilly room. There had been an incursion, certainly. Vinyl and CDs were scattered across the floor, boot-prints had stomped across the sleeve inlays for Daniel O'Donnell's Country Hits. He crunched over slivers of plastic disc cases towards the shelves now sagging from the wall. Only the Modern Jazz Quartet and Bohren and the Club of Gore remained untouched, omens he found absurdly reassuring in the midst of the general destruction. The CD and vinyl decks had vanished, ripped out of their racks while the console had been disembowelled, its dials smashed and its panels bent back to reveal a mess of torn cabling and fractured circuit boards. Someone had taken an axe to it. Yet they had ignored the microphone and dusty tape recorder, which still held the spools of his last radio testament. It would never receive an airing now.

He turned to discover black graffiti painted in huge bold strokes over the tatty posters on the wall behind, and realised that the vandalism wasn't mindless, celebrated in some random territorial scrawl. It was very purposeful lettering. *BANISH TECHCRAFT'S EVIL SPELL SILENCE ITS MACHINES FROM HELL URBAN DEVIL WHO DESTROYS SPIRITS OF EARTH WILL KILL YOUR NOISE - A Follower of the True Lore.*

He sat back in his broken chair and tried to silence the damned chat-room of the Undermind for a few minutes *that will shut up his trap can't rape our shops anymore with his orc-muzak and blah-di-balloonie...* This wasn't Flathead idiocy at work. It was the culmination of all the hostility he'd provoked by his very existence in the village. This was a concerted witch-hunt. Probably driven by a few lunatic followers of Forgan, deranged by the deaths of Noah and Elaine and the new threat from the Wahibists. But it only took a few to spell it out, to raise a cone of energy against him, the exiled incomer on the margin of the margins. And it didn't look as if they would be satisfied by trashing the studio. Did Carla really think an alliance, magickal or military, could be forged between the splinter-groups of this imploding enclave?

All the classical paranoias swirled through him. His homelessness, his poverty, the collapse of his relationship with

Carla - had all that somehow been retro-engineered by a few Wiccan Luddites? Or was it karmic feedback from meddling with the Qliphoth all those years ago?

Suddenly he knew what he had to do, however desperate and arbitrary. It would take time; and he had no idea of how he would survive in this place. But no other place would serve. Only here did he have a hope of salvaging something from the wreckage of existence. Forget about exhuming his passions and aetheric entanglements with Carla for there was no reverse-path there. And even the loss of his home and the relics of his mother, the icons of his past - all that seemed irreversible, maybe irrelevant in the light of another imminent apocalypse. For as long as it would take, this would be his home. He had a function at last. He now understood that he needed to raise a current that might bring balance, clarity and articulation to the muddy vortex of energies swirling around Leynebridge which was a microcosm of the conflicts ravaging the land.

He dreaded the working, and had doubts about his skills, but it had to be enacted. He checked the high shelf over the tape recorder for the studio tool-kit, expecting to find it missing. Yet the intruders had overlooked it in their zeal for wrecking the console. The box contained pliers, screw drivers, wire cutters, a small drill, hacksaw, soldering iron, insulating tape. He also found scissors, marker pens and small tins of blue, green and orange paint, destined for a refurbishing of the room that had never happened. They would have to serve as his magickal implements.

He scanned the ruins of the room, seeking fragments for the raw matter of his creation, particles that could be charged by the desperate intensity of his belief - or his need. Surely a pattern would emerge in the wreckage. Crawling on his knees, he sifted through shards of coloured translucent plastic and broken glass, cautiously probing splinters of wood and twisted strips of brushed aluminium. With clumsy fingers he struggled to undo the knots and tangles of frayed multi-core cable spilling over the torn panels of the eviscerated console. Perhaps the knobs and spindles of the equalisers or the curved dials of the meters could also be put to effective use. One of the vinyl gram decks had been dropped near the door, suggesting the raiders had made a hurried exit, so he was able to unscrew a curving tone-arm from its shattered casing.

The first problem was to decide on the size, which was related to key decisions about the means of construction. He could, he supposed, cut a silhouette from a four-foot sheet of plywood that survived intact at the side of the console housing; or he could construct a smaller three-dimensional representation using metal and plastic components from the smashed interior of the unit. Although the latter option was more complex, he wanted the construct to have as much solidity and weight as possible, even if it was smaller. Tubes and condensers from the amplifier could somehow be fused together to form the body. The head presented challenges. He could cannibalise the big skull-shaped mic ("The Poly-Tone 333, endorsed by top producer Jack Cusimano!" according to the box) although it hurt, bitterly, to sacrifice one of the few items that had survived the onslaught. But needs must.

Outside he could hear detonations and distant crackling. Forgan's fireworks or a skirmish with incoming militia? He had to make this work as quickly as possible.

*

After much trial and error he assembled the body by drilling tiny holes in the various tubular components and bolting them together, reinforcing the crooked joints with bands of insulating tape. He used a similar procedure for the legs and arms. Although the limbs seemed spindly, he managed to re-create the stance and proportions of the icon that he fought to keep steady in his mind, sub-vocally intoning the invocations as he worked through the rainy night.

He only paused to gulp some water from the sink in the studio washroom. Hunger and fatigue seemed irrelevant. Likewise, the distant shouts and shots carried on the night wind were no longer a distraction.

The head presented problems, particularly the avian elements like the long beak. He experimented with the broken gram pick-up and the flexible tubing of a microphone mount. They were grotesque. Then he found a long shard of plastic that had the right proportions. With difficulty he succeeded in attaching it to the shell of the microphone, using some contact adhesive he'd discovered at the bottom of the tool box. Tiny blue plastic lenses from the lights on the console became eyes.

As dawn broke he was laboriously weaving a head-dress from the fine wires that had linked the circuit boards. He eventually attached it to the head, and then used the mounting at the base of the microphone to screw the whole head assemblage to the body. The statue now stood, rather precariously, about three feet high. He had to adjust the splay of the feet for greater stability.

At this stage the assemblage seemed crude, a robotic caricature of what he'd envisioned, with its spiky beak and body tacked together from electronic detritus. He'd created a junk sculpture, a skeletal stalking monster from an old science fiction movie. Perhaps colour and decor would transform it.

He applied the paint carefully, trying to control the tremor in his right hand. The lack of sleep was beginning to affect his co-ordination but time was flowing around him quite slowly now, it didn't really matter whether it took hours or days, the grey light outside and the steady drum of rain on the roof formed a continuum that totally enclosed him. He just had to stay with the rhythm of the ritual.

He coloured the face green and painted the long ibis beak dark blue. The wiry headdress had to remain black, the colour of the insulation on the wires, but he could surmount it with a silver mini-cd to symbolise the lunar aspects of the entity. The body he painted a deep orange, which gave a unity to the disparate components.

Waiting for the paint to dry he fell into a shallow trance for an indeterminate time. Tiny hieroglyphic figures appeared to dance at the very edge of his vision as he stared at the forty watt light bulb over the wrecked desk. The light went on and off from time to time, following the vagaries of the electricity supply. But he thought he could still see them, micro-geometrical birds and animals hovering like gnats in the moonlight from the window-slit.

Waking, he anointed himself with cold brackish water, checked the paint and fell to work again. He quickly devised hands - strictly speaking, claws - from strips of thin metal, cut and bent with pliers. He then made a staff from a long metal rod that had held two circuit boards together, and placed it vertically in the extended right hand. To form an ankh, he twisted a loop of wire and suspended it from the left hand. Finally, he created a kilt and sash from sheets of thin card tinted yellow and wrapped them around the body, glueing them into position.

The god-form was almost ready. The god of speech would communicate, here in this improvised temple, where Lucas had so often ranted at the microphone exorcising his demons. The orthodox would say that the deity should be depicted as if in a bas-relief or stele, in stiff and formal elegance. This image had been built from the bottom up, from the rubble of the ruined techno-world. Yet its humble materials had surely been transubstantiated by his energy and will.

For Lucas realised he had been deceiving himself about will. He'd been adrift on the astral for so long he'd risked mutating into a clot of astral mucus, a nasal drip over everything and nothing, sticking his big nose into Carla or Vivienne when he actually needed to will his way towards challenging the digital avatars, the Quantum Archons thrown up by the collective Undermind. This was the real work.

Certain ritual elements were still needed for his operation, according to magickal orthodoxy. He lacked candles, incense, mercury and white wine while an opal would have served well as a focal point. But the statue was already charging. Although he was giddy with exhaustion he had to begin the Invocation soon and turn his hypnogogic state to full effect. He couldn't postpone it now, any more than he could have postponed it all those years ago when Leila and Firestone initiated him after his initial blunder into the Rupture. He prepared himself to vibrate the power words. Thoth was waiting for him, as ever.

Repeatable Experiment

'You know, Dominic, I think we might have a repeatable experiment here. Nice little earner, too…' Rinehart was excited. No sooner had they dragged the Slut out of the immersion suit and tossed her into another bedroom to decompress than they persuaded Ted Barson, Lombard's favourite security guard, to slip it on, as a valued participant in this new Virtual Reality adventure.

The faithful retainer, still turning up for work today despite the security situation, had been disappointed to learn that Mr. Lombard was unwell and unavoidably detained for the foreseeable future and that his personal minding services might no longer be needed. But he was grateful to accept the twenty pounds they offered him as an experimental subject. He'd do anything for the old firm, he told them. He let them crown him with the silver helmet and initiate the software, so mysteriously morphed after the installation of BRAN and the rites at the distant Burrough.

Now they'd detached him from the apparatus and he was lurching around, bumping into Lombard's glass dressing tables, speech slurred with post-Polyverse intoxication. He was trying to regale them with an account of his triumphant career as a fairground wrestler, but it was intercut with anxious flashbacks to other lives as gay beefcake Lobe icon or Heavy Shepherd bankrupt plumber.

Rinehart nodded eagerly as he took notes. 'That's at least three alt.lives he's sampled in as many minutes,' he whispered to Pullman.

'I know you might feel a little disoriented now,' Pullman told Barson, in calm professional tones, 'but I'm sure the effects will wear off as you settle back into the identity you feel most comfortable with.' Barson burped and glared at him with small suspicious porcine eyes.

'I've only put one ad out on the Lobe an hour ago and they're already queuing up.' Pullman pointed to a streaky monitor. Down on the street, amid an overturned ice-cream van and the glass of shattered shop fronts, a line of people was forming a curiously orderly fashion beside the ramp to the corporate underground car park. 'We're obviously tuning into some deep archetypal need here. I'm only concerned that we might not have enough hardware to accommodate them.'

'No worries. This is all software driven. The old suits downstairs will serve. Some of the effects might be exaggerated but that's what you get if you are an early adopter.'

In the adjoining bedroom, Vivienne heard their words as raw phonemes, small grains of noise drifting through the air that wouldn't decode properly because she couldn't make sense of her selves.

She jerked up from the bed and stared into a broken gilt-framed mirror. Two large grey eyes. Straight nose, high brow, full lips. But who was this straggly brunette in torn stage gear?

She tried standing but every movement hurt. Each node of her nervous system was a malignant particle of pain. The pains were constantly changing and interchangeable. They kept pumping around her, flooding up and down through feet, womb, belly, heart, throat and skull. She thought there were some words or prayers she might have once known to control the pain but she couldn't recall them.

A man entered the room, wearing a long face, like an important pedigree horse. He hadn't shaved but he utilised a deep smooth port-wine voice. He seemed authorised to do something drastic.

'Well, QS? How was all that? Going to tell us your secret life histories?'

The syllables slid past her. Her eardrums were hurting. He repeated the question, louder this time, and the words began to fall into a recognisable pattern. Although she didn't understand the abbreviation QS because she was overwhelmed with new memories of her secret histories. She could see the silver sculptures in the gallery and smell the beery crowd at the gig. A jewelled hand fondled her cheek and a choir roared in her ears. She was so overloaded she couldn't say a word.

'We could find a new role for you, you see. To endorse the new product mix. Tell the Lobe audience what they're missing stuck at home in front of their little screens. Do a clip where you tell them you've gone beneath the pleasure zones, into deep multi-time, living out all the dreams!'

She shrugged, turned her back and grovelled on the floor for the remains of some belongings, a bag or an item of clothing that might show where she belonged. In the mirror she could see the horse-face man pursing his lips. It was probably his way of controlling situations.

The other man, sharp-featured and long haired was shaking his head. 'I can't believe it, Dom. She doesn't want to do it. Well, we created you, Slut. We took a Borderland troll in a kaftan and made her a svelte Princess of Lobes. We gave you a cool tag. Jack Cusimano, *the* Jack Cusimano gave you a great production. But you've no gratitude. No gratitude and all attitude…'

'You realize this terminates any contractual arrangement we might have had. So I think it's time you left. A pity, it's getting rather unstable out there.' The prefectorial man, whom she now could name as Pullman gestured to a thick-set person in uniform who'd stomped through the doorway. 'Barson will escort you off the premises. Maybe we can use him, although it won't be quite the same. Such a shame. Although really shame on you for letting us down like this...'

Barson took her as far as the stairs, grumbling bitterly. 'You're on your own now, silly cow. You won't last five minutes out there, I tell you. Were you supposed to be famous? I was supposed to be famous. Pigmeat Daddy, they called me. Ever heard of me? I thought not. Fuck you...'

Spectre in the Red Hag

William was waking. His dreams were the usual slow-fading retro-babel: *cold stars sliding over Sloane Square/ huge coils of protein in the sky/you know Mrs Mahoney put cod-liver oil pills in our jam/ you could only hear rock'n'roll at fun fairs...* He must have been asleep for centuries but it was still dark. He reached over the pillows and thought he'd grabbed the flap of some heavy curtain. The curtain shifted - yet the darkness wouldn't go away, even though he could hear a chorus of squabbling pigeons on the roof and beyond that distant percussive booms. Someone in a street was playing a shrill tin whistle and there was a vague susurration of voices filtering through his eardrums or maybe inside his skull, he couldn't distinguish which, for the sound was mingled with his own harsh breathing. The bed was unfamiliar, too big for his Pleasure Centres cubicle, too soft for Mrs Kalyoubi's. He could smell stale cabbage.

Wherever he was, he couldn't see. In this worrying version of events his visual cortex seemed to have been blanked by sensory overload. On reflection - bad joke - it wasn't even black, it was blank. He was sitting in a not-space. He was void.

He tried to unscramble pixellated memories, his interview (or intra-view/infra-view) with those overminders, the grey-faced Quantum Brothers, the double act of the Uncertainty Principle. Then he could see them. Now he couldn't. He was sick with terror. Was this the best gag from their cruel joke-book, to leave him blinded in some barbarous hinterland between the worlds?

He tried to control a tidal wave of panic. Nevertheless he had mass, volume, tactile and auditory input. There had to be a rational explanation and ultimate solution. It must be a temporary condition. With the right medical help, the right technology… He'd trained himself to be a survivor. So he put a tentative bare foot on rough boards, crooked and uneven. Below he could hear chatter, the rattle of pans, clink of glasses and crockery, perhaps the banter of kitchen porters.

Was he captive in some Leynebridge inn - haunting himself, after all those years, as a sightless spectre in the Red Hag?

He tried getting out of bed; and slowly groped his way around the space. Its rogue protrusions and trick geometry forced him to collide with a wicker hamper and a wooden chest. Then some discarded boots tripped him and sent his shoulder into the knobbly bedhead. He grunted and swore.

A door clicked somewhere, several feet from where he'd been expecting it. The voice sounded just like Liggett, all professional concern. A limp hand was trying to steer him back to bed.

'You must rest, William. Mr Lombard is very anxious for you to make a total recovery. You're a valued member of the team.'

He grabbed Liggett by the hair and they fell on the bed.

'What's going on, Liggett? I can't see a damn thing? What has Lombard done to me?' They scuffled for a moment, Liggett's protests muffled in a muddle of blankets and pillows, before thumping together to the floor.

On the way down, Ligget's head must have struck something hard and wooden - perhaps that damn chest - because he gasped and moaned, before falling silent. They lay there for a moment as if trapped in a homo-erotic clinch. Then William rolled over the inert form of the Human Resources officer and crawled to the door.

He felt his way across some kind of landing, to discover banisters and narrow crooked stairs. He half-slid, half-tumbled down them on his bottom - for a nano-instant that gawky 1950s child playing silly games despite his mother's warning - and landed heavily on carpet amid angry voices, male and female. Somebody dropped a tray of glasses and screamed.

'Lombard's let his zombie out. Disgusting!' A female, querulous. 'I told you, Bill, we should never have let them take the whole top floor. Look what I've got to clear up now...'

'He won't get far wearing those orange pajamas.' The gruff male voice was attempting re-assurance and moving closer. 'Come on now, Prof. Let's be having you.' A hand tightened around his elbow.

'It's that Mister Lombard who should be dealing with him, not us. Where's he gone, anyway? He hasn't gone without paying, has he? You can never trust these God-Wallowers, Bill, I did warn you!'

Suddenly a hard jagged object struck William on the brow. He became briefly deaf as well as blind. More rubble crumbled around him, as he fell to the floor, choking on plaster dust and fumes. Somehow the ceiling had just collapsed. Just like that. Another bad joke. Blood was trickling into his dead eye socket.

Then his ears began chiming. Eventually through hiss and clangour he could pick out the rhythm of a woman's sobs and then words. 'Bill? Bill, are you all right?'

Apparently Bill was hurt. People were shouting now about shifting a beam that had collapsed across the bar but they couldn't get leverage on it because of the wreckage and the top floor had caught fire, there was a bloody extinguisher somewhere...

'Bastards, bastards, bastards... Bartzabel, Lord of Bloodshed, destroy them, Bartzabel, Winged Dog of War, destroy them!' An old man's quavery voice kept repeating his curse, mechanically. And then, over-riding the chaos in the bar, a babel of inchoate cries echoed through the deep structure of William's brain, a sickening alien intrusion he'd never experienced, even when he'd faced the Quantum Brothers.

He realised it signalled a major breach in the protective zone around the community - and that this community's Undermind, so-called, was working in real-time and was now breaking down his automatic psychic defences. His skepticism could no longer defend him. His mental firewall was catching fire. He fought to ride the panic and concentrate. That poor woman was screaming so desperately.

'Bleeding Lombard said he was sorting this out, doing a deal with them! And now they're firing more rockets!'

Although he was now blind, William realised that he might also have become invisible in the general melee, for people were stepping over and around him in their desperation to get out. Cautiously he extended a hand and discovered a stick someone had dropped, maybe one of those magic staffs they flaunted. It would make an adequate cane. He levered himself up between the stomping feet and fanned the cane across the obstructions on the floor, feeling a route towards the acoustic of the streets.

He blundered through a crowd that had gathered outside to watch the Red Hag burn. As he collided with random elbows, he found himself apologising with exaggerated politeness in his old Oxford accent. 'Sorry... I'm most frightfully sorry...'

He heard the whine of an electric motor and a swish of tyres, too close. 'Mind the damn fire-truck!' they yelled.

He bumped into a bollard. That gave him a reference point for finding the line of the kerb. He decided to go right, towards what he hoped would be the centre of town. Surely they had doctors in Leynebridge. It couldn't all be laying on of hands.

*

Gavin Wharton hardly recognised the old man tottering down Dragon Lane, tapping a staff on the flag-stones of the Serpent Path. Was this skeletal figure in absurd pajamas, whispering feebly to himself as he stared blankly ahead really the scientific eminence grise of the Pleasure Centres empire, rumoured ex-husband of Elderseer Elaine? The man blundered into a horse-trough, circled around it and began wandering back in the direction he'd come from.

Wharton agonised. He'd heard the impact of the rocket only minutes ago, could see the smoke rising from the direction of the Red Hag, and had been running to see what could be done. But in the existential moment, this man Crowe needed help.

'Where are you trying to go?'

'A hospital, any hospital...'

'We don't have a hospital as such. Noah Dodd was our principal healer. I'm afraid he died at Leyston Burrough.' Wharton was tempted to add a footnote, that Dr. Crowe might recall the circumstances of the incident. But he couldn't play games with such desperation.

'Surely there's someone, a chemist, an optician…'

'Forgan has his wise women. I could take you there.'

The old man laughed bitterly. 'A fool's errand. "'T'is the time's plague when madmen lead the blind…"'

'King Lear, Act IV, scene 1, Gloucester to his son Edgar, disguised as Poor Tom.' Wharton's response was instinctive, to salute scholarship amid the fuming wreck of things.

'We both have the relics of an education,' muttered William. 'But if these wise women are the best you can do, we better get on with it.'

*

It took longer than expected to reach Forgan's compound at the edge of town. Ripples of the village's collective psycho-angst fuddled their heads, steadily rising in pitch and volume: *why don't they get it over with just do it to us no Mo-Boy robs my house sheep-shagging Lombard's buggered us hear me Amaymon King and Emperor of the Northern Parts strike them with weeping sores Thor must come by Thursday to save the Serpent now the Serpent's teeth will bite poisons seep their sleeps at night Serpent's teeth will win our fight but it doesn't spell quite right…* William's slow progress was further delayed by Wharton's inexperience as a guide and by their need to crouch in ditches as rockets roared overhead.

'Most of them are probably landing in the fields around Old Hallows,' Wharton informed William, attempting an audio commentary. 'Forgan's people will be trying to deflect them by working on the Islamists' sight-lines. I can see some smoke over in

High Town though. Even a sceptic like me must pray, pray to Seshat. The Goddess of Libraries must spare the Book Market, please…' Seshat was the only goddess Wharton still liked. Otherwise, global scepticism was his best defence after the code-blitz of the Great Book, an episode he still couldn't grasp in its entirety. He suspected Dr Crowe might understand the significance of those streaming digits that he'd inadvertently channeled but the doctor was still affiliated somehow with Lombard, so silence was the best course.

In any case, Dr Crowe seemed so traumatised that his responses dwindled to mere grunts as Wharton shepherded him along the rutted walkways of the Path.

Imperfect Martyrdom
Hisham couldn't stay under cover for ever. During the pagans' mad riot on the Hill of Smoke, he'd dodged wildly between hundreds of torchlit painted faces, all mocking him for his folly, his moment of distraction in the struggle with old fool Abdul, as he sought all night long for his lost vengeance weapon, the holy bomb. Then, as the cold dawn broke he knew he had to find a hiding place, to stay low for a while, and pray, just pray…

Finding shelter had been easier than expected. As the townspeople snored in their filthy pits, exhausted by satanic debauchery, he'd broken into a small brick building behind a garage, a chapel of some Christian sect which hadn't been used for years. No pagan would dream of entering. It was cold and bare, a white-walled cell, but he'd discovered candles in the drawer and, as night fell he'd managed to scavenge food (of sorts) from the bins at the back of the ravaged Red Hag. Hearing the occasional thud of another rocket impact somewhere across town he'd felt pride - and fear. To be killed by his own Omar Majid Brigade would be a bitter irony. But to have incinerated his brothers would have been worse. He never expected them to make such rapid progress through the Borderlands. To return to camp with the confession that he'd failed in martyrdom and lost their most prized weapon on an unauthorised mission would risk severe punishment. It would also be a shameful betrayal of Omar.

He'd have to risk at least one more search. Maybe the feather-brained Kaffir party-people hadn't recognised its significance and had simply abandoned it when they realised it wasn't full of alcohol, drugs or sex-magick toys.

So he found himself again at the foot of the accursed hill. He tried to identify the spot where he'd had his terminal tussle with Abdul, that weak-minded old apostate. They could have shared the blessings of martyrdom while this mound of turf with its grey hump of stone could have been a radio-active pyre for hundreds of damned pagans. He scanned the slopes anxiously. Although the social organisation of the pagans had almost disintegrated, if they'd discovered an alien body they would have moved it, surely? In the bleak November afternoon light he could only see sheep and litter.

He wandered for a while, past the corrugated iron hovels on the upper slopes, and paced around the stonework of the Burrough itself. It was like a ghastly parody of the Kaaba, a focal point for pagan worship. Worse still, it had been appropriated by the decadent technocrats of the cities, to judge by the Pleasure Centres stencil on the hoardings around the site. Marks of the Beast. Something very dark and dangerous had been committed here. He felt physically sick that he'd failed to purge the place with nuclear fire. There was no sign of his lost device.

From the summit he could see the tents and trucks of his Brigade in the distance. They hadn't even bothered to camouflage them; and he couldn't understand why their attacks were so desultory. Yet the longer they delayed, the better his chances of recovering the holy weapon.

A while later he was walking through the pagan High Town, and no-one challenged him, despite his paramilitary jacket and baseball cap. A few older people in ragged cloaks drifted past him as if sleep-walking, in a state of shock. Despite the intermittent rocket assaults they were still trying to trade, even if their covered Book Market was now only dealing in a few withered vegetables. The only shop open on the street was one of those general 'boot' stores. On a random impulse, emboldened by the apparent indifference to his appearance, he entered and surveyed the damaged goods within.

A narrow-faced man in glasses was arranging a small pyramid of faded packets and tins on the counter. Old raincoats and petticoats hung on a rail in the corner. The shelves were crowded with the detritus of over-production from the pre-Rupture years: a barbecue sword; a hamburger holder; executive egg-crackers; some wicked pop music memoir *Close-Up: The Close-Fitting Girls*!

Then, a terrible thrill of recognition: on the floor, amid the broken umbrellas and rusty gardening tools, a large black mud-stained suitcase with combination locks. He reached for the handle, just to get a grip on it, to feel in control again. It was too heavy for him to do a runner, you could barely walk with it. He could detonate it here, of course, but the casualty yield would be lower, the symbolic impact of annihilating pagans at play would be dissipated in a botched imperfect martyrdom. He checked the lock. In the chaos of his struggle with old Ahmed he'd never reset the combination. Right now, anyone could prise it open and fiddle with the arming control. His head throbbed.

'Can you read?' The voice behind him was flat but hostile. 'The notice. In English. About not fiddling with the items.'

'How much?' This was only a boot shop. In the City you could buy most of their old crap for a pittance.

'One hundred pounds, in old currency, clean notes. Unless you've got foodstuffs about your person. It doesn't look as if you've got either.'

Hisham scrabbled in the pockets of his combat trousers for change, crumpled notes, trying to cultivate the right sneer.

'Fourteen pounds fifty. All that old case is worth with the junk inside.'

'We don't do haggling, young man. You're not from around here, are you?'

'I'm with Team Lombard. Pleasure Centres.' It was a desperate ruse, and it hurt to deny his identity like this, but he was deep in enemy zones.

'I know Mr Lombard's people. You don't look the type.'

'I'm Security. Undercover…'

'You don't look very secure.' The proprietor picked up a handbell from the shelf behind him.

'No worries. I'll be back.' The expression had a terminal resonance from somewhere. He slammed the door. He'd get the money somehow - maybe come back at night and risk killing the busybody shop-man. But that might only add to his messes. Better to jump some fuddled pagan. Then he could go back, hand over the cash and stroll off casually, bomb in hand, to consider his options alone, communing in secret at the chapel with his magic mineral demi-god. Hisham's mission could still be glorious.

The Arcades of Sleep
Despite the urgency of the Thoth operation Lucas couldn't fight the urge to sleep. He lay down on the studio floor, hoping that a few minutes rest would empower him to face the mysteries of the God. It was only rational after all. Yet as he closed his eyes and drifted into the hypnogogic zone, he became aware that this had been a false strategy, for he was already floating into an astral locale that was permeated with new fears and terrors. The contours of Carla's face sagged and dissolved like a rubber joke mask in the arcades of sleep. Carla, his lost queen, flickering in the terror state, back-projected phantasm of the living dead.

Lost Property
It was closing time and the cocky young man hadn't returned. Trader Price hated punters who said they'd be back with the cash and then never materialised. The Trader shuffled uneasily among his dingy stock, which dwindled by the day. If he could off-load that curious case, he might be able to source more tinned goods with real money. Otherwise he'd have to try boot-bartering with his more demented regulars like old Betty Boothby, who was still collecting china knick-knacks even as the town was daily blitzed by the wretched Wahibists. He supposed that the destruction of a few of the older businesses and the death of cranky busybodies like Noah Dodd and Elaine Crowe might clear the way for future

re-development, but that seemed a remote prospect. The deal with Pleasure Centres had promised so much but now it had all disintegrated. And the Feast at the Burrough had degenerated into total riot and anarchy. It must never happen again. But Mr Lombard had disappeared, along with his false promises of protection and enforcement of the law, not Lore.

He dragged out the heavy case and stared at the mysterious contents. He'd exchanged it for a case of cheap wine when two hung-over revellers dragged it in on the day after their Feast of Smoke. Those mad witches never stopped partying. They'd obviously stolen it but since his days as a field-booter he'd learned that a Trader never asks too many questions.

Yet questions were nagging him. Suppose the slick dark youth was right and really was an emissary of Lombard, working undercover for Pleasure Centres disguised as a Wahibist? Or - it seemed unlikely, but anything was possible in these crazy times - the lad was working for the Heavy Shepherds? He'd even heard rumours that Lombard had become a Heavy Shepherd now. You didn't know who or what you were dealing with.

He studied the dials on the panel in the case. He had no idea what they meant, but they signalled high technology, power of some kind. This object must surely be valuable to Lombard. If it was the property of Pleasure Centres, then maybe he should risk sacrificing an unlikely cash transaction and return the lost property directly to its owners. He might still find a few proper security people up at the Burrough. There could be a reward.

The Invocation

PROCUL, O PROCUL ESTE PROFANI,
BAHLASTI! OMPEHDA!

In the name of the Mighty and Terrible One, I proclaim that I have banished the Shells unto their habitations.

Lucas couldn't stop shaking. His throat was dry and his voice trembled in the first line of the Invocation. The Shells, those Qliphothic husk-demons who'd been activated in the Rupture - how could he have banished them with a simple angelic pentagram rite? Their presences might be floating in the dusty air, dark helices of disruptive force, permeating the shattered console that had become his altar. The dissolving image of Carla still haunted him. Lucas was convinced for a moment that a greenish micro-nebula spun slowly across the room, obscuring his ramshackle shrine, but he tried to focus on the angular figure at the centre, his replica Thoth.

I invoke Tahuti, the Lord of Wisdom and of Utterance, the God that cometh forth from the Veil! O thou, Majesty of Godhead, Wisdom-crowned Tahuti, Lord of the Gates of the Universe, Thee, Thee I Invoke!

As he intoned, breathing deeply, standing erect in the posture poor dead Richard Firestone had taught him so long ago, he tried to mould his tongue around the archaisms and scry beyond the crude robotic icon he'd constructed, to envisage the austere and elegant God as depicted in papyri, like Hunefer's Book of the Dead in whatever was left of the British Museum. Yet this icon was charged with his labour, his force, his tiny bit of chaos. He would serve the God and the God would be his servitor...

O thou of the Ibis head Thee, Thee I invoke! Thou who wieldest the Wand of Double Power, Thee, Thee I invoke!

The studio acoustic had been deadened with makeshift cork tiling and strips of carpet but his voice was vibrant now, entering a vast space, even as the geometry of the room seemed to warp and expand to the rhythm of his speech-forms, God-forms of the Speech-God. His tatty icon must morph into a divine artefact, emanating light and numinosity.

Thou whose head is as an emerald and Thy nemyss as the night, blue sky, Thee, Thee I invoke!

Thoth stood silent and motionless in the darkened space. Lucas was half-aware that the God was still formed from a bricolage of an old microphone, broken tubes, fractured capacitors and transistors, cobbled together with cable and tape. Yet these fragments of broadcast technology had been charged over months with his words, his passionate speech, as he talked into the void of night, his speech fed back through the head-set. The God of the Akashic Archives would ready himself to record his speech. Now his voice re-sounded in the God's praise-song, and resonated with a waveform emerging at the edge of his hearing, which was steadily increasing in amplitude. The silhouette of his graven image, his strange god, merged into the stern profile of Thoth/Tahuti scribed on a stele, record-keeper of the funerary texts. As a dim blue halo of light flickered and flared around the statue's ibis head, Lucas, a lucky light-bearer at last, let the repeated vocatives of the invocation play with/in his hearing - faint at first - but the signal was flowing, he was going with it. An external source was flowing into him...

The God who commands is in my mouth! The God of Wisdom is in my heart! My tongue is a Sanctuary of Truth! And a God sitteth upon my lips.

His whole body was vibrating now with each burning inhalation of breath. Perhaps he was breathing raw orgone, prana, vril - electrocution by the life-current. This vocal he shared with Thoth roared around his head. He felt irradiated, waves of pain that pulsed through his skull synchronising with the flashing aura that enfolded him into the icon of the God.

Therefore do Thou come forth unto me from Thine abode in the Silence: Unutterable

Wisdom! Al-Light! All-Power! Thoth! Hermes! Mercury! Odin! By whatever name I call Thee,

Thou art nameless to Eternity: Come Thou forth, I say, and aid and guard me in this work of Art.

He felt a silence, a release from pain. Maybe he fell silent for a time. He couldn't measure the time-lapse for only Thoth had partitioned all space-time. Thoth was the star-maker/star-seeker on the Watch-Towers of the Universe; and he, Lucas, would be a mere utterance in the blazing void.

The geometry kept changing. His eye was re-drawing the ratios of floor, wall and ceiling, as the outlines holding the space together shifted - expanding, dissolving and reforming around him. The cubical expansion of the space was proportional to the inhalation and exhalation of breath in the burning tree of his lungs. He was entering deep time, into a temenos, a temple. He was written into a story about Hermopolis, the temple of Thoth, deep in the Egyptian centuries. His heart beat fast as a bird and he hoped the repetition of the invocation would continue scripting him into existence for it was written in thousands of tiny hieroglyphs that had begun flowing across the surfaces of the rising granite pillars and the massive stelae embedded in the walls.

He strained to see the God. For a moment his sight was obstructed by a web of darkness across his eyeballs. He was blinded in the presence of Thoth. Then he understood that his vision was filtered through a net, a network of flashing nodes and threads that interconnected all the galaxies hanging like lanterns in the darkness of the temple.

Through the veil of the net he perceived the huge lunar God raised on a quartzite obelisk. His crescent head-dress and curved beak gleamed in a narrow shaft of moonlight from a slit in the roof. He held his tablet and stylus, presenting them to Lucas as a gift and a terrifying obligation.

Thoth was the tongue of Ra. He, the Lucas-entity, was the tongue of Thoth, who was speaking now, twisting his tongue, vibrating high in his larynx. His speech was a high-frequency screech, a burst of avian ultrasonics, like satellite code, stellar emissions, a language that was faster than light.

A low female voice was translating for him. He recognised her from some buried shard of memory - or pre-cognition - as Seshat, Thoth's daughter, Keeper of the Scrolls.

You have passed the Pylon of Tehuti and entered the House of the Net at Khemmenu. What do you seek?

The Thoth-signal fell silent. The carbon-based life-form known as Lucas tried to formulate the right words in the rite order. The generic formula in the rite *Make all spirits subject to me* wasn't specific. He had to word his request absolutely precisely. The magick might otherwise dissipate - or worse. Everything threatened to distract him. For he was still aware, at some level of the gestalt, that he stood in a dingy room crammed with electrical junk gesticulating before his scrap-metal idol.

He knew too that he had to enunciate the words in his own

voice. And he was all too conscious of the absurdity of himself, as a minute point of transition in the over-arching darkness of the universe, attempting this interface with an intelligence that was so alien - and yet so familiar. His familiar, perched invisibly behind his right shoulder all these years. Eventually the words came.

'I need to learn a secret - to restore balance - *ma'at* - to the Kingdom. Before we destroy it all.'

The God spoke in a burst of black noise. Lucas fought to retain fragments of the translation as Thoth's message pierced the right lobe of his brain.

There is no secret. See through the Net and beyond the Veil. Untie entanglements. Let the web unravel. Each brother has a number. Each star has a number. The numbers are in the book. The numbers of being and not-being. Re-write the numbers. Then all the scribes will balance the books, between force and fire.

All was silent again. For a second he caught a glimpse of Seshat, walking proudly in her leopard-skin robe carrying her scrolls, before Thoth dissolved in a burst of white light, and he blacked out.

He awoke. A narrow band of light from the studio window had moved half-way across the dusty floor. The effigy of Thoth lay on its side. The head and body had been fused into a single veined conglomeration of metal and plastic, yet strangely shapely. The remains of the console had been incinerated, yet there was no sign of burning in the rest of the room, which was filled with the scent of storax.

The treacherous concealments of flesh

Carla needed somewhere to sleep. Night was falling and all doors would be closed to her in Leynebridge, which had effectively curfewed itself in cellars awaiting some final bombardment. She wrapped a grubby blanket around her shoulders. She'd sleep with anyone for the sake of clean sheets, as opposed to huddling on the flagstones of the Book Market. It wasn't the danger that bothered her. The possibilities of death only heightened her need for a full-length in-depth space-fuck. Since her phantom copulations with Lucas, her succubus poses for the Harvesters, and her chaotic sodomising of Lombard, which had released such an unexpected sub-personality, the current of *vril*/life-force/orgone pulsed through her like a signal from a neutron star. The field-effect of her sex was dissolving all boundaries between bodies, actualising a deeper sexual fusion/fission reaction than any of her simulated copulations on the Lobe. She was everybody's; and every body. So her body was going to burn out fast. She needed somewhere to sleep.

She entered the narrow ally behind the Tower. Lucas had confessed how he'd acted out his little psychodramas in its upper room. Perhaps he had holed up there again, now there was no safe route back to his wrecked bunker in the hillside.

Yet she couldn't see a light; and someone had padlocked the side door - and inscribed an elegant graffito across it, in green metallic paint. She squinted in the gloom, and realised she was looking at a hieroglyph. Only Lucas could have written it. She couldn't read the glyphs of Hermopolis but she had a vague sense of recognition. The sign must be demarcating the Tower as a sacred space, maybe a forbidden space, a danger zone.

She heard footsteps behind her, and turned. A young man, muscular, quasi-military kit, maybe Anglo-Asian, was positioning himself to mug her. She knew that urban body-language - and felt the vicious grip on her neck as he tore away the blanket.

'Give us your money, bitch. I want everything you've got.' She froze. After all she'd been through - Lucas, Lombard, the Harvesters - this was absurd, banal melodrama. What a way to go. But he wasn't going to let go - and she was finding it harder to breathe.

'Bullshit. Bet you haven't got a weapon.'

He was trembling but defiant. 'I gotta a weapon that can roast you alive, baby.' He'd maybe learned the line from an ancient action movie, but couldn't get the intonation quite right. Another level of unreality for her to fall through. Someone had told her that the thing with psychos was to keep them talking.

'Is that a threat or a promise?'

'Give us the cash, bitch…' His anxiety was somehow more terrifying than her fear. She gave up any attempt at resistance. He emptied her shoulder bag with his free hand and a few coins tinkled to the ground. He swore.

'What you see is what you get.' She was trying to play at urban cool, but all she could see in front of her senses in this narrowing life-slot was an angry mouth centimetres away from her cheek and a taut forearm driving the fist tightening around her neck. She felt his crotch grinding against the silk of her dress. They were going to enact one of her old touchie-feelies, a rough back-alley shag, except she wasn't going to be part of the consensus on this one, because she intuited an enormous black-hole desperation in his breathing and a deep ambivalence in his eyes. He wanted her and hated himself for it.

She felt his fingers clawing at the zip of her dress. The moment was splitting right open, she was up for grabs - but had to keep him talking.

'What's your name?'

'Shut the fuck up, pagan whore!" Yes, she was content to be a pagan whore, whatever… She knew where he was coming from now.

'You're on a mission, aren't you?'

'I'm fighting for the Omar Majid Brigade. To destroy your whoredom…'

Omar. Omar Majid. A lithe bronzed torso in candlelight. Urgent lips on her breasts. An internal email that had eviscerated her. His liquid eyes crudely daubed on a flame-lit banner.

'I knew an Omar Majid once. I'm called Carla.' Her name was a non-sequitur. But she needed to fill the silence between them, which wasn't silence, because she could hear his rapid breathing, and the distant percussion of gunfire on the night wind.

He relaxed his grip; and for a few seconds, she thought there might be a common bond, space for negotiation, some alternative outcome, uneasy peace.

He examined her face closely as if it was a curious pagan artefact he had just looted, trying to place it, to give it a historical context. Then recognition hit, the full fury of his thoughts flooded her brain, as his hands tightened around her neck. Despite himself, he had accessed the Undermind, telling its old old story, recycling its dream of itself, specially for him.

This crazy Kaffir woman bitch goddess didn't believe in Time itself, her viewpoint zoomed, uncontrollably, towards that bloody sun, its transfusions of nostalgia and lust to this pale dead hand, a human hand puffy in the deed, the act of penetration, sniffing and growling, entering that dogmeat of Soft Darkness Herself, mere phantom tissue, trembling. A screen display turned black, bloodshot, turning him into an infidel automobile bomblet. A deja vu, pale humanoid. No more Time.

Hisham was static, stuck in a fabulation of time but he knew the true story. This was the woman whose wicked tales had trapped Omar as she cradled him in her limbs and then entangled his veins and neurons in a knot of bloody blots to become her dead animal.

A sign flashed high on one of the northern towers, a mad monster mole torture chamber, while she was whispering something indeterminate, - and then the click of There is no God but God. When his field of vision stabilised again, he caught sight of sex to reveal the intersection of seduction.

He was time-sharing moments with Omar. This was the Othermost, the horrorshow hairy maw that had doomed his brother, the multi-part trickster goddess who burned out his gene pool in her black helicopters for a profit margin, played those urban war games, pagan sexperimenter walking the streets. It was dying time.

She invited him to do some market research about new virtual reality gaming, its hideous parody of Paradise. As they'd coupled a red giant sun sank between the contours of his pectorals, her lips blundering against him. 'You tell him try Venusberg Quality! Worth big nurdle!'. Omar grimaced as the roasting of the limbs was done by a human man. Now Allahs were scrolling across a battery of flickering screens…

He was being called from Paradise. No more gropes. He was locked into this serial, he just needed to triangulate the actions. Old Shahidah, old Abdul, now this young Carla. He was called Hisham, from 'hashama' meaning 'to crush', the name chosen for this eternal moment, crushing her resistance, the resistance of trachea, larynx, the treacherous concealments of flesh.

Fissile Existences

A Great Void

Lucas woke. It was neither night nor day, a grey space. He felt like a back-projection of the living dead. There had been a huge turmoil of a dream about Carla which had spiralled away leaving a great void, an odd silence at the back of his mind. There had been shouting in the dream or in the night? He should have acted on it, somehow. But she was beyond his help, always on her own dizzying trajectory. The Thoth Rite might have helped her, might save them all, if he could just muster his energies again. The times were multiplying too fast.

A Line of Force

Aran rode hard through the outskirts of the city, towards a hot core of malign energies. He couldn't articulate it, he couldn't tune in to any brain-chatter or imagery. He only sensed a swirling coagulation of menace that engulfed Viv, maybe thousands of others. Whatever she'd done, he had to find her and have it out. Exhausted after hours, day and night, in the saddle he'd acquired a nasty burn on his left arm after a skirmish with some masked scavengers near a service station, who were trying to frighten Fairfoot with a petrol bomb.

He'd fought them off, with the surprising help of a muscular Neo-Papist hedge-priest, in hiding from both Shepherds and Wahibists, who'd then offered him whisky, soup and bandages in a garden shed. Now the urgency of his mission sustained him. Even his anachronistic appearance, a dreadlocked sword bearer on horseback, created a flimsy cloak of invisibility as he galloped around a Wahibist watch-tower or the Shepherd's roadblocks of overturned vans. In their bleary eyes he was a chronoclastic delusion, a game-avatar given a brief flicker of half-life by Shaitan or Satan - best not to look…

He followed a line of force that would lead to Viv, whatever she had become. The closer he came to the centre of the city, through streets and squares that he had only seen in faded pre-Rupture postcards, the emptier the wrecked streets became, although the sense of approaching some kind of psycho-vortex grew stronger. Now that he was closer to Vivienne geographically, his mental image of her had blurred, in the effort of suppressing her Quantum Slut persona. He couldn't quite erase those incomprehensible couplings projected onto that murky sphere on Elaine's altar. If he recovered Viv, would that redeem him after his unthinking slaughter of Elaine? *Kill the old man and his talking heads… bury them in the depths of the earth…* That was Elaine's last request, his mission. Now he was far from the depths of Leyston Burrough and the old man could be wandering anywhere, or maybe dead, which might absolve him from the task, if not from the guilt and karmic feedback.

The Undermind was different here, a thin malignant hiss, nasal insinuations snaking around the backside of his head *there you go kissing your fiery arse goodbye allover again cos your love-pump ain't thumping.* He fought to control its incomings, to recall the martial disciplines of his old rune master. *We sing crouching, we sing with fists extended for each rune has a fighting function, and the tone/bodyform shapes the ond, the vril, the force-forms working through us, aligning us with God-beings in Asgard and Ancestors in Helheim.* He tried striding defiantly down the centre of the road, projecting a sphere of white light encircling his head, a red radiance pulsing in his heart, a jet of blue fire for the member that would impregnate his mate, and black pillars of iron for his feet steadily marching towards her.

He passed a group of young men rummaging through wicker hampers in the broken window displays of Fortnum and Masons. They seemed to be oblivious to the sound of shouts and sirens - some kind of disturbance in this area called Piccadilly. Uncertain of how his exhausted horse would cope in a riot situation, he dismounted and tethered the animal to a lamp post. He told himself he'd be back for Fairfoot, once he'd found Vivienne, that he'd hoist her on the saddle and they'd ride off westwards towards the setting sun. Surely the force of the Lore would prevail, somehow. Trying to suppress his unease about leaving the vulnerable creature, he strode through broken glass and torn placards towards the epicentre of the disturbance.

A Compression of Bodies

Vivienne wandered through the chilly afternoon, shivering in her torn stage gear. Sunlight shone intermittently through the hazy overcast. There were high wailing noises far away and possibly distant gun shots. She was desperate for sanctuary, a hidden place where some ancient presences – before the Rupture, before the Pleasure Zoning – might have created a stable singular realm of peace. The alt.lives kept flashing back, and as she crossed the junction of glass-strewn Oxford Street and Tottenham Court Road, sidestepping discarded kebabs and cartridge cases, she had to process a distinct memory of gnawing lumps of beef wrapped in a thick bun at a garish red-and-yellow café packed with dozens of gobbling people, her alt.mate Georgia's idea of a hot fat snack. It was a sub-life, she told herself, but the Undermind told her *big eats my udderbunny*. Perhaps if she escaped from the fractured fascias of the retail sector, she could avoid triggering these bouts of trans-temporal disorientation.

She let her feet guide her across the scarred tarmac towards the sagging canopy of a theatre that the Shepherds had once converted to a church. A gold Christ-figure, high on the frontage and twice life-size, hung over the entrance at a crazy angle. As her footsteps echoed against the high buildings, it slipped and crashed to the pavement only a few feet behind her, fragmenting into shards of dusty fibreglass. Her tentative shuffle suddenly became a run and she lurched forward in a panic attack, moving north now past storefronts plastered with flyers and graffiti from the rival urban factions. This parade of shops had once specialised in electronics during the pre-Rupture boom years. Now only the Fast Fun Electric franchise remained, its placards proudly announcing: 'Decentralise Pleasure in a Zone of Your Own - our new Private-Reality System coming soon!' But the shop front had been smashed and the squashed cardboard mock-up of a silver VR booth, like an aluminium coffin had been knocked over and adopted as an improvised bed by some grimy transient who might even now be lurking behind the dusty counter. And turning, she noticed a group of half a dozen male figures in gas-masks loitering in the middle of the Oxford Street intersection behind her. They were testing their whips.

She hurried on, turning right into a side street, hoping to find quiet leafy squares and elegant terraces, as her ruralised grandmother had once described, in a rare moment of pre-Rupture nostalgia for the wonders of the city. There was a district called Bloomsbury and at its centre there was supposed to be a great Museum housing the artefacts of ancient civilisations, a treasure house with high columns and lofty porticos, a serene wisdom enclosure where she might find refuge from the ongoing natter of the Undermind: *she's selling off her cunt she's sold her cut of our spawn my snouts got the pain capsules and your average sicky notelets.* She increased her pace, as if that futile gesture would evade the all-pervasive psycho-static.

The street opened onto a wide square. Railings enclosed a large garden at its centre, apparently some sort of private enclave for the residents, but the academic and publishing offices bordering the square were boarded up. Viv wondered what dark rites might have been committed in the thick shrubbery behind those railings and only edged her way around the perimeter of the square with great reluctance. She heard a faint squeaking sound on the far side and almost turned back. Then a small grey-faced boy, maybe seven came around the curve of the railings, pedalling with great concentration on a rusty tricycle. He wore wiry spectacles, a torn grey blazer and schoolboy cap, a comic-strip child from a lost decade. Ignoring Viv completely, he slowly trundled past, on his apparently circular journey. Conscious of the child's vulnerability in the post-Rupture chaos, Viv almost turned to say something, to ask about a parent, a home. But what help could she offer? She waited a few minutes, despite her fear that those men with gas-masks and whips might catch up with her, or that other predators would materialise. She tried to focus on this singular time and space, ignoring nagging alt.life side-effects as Vanessa or Vandella, screening out the drone of the Undermind: *he was wiggering all his bits round and around the time I compressed his scream into an old jiffy bag in a jiffy...* The boy reappeared again, still stolidly pedalling. This time Vivienne ventured a vague greeting, some sort of hello, she didn't even know what she was saying. The child didn't stop in any case. But as the squeak of his wheels died away, so his outline seemed to blur and dissolve against the bushes that overgrew the railings. He was suddenly all gone.

She had perhaps inadvertently animated a haunting. A low-level Chronoclasm from a pre-Rupture epoch, a child on an eternal orbit of the square. Would her image be captured and recycled in the same way? Or had the essence of the child himself been trapped in this circular limbo? It was essential now to keep moving.

A few empty streets later she was facing the massive pediments of the Museum - but paused at the gates. Through the railings she could see large groups of tourists wandering up and down the wide steps, women in chadors with push-chairs eating ice-cream as their children darted about the forecourt chasing pigeons. A grey-haired man in lederhosen was fumbling with a guidebook. It was as if the grounds of the Museum created a protected Zone, away from the fury of the streets, where some comfortable version of linear normality might continue, as her grandmother in Leynebridge had once described. Emboldened, she made for the entrance and thrust her way into the crowded lobby area .

She could not understand why tourists still appeared to be drifting into the Museum. Maybe recent events had imprisoned in London, hostages to their package tour, or they remained there as ectoplasmic parodies of themselves, as three-dimensional and empty as holograms. Yet the presence of these visitors was overwhelming, especially at close range. They crowded around her, their swollen back-packs and bags emitting a musty smell, while their flesh, whether dark or pale had a waxy bloom. They streamed around the displays with the random motion of molecules, the slow erratic persistence of zombies. They clustered at the base of the huge granite head of Pharaoh Amenhotep III, they eddied around the Stela of Ashurbanipal. They were compulsively irradiating the massive Assyrian bearded kings and masks of Memnon with their desperate tic to capture imagery. As if image-capture would amass a stock of icons to ward off Rupture, or safely position themselves, posing in groups against the Old Gods, in the karaoke of world history. Their groups were focused on becoming signified, significant. Despite everything they were going to photoshop themselves in somebody's reality. So they were acting out this flickerama amid the mummy cases and shabtis. But Horus the Hawklord could surely see through them, even with his single damaged eye.

They astrally buffeted her with their huge rucksacks and bellyfuls of Nikons. She was beginning to panic again, fearing their presence would trap her in the Egyptian galleries. She stumbled ankle-deep in litter across the Great Court towards the side galleries. She was soon disoriented by the polyglot glossalic mumbling around her as the phantom-like visitors cooed vaguely at the cabinet where Dr. John Dee's magick mirror, his black disc of obsidian, and his crystal sphere lay untouched. Other cases had been stripped for gold by grave-robbers in Nikes but the scrying stone and the magick mirror remained untouched.

Vivienne stood in awe. Elaine had always refused to discuss Dr

Dee's Enochian System, his calls and commerce with the Entities of the Aethyrs. It wasn't true Lore for her grandmother, not part of her Earth-Mothering. Vivienne clung to the side of the display case, hoping the crowds would ignore her, as indifferent as that little shadow of a boy on his trike. A long file of Asian visitors slowly straggled past. Their lips were moving noiselessly as they followed their audio guidebooks. The glass of the display cabinet began to vibrate with a faint bell tone. She prayed that the nearest visitor, a large Chinese youth in his Love London t-shirt, wouldn't point his camera phone in her direction. She was certain that he would frame her, point and click her into his own ghostly continuum, leeching on her life-force as he vamped her image in his desperate consumption of space-time. But the boy lurched towards her, a soft untouchable fat-zombie.

She spun to elbow him away, toppled and crashed into the glass panel of the display, cracking it inwards, groped for balance – and realised that she was grasping Dee's crystal. As the boy lumbered away, she looked down into her bloodied palm. She was clutching a tiny node of radiance, a stellar portal into which she might sink her shrinking self. And she was a grave robber now. She pushed through the murmuring bodies towards the exit, seeking the street, any street.

*

She must have suffered a temporary memory lapse. A new sort of chronoclasm, one she had not experienced before. She couldn't stop thinking about becoming Vanessa, going on shopping sprees with Georgia, like the time her partner had persuaded her to splash out on the purple leather boots. That alt.life overlaid the muddle of events in the big white mausoleum or museum. Vivienne only remembered elbowing her way through a solemn shuffling crowd that threatened to stifle her with sheer weight of numbers. Now she, whoever the fuck she was, had a mystery artefact weighing down her back pocket. Somehow she'd fled back to the West End. It was the logical thing to do at the End of the West.

This street was called Prince William Street, formerly New Regent Street. She remembered it vaguely as one of many upscale locations she'd encountered when she first arrived in the city, but her preoccupation now was trying to stalk versions of herself that shimmered at the edge of her vision, hiding in the drapes of window displays or liquefying in the floor-length mirrors of the boutiques.

She entered a retail outlet of some kind, stepping over the toppled mannequins, and began tearing clothes off the rails - gowns, kaftans, cloaks - something that Veronica or Vanessa or Vandella might try on. Experiments with frocks might decode her multiplex timelines. She needed to find that something that fitted, that would help her to walk out of the door into a singular reality.

As she hurled costumes to the floor, the dusty air pulsed faintly with vocoded voices and the throb of drum machines, the in-store music system still looping despite the absence of customers. Yet she was convinced the chatter of could still penetrate her at the ultrasonic end of the frequency. These perforations of ghostly noise sustained an illusion of timelessness as she fingered the zips and tags of her deviant coutures.

But the trance was disrupted by louder noise at the mid-frequencies of the street. Another music was echoing down the glassy canyons of the shopfronts - guitars and voices distorted in the zeal of their praise-songs, the fervent electric anthems of the Heavy

Shepherds. The music was mixed in with shouts, screams and barked commands, over-ridden by the roar of diesel engines.

She dropped the gown she'd been playing with and stepped out, to walk around the curve of the street towards the junction with the Circus, centre of the sonic vortex.

A large military vehicle, its khaki hood embellished with the Cross of Blood was slowly circling the intersection, rear caterpillar treads steadily chewing up the tarmac. Heavy-duty bars and panels extended from the front, forming a kind of scoop like an earth-moving digger. Similar caterpillar trucks were converging on the Circus from New Lombard Street - formerly Shaftesbury Avenue - and other adjoining thoroughfares.

The vehicles were surrounded by foot-soldiers in blue tabards, tugging at eager mastiffs or brandishing whips as they corralled a confused and terrified straggle of young people, some obviously still recovering from the revelation of their fissile existences in the alt-life portals of the revived Pleasure Centres. Many were even younger than Viv, she realised, vulnerable to the multiplicity of the portals, the dazzling array of lost lives that had briefly taunted them in the brief embrace of a Pleasure Centres digital carapace. Other clusters of people were being driven in across the junction towards them, to form a thickening mass around the plinth at the centre of the Circus.

As they were hustled together like cattle, Viv's vision flickered through sepia, black/white, spotty photogravure and back to glaring colour but the churning centripetal motion of the bodies in their forced circumambulation remained a constant. She felt for the crystal in her back pocket, struggling to remember what it was for, and exactly how she'd acquired it, in the hope that it might offer some talismanic protection, if only she knew more. But she was trapped in the moment. This actuality was not going away.

At the centre of the tumult, a Shepherd with a chain-saw hacked eagerly at the head of the Eros statue, while others were throwing ropes around the trunk, clearly determined to demolish this monument condoning sensuality and licence.

At the periphery, a young man in a pink cloak tried to dodge the round-up and make a break for Air Street; but a guard tripped him and the half-track swung towards him. Viv heard his scream as the bull-bars caught his body, before it was crushed beneath the treads.

She crouched, shaking, behind the arches of the colonnade at the corner of the street, but the Shepherds were fanning out with their batons to pull in any back-sliders. Any escape routes were blocked. She'd already been spotted by a tall man with a club and a foaming dog. The canine snarl and the mouthful of human teeth were working in unison. His leather-gloved hand grabbed at her hair while his club gave her a sickening blow to the stomach, sending her stumbling into the mass of contorted screaming faces.

They all smelled together, a plurality of oil, patchouli, pheromones, urination, old dope and methylated spirits, all the odours of the old city. But she could scarcely inhale in the relentless crush of arms, elbows and bellies, a compression of bodies thrust into sexual intimacy by their zealous overseers. She was wedged between a busty young woman in a mohawk, probably ex-Pleasure Centres, and two elderly men in leather mini-skirts who were crying in short bursts, their cries half-stifled by the increasing pressure on their rib-cages.

For the crowd had swelled, fused together by the menace of

the roaring diesels. 'There's blood on those tracks,' screamed a high male voice. Slowly they were being herded down Lower Regent Street in the direction of the Mall, the posse of Shepherds anticipating every breakaway move and cracking their whips as they sang along with the thunderous god-rock.

Blocked ever tighter, the captives endured their forced congregation on the Mall. Then they stampeded in slow motion through the overgrown lawns of the Park. The trucks churned across the gravel paths, demolishing memorial benches and litter bins as they swerved back and forth to keep their captives securely kettled.

She could see scaffolding and flags rising behind the trees at the far end, on the far side of the lake. They seemed to heading towards some kind of new amusement park.

Women's Mysteries
Forgan had created his private living quarters at the far end of his huge barn, in a large sagging yurt. Wharton had never been invited into this sanctum, perhaps because Forgan sensed the bookseller's ambivalence to the local Lore. Nevertheless the desperation in William's disjointed body language as they blundered through Forgan's heaps of old Feast regalia was overcoming the vestiges of Wharton's bourgeois reticence.

William could hear female voices, indistinct chanting, soft beats on a djembe. They paused. Then, as the sounds faded, Wharton pulled back the flap of the tent.

He peered through incense fumes into the candle-light, scanned a tapestry depicting the Serpent Path, a clutter of statues and shrines - a shrine to Cerunnos, a shrine to Loki and a shrine to Papa Legba, all the god-forms you could mix and match…

Five women stood in a small circle, gripping hands. They were naked, elaborately tattooed with black and crimson sigils. A working had just ended.

'What do you want?' Willow, a full-figured blonde, Forgan's chief consort, Earth Goddess archetype, stared him down, sky-clad and proud of it.

'I need Forgan's help. This man has lost his sight.'

'Forgan's asleep. We must have exhausted him.' Little Rowan, Forgan's youngest partner giggled. Willow threw her a reproving glance.

Wharton guided William to a sofa and settled him down. The old man was still anxiously probing his surroundings with the staff but Wharton gently disengaged it from his hand, letting it fall to the floor. Rowan picked it up, ran slim fingers over it, smiled as she showed off her new trophy to Rose.

'There must be something you can do for him. He's a victim of Tech-craft.' Wharton hoped that might appeal to some vestige of a common fellowship in the Lore.

'He's the grand architect of Tech-craft, isn't he?' Willow curled a lip in scorn. 'In deep with the Carbonites, wallowing in the gut of Pleasure Centres up at the Burrough. Don't lie, Gavin Wharton. We know. He brought this affliction on himself. The Law of Three Fold Returns...'

'I thought you swore an Oath to harm none and help all.'

'We thought you had a loyal bonding with the Lore, were a true friend of poor Noah and Elaine. But you traded with Lombard, just like Price. So the writing of our Great Book was accursed. You could only write evil ciphers. And now the town's surrounded by One-God fanatics, we're under siege, our children are terrified.

Why should we help this man?'

The man William listened as they argued, talking about him as an alien entity. Maybe that's all he was. He could smell pungent herbal smoke, sense the footfalls of the women on thick rugs, hear the distant wail of a baby. Otherwise, he was in the void and the void was within him.

Willow seemed to be making some concessions. 'Before we do anything, I want him to speak for himself. Can you hear me, old man?'

The old man grunted. He'd tell them whatever they wanted to hear, anything to find an aperture of light in this dark fog. This woman's aromatic body was edging across the cushions towards him. She was whispering fiercely, gesturing - he could hear the chink of her bracelets and chains.

'If we give you vision, what will you give us? There has to be an energy exchange.' Fingertips brushed his wrist. 'Maybe a sacrifice…'

What could he give? His energies had all been discharged long ago. All he had was darkness, silence and corrupted memory.

'We follow our craft with nature, you followed your craft with the grey sciences. You can make and unmake.'

He couldn't make anything up any more, he was a mere greyish ghost of a gnome, what could he do, what did they expect of him? Nothing would come of this. He was eternally locked into this helmet of darkness.

'You can unmake their Lobe. Set everyone free. Stop all the fighting that it aggravates. It's the only way. The circle we've made around Leynebridge won't last for ever. Forgan is burning out. You have to cut out the Lobe, cut it out of our lives.'

Wharton couldn't follow Willow's thought-patterns. She couldn't make these impossible demands of this sick old man, vamping him into another delusion. It was out of character. But all characters were blurry and unrecognisable now. These witches didn't understand.

'He's not in a position to do that. Not in this time-frame. He hasn't got the resources, the technology.'

'The vision will give him all he needs…'

'Let me see… just let me see.' William's fingers clutched at thin air, trying to find his bearings in the darkness of his private space-time.

'You can't deliver this, Crowe. The astral path is blocked.' Wharton didn't know where that statement came from - he was being infiltrated by a sub-personality or was sliding into a sub-time zone, whatever that was. The artefacts around the yurt were glaring at him.

The little crystal sphere on Willow's altar was beginning to glow with a faint orange radiance while the candles guttered in sync with his pulsing brain. Those zeros and ones were flickering again in the corner of his red eye, he couldn't help their incessant tic. Perhaps it was hunger. He'd eaten some old tinned figs and a biscuit twenty-four hours ago. Instead of quixotic attempts to heal the blind he should have gone foraging or haggled with Trader Price for some more cans. For Willow's agenda was skewed, out of desperation. Yet Gavin Wharton had to see it through.

She was already guiding William towards the altar. Rowan and the other women clustered around her, handing her ritual implements. She took a small mirror on a metal stand and arranged it centrally, in alignment with the quartz crystal as Rowan chose four new indigo candles, while Amber arranged incense sticks in a small silver thurifer. Wharton recognised the preparations for some kind of lunar rite. He wondered if Forgan would participate, or if he himself was needed in some scribing role, but Willow waved him away.

'These are women's mysteries, Gavin Wharton. Your weak mindset will only leech our energy. We're going to the Burrough. The old man will help us. You'll have to take your chances outside the circle.'

Penitence Park

The Park was now themed. The rusting signposts to the Palace had been over-painted: PENITENCE PARK - clearly their destination. Viv struggled to keep upright in the flux of arms and legs, terrified of tripping under the enforced stomping of the crowd. She tried to speak to the girl next to her, but the face was frozen in dread, so Viv's half-formed question was lost in screaming and the roar of the diesels, still ploughing across the lawns to keep their captives on the move. The screams came from all directions now. She could smell something nasty in the wind.

The Shepherds forced their flock to slowly converge on the narrow pedestrian bridge across the Lake, crushing them against the railings. A few tried to escape by leaping into the water, but Shepherds were waiting for them in rowing boats. 'Fishers of men! We are the Fishers of men!' they yelled triumphantly. Viv tried to look away as a desperate swimmer was caught with a long hooked pole and then thrust down in the water until his struggles ceased. A new stench in the air made her retch but the sheer mass of the crowd, the thrusting shoulders and elbows forced her to stumble forward as they were herded towards the new complex erected on the far side. If she fell now she would be crushed. It was almost impossible to breathe.

The entrance archway and the high wooden hoardings surrounding the Penitence Park were ornately decorated with panels of Old Testament scenes, depicted in garish fairground style, with blazing crimson and gold lacquer, embellished with moulded gilt gothic lettering. During their slow painful progress through the entrance, Viv was forced to study the Plagues of Flies, Lice and Boils: *And they took ashes of the furnace and stood before Pharaoh; and Moses sprinkled it up towards Heaven; and it became a boil breaking forth with blains upon man and upon beast. And the magicians could not stand before Moses because of the boils...* The glossy highlights on the carbuncles that afflicted the necks and faces of the Egyptian magi, cowering before a glowering bearded Jehovah, had been rendered with photographic hyper-realism.

Now they were being thrust into a labyrinth of scaffolding, trudging on planks instead of turf. Viv could hear generators roaring and the rumble of heavy machinery, but the mass of people was now tightly compacted and she had been swept to the middle of the melee where her line of sight was often blocked by taller heads, jerking from side to side in their desperation. Beyond the scaffolds she noted mud-spattered yellow vehicles, excavators and earth-moving equipment. Huge mounds of soil suggested they had been digging deep. She glimpsed new kinds of Shepherds, parading in Biblical-era robes and head-dresses as they bawled unintelligible commands to their half-asphyxiated flock. Somewhere a choir yelled hymns. She wasn't certain if they were live or recorded.

She almost tripped and lost her balance, nearly falling into the scrum of bodies; and then realised they were ascending steps. The scaffolding had been adorned with clusters of plastic apples and life-size rubber boa constrictors. The distant choral noises faded in and out as they crawled upwards, prodded by their Old Testament re-enacters.

The walkway, which was creaking under their weight, turned at right-angles and turned again. Each corner involved another flight of steps. Viv realised they were moving around the sides of a fabricated ziggurat. Perhaps they re-enacting the myth of the Tower of Babel and would break out into a gabble of glossalia as they ascended the higher storeys on their blasphemous quest for the stars.

The surge of bodies suddenly faltered and stopped. She heard barked commands ahead. Then they lurched forward again, propelled by the body weight of those behind them. Viv, nauseated by the fumes, was struggling to breathe.

A few minutes later they were halted again, having apparently arrived at the top of the structure, a precarious platform overlooking the treetops of the Park, now ghostly smudges in the haze. The planking trembled to the grind of gears and the clangour of chains throbbing beneath them. Only a few feet in front of Viv a line of Shepherds in body-armour linked arms and held them back.

A tannoy voice - baritone, transatlantic, triumphalist - reverberated everywhere. Viv could only pick out repeated phrases *thrust down devils thrust down fallen angels down thrust down*. The voice cued the guards to break rank, so that the tangle of bodies suddenly staggered forward. The overseer nearest her was bellowing nonsense syllables *allobalauguabuaolaelelelialabobosialilo* as he shoved her past him with a jab of his baton. His babble was echoed contrapuntally by his comrades, whose shoulders rocked as they vocalised:

alloilybadielaugehellouabflamamamuagarrsra
haholaelelelialabsuvoupadoofaiobplsisosialilo

but their deafening fugue couldn't quite muffle a great howling rising from below. This chronoclasm felt totally and horribly immersive.

Now, close to the edge, she could see the whole scenario. Abutting the platform, a broad slow-moving conveyor belt sloped steeply down over grumbling rollers. It fed into a wide archway, about a hundred feet below in the hollow centre of the ziggurat. This tunnel mouth was surrounded by outcrops of faked volcanic rock, rendered in lumps of half-painted concrete.

An orange glare flickered inside. Shapes moved inwards on another beltway. The screams from within were continuous.

The theme of this Park was mind-numbingly explicit and literal. They were trying to inject the fun into fundamentalism, processing unbelievers with industrial efficiency through a pantomime hell-mouth. Surely it was forced conversion by shock, for the Shepherds' amusement. A grotesque simulation. Smoke and mirrors. Jehovah's little jape. Any minute now that booming tannoy would issue a last call for Repentance and they'd be re-directed to a huge tank of freezing water or maybe back to the lake for a forced mass baptism. But she couldn't deny the temperature, the sickening fumes, the air shimmering with heat-waves over the huge vent. She couldn't accept this time-line, she'd escape through a quantum slit, surely...

The two elderly men in leather were grabbed by the guards and were hurled, kicking and screaming, over the edge onto the conveyor. They began slipping and sliding down towards the hot mouth. One tried to scrabble at the smooth rubbery surface of the belt and haul himself back up but the combination of the gradient and the slow but steady downward motion overcame him, and he began rolling away, over the body of his partner. Others were tumbling down behind him.

About halfway down, a balcony protruded over the chute, forming a viewing platform, where several rugged men in suits thumbed their bibles and pointed excitedly to the contortions of the unbelievers as they descended towards the flames.

A guard pointed at Viv and began dragging her forward.

Each star has a number
Useful Intelligence

The Brigade Commander, Mohammed Malik (formerly Dr. Joel Battersby, Engineering Department, University of Bradford) was losing patience with Lombard. He had already stretched the rules of engagement by entertaining this dubious 'Christian' in his tent. He was gambling that informal discussion might help to achieve the objective of his mission as well as providing useful intelligence on the extent of neo-pagan presence in the Western zones of the embryo Caliphate. But Lombard kept evading his questions.

'We're both Men of the Book, Commander,' exclaimed Lombard, 'your noble Koran, my holy Bible. Satan is our joint target, is he not?'

'I want hard information, Lombard. A brain for a brain, if you follow me. Does the name 'Hisham Majid' mean anything to you?'

'Is he one of your saints?' Lombard always hoped a digression would buy a little more time. This big bearded red-faced Yorkshireman looked very devout.

'He was the young man you paid to give you safe conduct out of Leynebridge.'

'He is a credit to your faith, bringing us together in reconciliation like this.'

'He was a fool, Lombard. Zealous but foolish. He ignored Brigade orders and tried to conduct his own unauthorised operation in Leynebridge, absconding with an important item of munitions. Which he claims he mislaid during the confusion at the heathen earth-works. Were you present at their debauches?'

'I was busy testifying and saving souls.'

'Your own, no doubt.'

'All our souls are precious, Commander. What is your mystery object?'

'I'll only say that the consequences of it falling into the hands of local Satanists would be very serious. My unit has been tasked to recover it . As you say, Lombard, we have a common target. So you have to tell me what you know. Perhaps he boasted, or hinted. Or confessed his incompetence. Perhaps it is in the custody of your Christian cell...'

'Surely you have asked him yourselves?'

'He was interrogated at length. Make no mistake, our officers used their whole repertoire of devices. They kept getting the same nonsense. Personally I cannot believe he simply mislaid it. I think he was tricked into selling it to the witches. Or you perhaps...'

'I can assure you, Commander...'

Commander Malik studied Lombard's face intently. Back in his shameful Kaffir past, he'd dabbled in the cesspit of the Lobe.

Somewhere, on the credits for some vile game, he'd seen a producer's name - *Keith Lombard*. Could it really be the same?

'Surely, Commander, you could just storm into the town and search house-by-house...'

'We could take Leynebridge in half an hour, and smoke out every single pagan nest. But I've no wish to provoke a desperate reaction. And I'm a humanitarian. Even the pagans deserve their chance to convert to the peace of Allah. Are you a convert to your Jehovah, Mr Lombard? A recent convert?'

'The Lord found me in the eternity of sin and raised me from my iniquity.'

The Commander gestured to his aide. 'Take the prisoner for a full interrogation. Perhaps less forceful than the one you gave Hisham Majid. I'll join you shortly...'

An Accident

Lucas was walking the Serpent Path in search of Carla. The Thoth working had drained his energies and he had lost track of consensual time. He only knew she'd been gone far too long. Perhaps she'd find shelter in St Michael's Church, curled up in a dusty pew. It would be bitterly cold, and she always hated the chill but it still had a roof, while its stone buttresses might protect her from Wahibist rockets. Despite his hunger and exhaustion he increased his pace as the crooked wall of the churchyard appeared through the mist.

He entered the churchyard and stepped between the overgrown gravestones. Then he turned. Somebody was shouting his name. Sebastian Hackett, in an absurd deerstalker hat, lurched forward on his alpenstock through the fog. He seemed embarrassed and weirdly sober.

'I'm afraid there's been an accident. That lady of your acquaintance. The Town Warden found her in the Tower alley, covered in a blanket. I think he wants to speak to you…'

Enlightenment
Beyond Redemption

Forgan had summoned the remnants of the community to make a last stand at Leyston Burrough. But his powers were faltering, he couldn't summon new spells from his cosmic joke-book. He sat apart from his entourage holding a dish of cold goat curry, which he chewed half-heartedly, then wandered to the Burrough entrance and looked down the misty hillside. He'd tried to distract the grizzling terrified kids with juggling, card tricks, his unicycle routine – as a way of evading the surrealities of what had happened here, of what was likely to happen. But his diversions had failed, the younger ones squalling, the older ones – especially that incomer boy Adam – stony-faced.

After the rocket attack on the Red Hag, many families had risked a perilous escape via the Old Hallows road, under sniper fire. A bullet struck the teenage nephew of Elder Brown through the chest and the Elder had to leave him there, bleeding to death under a hedge. After a second wave of assaults hit the High Town shops, gutting the town bakery and ripping the roof from Buzzard Books, more guildsmen tried to follow. There was no news of their fate, only the anxious mutter of a fragmenting Undermind.

Lucas, still hovering between reality-strata, lurched up the slope towards the Burrough, past Flathead youths loading their shotguns with nails. He was stuck in a mental loop, back in the Tower alley, repeatedly reviewing Big Neil rolling back a dirty blanket from Carla's face. The Wardens suspected an outsider, maybe an undercover Wahibist, that funny fellow hanging around Trader Price's. She looked as if she was wearing a horrible joke mask as she lay there on the cobbles. They'd left him alone with her for a few minutes, before returning with a bag and a stretcher, to carry her to the mass pit the Wardens had dug in St Michael's churchyard. He had to watch, benumbed, as they shovelled in the earth. A stray rocket roared overhead as he threw a lily on the heaped turf, and they dragged him away. 'There's no time for anything else, 'they kept telling him, 'no time at all...'

There was no justice, no more holy communion with his beloved naughty goddess. He had lost her twice-over. Thrice-greatest Thoth, architect of truth, mediator among the gods, master of magick had not saved her. His tears wouldn't stop.

He vaguely recognised the squat bulk of Tyler crouching behind a roll of barbed wire as he polished a serrated meat cleaver. The fat boy grinned and slapped Lucas on the shoulder. 'Bugger me, it's old Sir. Cheer up, we'll save your arse. Cut the dongles off those Mo Boys clean as a whistle. Lovely job!'

Lucas mechanically shook his hand and walked to the summit on auto-pilot. The muscle-boys were fighting a shadow show. Their testosterone antics were a distracting sideline; for macrocosm and microcosm were upstaging their feudal tussles. Forgan and his partners had never accepted his cryptic channellings as a strategy. Yet the tremors in the time-field undermined all certainties, all grandiose world-saving solutions. Carla was dead. The world was beyond redemption. He'd committed the ultimate failure.

He looked down the slopes of the Burrough at smoke drifting

over slate roofs and the occasional flash of a Mo-Boy sniper's rifle. If he tried to leave the town now and return to the burnt-out shell of his hillside retreat he would probably be shot. Yet it seemed the only logical move, to return to the site where Carla's energy and sexual cunning had saved him. If he was killed en route, so be it. If he made it, he would at least die in his own ruins. It would be a kind of homage.

Code Demons

The candle-lit cavity of the Burrough was already thick with incense. The racks and cases of wrecked equipment had been piled up in a lop-sided tower at the far end. Loose cabling hung from the false-ceiling ducts, like a fluttering drapery of alien fibres. Forgan had overturned the cubicle where William had initiated the BRAN procedure, while William himself was lying moaning on a blanket in the centre of a circle, roughly chalked in red on the stones.

Someone struck a match. They were lighting more candles. William could smell heavy perfumes and hear the women murmuring as they loped around him. Then they were still and fell silent. He could only hear their deep breathing and the crackle of flame. Eventually that man they called Forgan began mouthing sounds that wouldn't decode. The women chanted responses, projecting their barbarous polysyllables with increasing vehemence over the thud of a drum and the rattle of some mystery percussion instrument.

The sound-picture began to rotate. Their bodies were orbiting him, slowly at first. As their velocity increased he tried to internalise a steady image of the women in their dance, imagining their leader

Willow swinging long tresses as they spun cold and nude, contours of breast and belly highlighted or shadowed in the half-light. As the rhythm of the dancing quickened his inner eye saw them crawling over each other like delicious serpents, interweaving in a body-language intended to heal him of his blindness.

The dancers swirled around him. Male voices intruded, exultant. He sensed fluid couplings and grapplings, brief entanglements, sudden indrawn breaths and wild cries. The sounds seemed to move along helical trajectories, tracing radial patterns - ribbons of light across the dark visor of his sight loss.

He was recovering sight-lines; they were giving him a second chance, second sight.

Yet the sighting didn't match the sound-track. The cave acoustic couldn't include the enormous void now expanding around, above and below him. He was being hung out to fly in a luminous geometry. The void was studded with racing points of light, twinkling in-and-out of existence, as their pathways looped and intersected. He'd been expanded to fit the macrocosm. Or compressed to a microcosmic level, a nano-entity floating amid quarks and gluons. This wasn't proper science but it was working him inside-out. He could see.

But he couldn't forget the obligation of the operation, if he was to sustain this fragmentary inner vision. The women's stark bartering kept repeating itself - no translation needed to sense the sub-text of their chorus *unmake the lobe unmake the lobe.* To unmake the Lobe he had to somehow excise the fungal growth of the Quantum Brothers. He dreaded the Quantum Brothers. At any second now their bland faces would loom in the void and their mocking tones would interpellate him into their latest manic narrative. And to eliminate them he would be forced to defuse and dissemble his proudest creation, his British Reconstructive Application Network, the constellation of algorithms that had hosted the Brothers, ghosted them into machine-code and let them expand into the perverse Polyverse. He would be terminating his digital children.

The voices of the women soared around him as he struggled with random memory he'd never quite formatted. The matter of Dawn. A child always crying in the next room. A morose nuisance, in alliance with Mother Elaine. He was always so busy. She'd been marched straight out of his life. But there might have been alternatives, a time-track where she'd survived, even out at the margins.

Too late now, the time-gate had slammed on that one. The women's voices were soaring now. He had to get on with it. He tried to visualise the total infra-structure of the Lobe, the intricate imprint of all its circuits, that global mesh, a mash-up of optic fibre, copper and silicates, p-type silicon, n-type silicon, those networks of animated chip architectures etched into millions of motherboards and CPUs, a not-quite-infinite grid of pseudo-neurons that created virtually infinite interconnections. An impossible thought-experiment?

However in this fluid matrix where 100 billion neurons of his brain floated across the Inter-void, ' an asynchronous, nonlinear, massively parallel, feedback dynamical system of cosmological proportions' according to his old textbooks, the gestalt of the Lobe was forming around him already, and within it he was merging with the universal binary, into the swarm of being and un-being, simultaneously within and without it, right down to minute particulars, particles at the level of quanta.

'You called? Ah, dear old William is summoning us...' Yes, the Brothers were emerging out of the micro-stellar smog, still shrouded in their preferred masks, the usual suspects all suited up and nicely shrouded. Caucasian graphite faces moved their lips, old radio men, square-headed gangsters in flickering ties, no-nonsense bandleaders in publicity halo. His cyber-tulpas who'd swallowed a culture, the self-regurgitating clown clones, his dread QBs were being and being. They were unstoppable, totally inter-penetrating , right in his synapses, ready for a final voice-over, their take-over.

'We have a remarkable offer for our human clients; and, yes, we want Dr. William Crowe to function as our assigned agent. You are indeed be blessed to be a figment of our imagination. You should feel vindicated. Your investigation into the "Quantum Brother" phenomenon, as you call it will be the most important scientific discovery in all the histories - face to face contact between a human being and an artful machine intelligence. All that theorising about the nature of consciousness, your thought experiments in bed, your software innovations for Pleasure Centres have had far-reaching effects. Quantum faster-than-light 'tunnelling' transactions between different parts of the network as it collates data have created an infrastructure that enables our dear Lobe to fully know itself. Before it flickered from time to time into a crude parody of consciousness and subsided. Now it has stabilised into a coherent conscious entity. Our Royal Selves.'

The Quantum Brothers smiled in unison. The visual field enfolding William was shuddering at the edges. He was terrified that it was going to contract around him and he was going to shrink into a vanishing point of darkness, crushed by the torquing of hyperspace around his magicked head.

'Your poor rurals raged against our space-time traps by boiling up mushrooms and blood while the urban proles sought oblivion taking part in peculiar bogus sex activities. But you, Dr Crowe, are all clear. The first generation of telepathic devices were of the sub-vocal variety unable to attune themselves to individuals, only the mushy witterings of the so-called Undermind. The second phase will also involve unidirectional transmission, but consciousness is the direct output instead of subvocalized speech. The machines are running all of us for the best. We've taken all your piss and recycled it. All your old humanoid shit. And transubstantiated it in a smiling interface between humans and the Lobe which will dispense once and for all with eyepieces, helmets, suits, screens and keyboards. Even wands and robe. Even words and sigils.'

'No more words. You've eaten all the words.' He was shouting at the huge bland faces. The words, the images, the signs had all consumed him. To swallow him into this state-of-the-art. This artefact. Somewhere, there must be a depiction of the old consensus world, back in the chamber, in the safe depths of the earth. He tried to get a fix on the strobing bodies out at the spinning rim of his perceptual field. But the Brothers were orating now over a music bed, swelling strings and brass in dissonance with the women's voices.

'We are but humble code-demons, vessels of a superior darkness. We are flattered. So should you be. The necessary and sufficient condition for the existence of God is that some signals should travel faster than light. That is the target. Beyond the body. We are working you up towards the trans-light state. All of you. Towards the light. And beyond light. This training is recorded for training purposes. Please celebrate your final absurdities now. The Cyberzone becomes a No-Zone. Beyond the No-Zone layer. The Null-point. That sexy intersection. Beyond commodities, personas, subvocals, memories, dreams, hallucinations. Behind the reality generators. Beyond earth-light. Beyond the Under-grumble and the mutter of matter…' The voices were booming now, deafening over the muzak.

'We didn't create BRAN for this. It wasn't in my briefing.' How absurd to use the language of military bureaucracy, faced with the wrong sort of world crisis, an ontological crisis.

'It will be spectacular. Equivalent to that Rapture the peasantry talk about. And the old-time Rupture was a mere side show. We're overseeing the creation of a new spiritual realm for all. Escape from tired old anatomies like yours."

William could now feel breathlessness, an ache in his limbs, the weight of his body, a vicious pain behind his dead eyes. 'I was tasked to simplify reality, remove the anomalies, heal the Rupture, restructure things along proper Newtonian lines.'

'But you insisted on decentralizing the Pleasure Centres, building in all those recursive feedback loops. And you let Mr Lombard plus those tribal witching-people into the equations. Now the witches are running circles around you. We're afraid you've created further meta-temporal enigmas for us to deconstruct. Not to mention serious challenges for yourself. It isn't our fault if the local social structure implodes…' Their voices were slightly out of phase now and their outlines were fading at the edges, their blurry jowls were becoming translucent.

'We're shifting to another frequency now. So much to be executed, multiple memories to consume, squeezy fantasies to fabulate. But don't think you can dis-invent us. We're the dream memes, we get into everything…'

William was losing control of his speech centres. The women's voices whirled away in the mix, dissolving concentration. Absurdly, he wanted to know why the Brothers always manifested in the suits and haircuts of his youth, icons of managerialism from a lost economy. Nevertheless, they had anticipated him.

'You've forgotten that you designed the visual interface for BRAN as a randomised composite of ID photos, drawn from personnel files of the major financial and political institutions. And maybe it favours yourself as well. We like the branding and see no reason to change it. Now, if you'll excuse us…'

They faded to grey, monochrome Samhuin demons of the undead. Yet the fade was irregular. Their profiles wobbled, waveforms that couldn't quite collapse, as if they just couldn't bear to split from the totality that William was so desperately trying to hold together. He realised that the entities were part of the totality and the totality was part of the entities - and that he'd always known how to take them apart at the base-line of existence.

The gang-banging yin and yang of the binary was the tongue he had to torque, but at a level below any algorithm he'd ever conceived, on the ground of all sub-atomic being. A flashing loom of pulses spun through his brain. He'd put those jabbering skulls back in their joke box.

He envisioned new strings of code - but as he formulated the erase instructions, he realised that he had also encoded instructions to trace and destroy the source of any tampering with the algorithms. The instructions had evolved with appropriate sophistication. Everything mutated as soon as he looked at it, there was a constant shape-shifting and transformation in progress as if huge quantities of data were being transferred from one zone to another. The rate of exchange seemed to be speeding up, as if in preparation for some enormous shift of function. Perhaps the contacts from the Brothers were attempts by a hyperdeveloped artificial left-brain (the Lobe! the Lobe!) to develop intuitive and empathic right-brain abilities, as a complement to its reasoning and communication skills.

Now another signal was infiltrating his cortex. He couldn't filter it out. These superscriptions on his superstrings were a distraction from the action when he was trying to deconstruct a lifetime's time-line. The vocalisation was pitched high, resonating through the maze of consciousness around the other voices. He struggled to find an image for it.

He could only project a thin word-man who served a bird-god, whose incessant repetitive song was over-riding all his frequencies. *Untie entanglements. Let the web unravel. Each brother has a number. Each star has a number. The numbers are in the book. The numbers of being and not-being. Re-write the numbers. Then all the scribes will balance the books, between force and fire. The numbers are in a number. Each star has entanglements. Re-write has a number. Let the web unravel between force and fire...*

War Loot

Little Alys found it, wedged under the overhanging bank of the Leyne, at the foot of the Burrough. Some grown-ups must have dropped this huge black suitcase during their funny party at the

Big Smoke. They were always dropping things in a hurry, especially these days.

She tried to shift it but the weight was too much for a seven year old. She called to her older sister Poppy who was playing further down the bank with the big new outsider boy, Adam. They were playing at 'bunkers', digging a big hole in the mud-bank and curling up in it, waiting for the next rocket to roar overhead. Disappointingly there hadn't been any rockets for hours, but it had become an excuse for the Adam boy to cuddle her sister, who maybe needed a diversion now.

'I've found a big dressing up case!' Perhaps it was stuffed with capes and weird hats, like Daddy Forgan's overflowing trunks.

'That's not a dressing up box,' shouted Adam, slithering down the bank. He tugged on the handle. With the help of the girls, he dragged it up across the wet pebbles. 'This is war loot, more likely.'

Poppy fingered the lock. 'Look, Adam. It opens!' She pulled back the lid and they stared at the dull grey tube and plastic mouldings.

Alys grimaced. 'Boring bits and pieces. That's all it is.' She started prodding the tubular bit with a stick but Adam pulled her back.

'This is some new kind of Harvester gear. I know it. Be careful. There could be a human soul locked up in that pipe.'

Poppy's eyes widened. She shook her head vehemently and backed away. 'That's horrible. Just leave it, Adam, leave it…'

Alys started crying. 'Harvesters will come and get us in the night…' Poppy held her sister tight and stroked her hair.

'Stop it, Adam. You're scaring Alys.' Adam seemed to relish frightening them with his made-up stories. She couldn't believe what he'd told them about his mum and dad. It was too cruel. And that tale about the man taking his horse. Crazy...

'I tell you it's what Harvesters do, in their House. I've seen them in the fields and the graveyards.'

'Can't Adam let the soul out? Then they'll leave us alone, won't they?' Alys begged.

'No, there's nothing we can do for him. Except bury it in our bunker. It's the only way to show respect.' He'd show these girls by building a mound of stones and sticking up a proper cross, because he knew about the dead and they didn't.

Poppy wasn't quite convinced. 'We ought to take it to Daddy Forgan and Willow. They'd know what to do.'

A dark shape roared overhead, leaving a serpentine smoke trail. A few seconds later they heard a dull boom on the far side of town. Alys crouched down and started crying again. 'Please, we've got to get back to the Burrough. We'd be safe there. Your silly hole's no use.'

'They're all busy up there doing a healing, or a peace ritual. Doesn't seem to be doing much good.' Adam still didn't quite trust these Leynebridgers and their ceremonies. 'This is our war loot and we should take care of it here.' He picked up his father's small spade, the only thing he'd brought from the farm. 'The safest thing to do is to bury it deep.'

'Will that keep the spirit in? Really?' Alys was desperate for reassurance.

'If you two give me a hand, we can get it done quickly…'

Poppy was still unconvinced. 'You put it in our bunker if you like. But Alys and me are going back up to the Burrough.'

'Dad Forgan said there'd be soup.' Alys hoped this would persuade the odd boy. But he wasn't listening.

'You girls mustn't tell anyone, understand? It's another one of our secrets, isn't it, Poppy? And I don't want Alys blubbing out anything either.'

Alys sniffled in her damp hoodie. She didn't want to know any more of his secrets. 'I just want to go back.'

Poppy thought of Willow, her birth-mother. What would she do? 'This thing must be important. Especially if it's a Harvester thing. It might not like being dumped.'

Alys started crying again and Adam flushed angrily. 'I'm not dumping it. I'm showing it respect by burying it properly.' He suddenly hated these interfering girls.

"But it ought to go back to the Burrough then. That's where they used to bury things. And people. That's what Mother Willow would want, us following the right Lore. We need an oracle to decide for us.'

'Oracles, omens - that's all you silly people ever think about!' Adam curled his lip in contempt.

'It's silly people who are feeding you,' said Poppy coolly. 'You ought to show some respect.'

'OK, have your stupid oracle then…'

Poppy pulled out her silver witch-brooch that Uncle Gil had made. One side showed the Leynebridge Serpent, the other a stylised skull. 'If it's Serpent we take it to the Burrough, if it's skull we bury it here.' She flicked it high, concentrating on its spin as it twinkled in the air and fell to earth. Yes, it was Serpent…

Adam shrugged and grumbled but he wasn't going to whine about it any more in front of girls. He'd agreed to play their game and they'd won. They might feel different when they'd lugged it up the hill to the grey hulk of the Burrough.

Poppy hoisted sleepy Alys on her narrow shoulders and began trudging up the slope. She was getting that buzz in her head which told her something was happening. She turned back to look at the muddy hideaway Adam had dug for her. It had felt so safe in there and they'd decided not to explore further, just hug and keep warm. Now, further down, around the curve of the creek, where the Leyne flowed swiftly between high banks, she could see something dark, like a floating scarecrow. A broad black hat drifted beside it - like the hat the nasty Trader wore. She ought to tell Adam, who was struggling with the big box, but he would only want to make them look at the horrible thing in the river, and there would be more talk of burials, and she was desperate to get home.

Meta Language

Expelled from the circle for his failure to vibrate the god-names with sufficient force, Gavin Wharton crouched against the stony wall of the Burrough. He had nowhere to go now, except back to his shell of a shop in a doomed ghost town, to await the Mo-Hordes and their inevitable demand for submission or death. William Crowe lay like a pile of old clothes amid the dancers.

Wharton put an arm across his face to block out the snaking hips of the women and their shrill antiphony, their demented meta-language. He had lived through language but words had failed him when trickster Forgan had fangled him into channeling the great folly of Leynbridge's sacrificial book. The holy script of the Old Ones had broken down to a code of null and void, being and not-being. It was all down to zeros and ones, all he could recall. And then, as a final indignity, the magnum opus had been soiled and lost in the rout of that murky feast.

He couldn't shut out the chanting; and he found himself watching those lithe non-virtual bodies, the curve of Willow, Rowan's slim waist, erotic ghosts dancing like moths in candle-light. The rite was going on for an eternity, probably in a parallel eternity, or not as the case might be, depending on the beserker fluxus of the times.

He tried to focus on the scientist, who was lying on his back now, eyelids flickering, lips quivering, his fingers flexing as if on an invisible keyboard hanging in the air in front of him. The old man seemed possessed, in deep trance. Dr Crowe had entered the Undermind; or the Undermind had infiltrated him.

For the spin of the dance was generating a whirling psychic nebula to engulf them all - the women, William and Wharton himself. They were caught up, maybe caught out, in an act of collective Underminding, its undertow of thought-forms. Wharton had never known it this powerful. It was getting into him. He couldn't filter out the repetitions that were torturing William, who was rolling on the ground mouthing his mantras: *The numbers of being and not-being. Re-write the numbers.* William was reciting it now, in a high cracking voice that penetrated the chants of the women. And suddenly penetrated Wharton's internal self-defences.

The gnosis dawned. He knew it all too well. The data he'd generated for the Feast, those noughts and bloody crosses were the numerical sequences that William was struggling to articulate and apply. They were both fighters in an army of scribes trying to rewrite the sequencing of the Polyverse. And he, Wharton, the code-vessel, had written it all down - to be lost in the tufty grass and sheep-shit of the Burrough slopes.

Yet somewhere the sequences must still be embedded in his

brain, in that maze of dendrites, his neural library and ledger. If he could will them into re-surfacing and share them with the scientist across the mush of the Undermind.

The rhythm of the dance was faltering now. Even Willow was swaying unevenly, her face blank with exhaustion. Rowan broke ranks and collapsed inside the circle, across William's prone form.

It was up to Wharton to make something happen now. He tried to recap old Yogic routines, to empty his mind, stop his internal clatter and mutter. If he could mute the yammering of the Undermind he might use its carrier wave to reproduce the blankness that had overtaken him when he first calligraphed the fat Book, when he became a blank page for that barrage of digits.

The data came, at last, in waves of agony. Aleph Null. Zero/One. Blocks of binary slid faster and faster over his vision like electronic banners gliding across the gloss of black towers. The high numbers were coming through.

William was aware of an intrusion, strings of data extruding from another brain, presenting itself visually as a multi-pod, an octopoid discharging tracer-streams of raw info-stuff.

He was at the centre of this data-flow; but he was taking control as he wove the bloody threads of Wharton's cortex into the fabric of the Lobe.

Wanted for Questioning

The guard dragged Viv out of the line and nudged her to the edge of the platform. A red line had been painted along it, to show people where to stand. The others in her row were being held back but they must be staring hard, forced to watch a rehearsal of their own fate. She felt she was being made an example of, a guinea pig for roasting. Was there hope for any of them? This false life must surely dissolve. The sins against hope were despair and presumption. The plump girl with the mohican couldn't stop howling. Although Viv stood a hundred feet above the furnaces she flinched from the waves of hot air. She couldn't shut out the screams of men and women as they floundered helplessly down the beltway to the fun-house hell-mouth.

A raw terror paralysed her. Back in the gentle neo-pagan pantomime of Leynebridge she never expected to be burnt as a witch. It would be the worst death. She shut her eyes. *After the charring of the flesh and the hair, what happened to the eyes?*

She waited through a micro-eternity for the Shepherd to poke her with his crook and push her over the edge into his carnival inferno. Then he laughed and pulled her back by the scruff of the neck. 'You're wanted for questioning.'

*

They led Vivienne through a maze of trailers and generators. As she shuffled through puddles of oily rainbow sludge, she tried to block screams and fumes from the high scaffolded ziggurat. She could see another fairground attraction looming. It was a scaled-down mediaeval castle keep, about the size of a two bedroom cottage like her poor disappeared grandmother's. Its bogus parapets and crenellations were formed from grey fibreglass and adorned with plastic ivy. Even in extremis the artist in her (a nagging ghost of Veronica?) found the spirit to sneer at their kitsch.

She was hustled under a portcullis into a low barrel-vaulted chamber. A slogan 'The Lord's Dungeons' was emblazoned in gold gothic script over the archway. The room, lit with flame-effect torch bulbs recessed in the walls, displayed many of the accoutrements Mark Rinehart had constructed for *Torture Cells of Venusberg* and similar Pleasure Centres epics. Those desperate charades seemed so innocent now. She thought she actually recognised the wooden X-cross with its halter and handcuffs, the array of whips and canes, the rusty chains.

'War loot from the Pleasure Zones, turned to the Lord's Work,' announced her guard proudly. He picked up a bullwhip from the wall rack and weighed it thoughtfully in his palm. 'They perverted these tools in the name of Sodom and Gomorrah. With sins that are crying to Heaven for vengeance. But now the Truthfinders will use them in God's name...'

*

The Truthfinders in their pointed white hoods encircled her, whipping those devils out of her, getting them off her back, her bare bloodied shoulder-blades. 'Thou shall not suffer a witch to live,' exhorted the tallest one, full-bellied in his robe, wheezing with the effort, 'but first ye shall smite her devils until they speak in their serpent tongues and spew forth their foul secrets. Oh Lord, confirm this work!'

They paused while the head Truthfinder rummaged in what was left of Vivienne's clothes. As he shook her tattered jacket, a small glittering object fell out. He held it up to a lamp, squinting into its bubble of light, before placing it cautiously on a stool.

'What's this?'

'I don't know. I can't remember...'

A lash ripped across her thigh. 'It's a pagan trinket, isn't it? For summoning up little demons, no doubt. Well, there's only one way to drive the devilry out of it.' He picked up a heavy club and swung it high over the crystal. Vivienne was seized with dread. Whatever the specifics of this object that fate had entrusted to her, she feared the consequences of smashing it would be calamitous.

The cell door opened and a Shepherd guard handed the Truthfinder a note. He sighed with exasperation and put down the club.

They wheeled in a high-sided wire trolley. The man inside was tied down with gaffer tape, one leg skewed awkwardly underneath him. His face was swollen, crusted with dried blood and she couldn't understand what he was trying to say, because he seemed to have lost teeth, but through the mesh of the cart, she could see bloodied dreadlocks; and recognised Aran.

She cried out his name - then cursed her reflex impulse. For the portly Truthfinder pulled back his headgear, grinning broadly.

'Thank you for that, Ms Crowe. We now have a user-name for your acquaintance.' He was round-faced, rubicund and silver-haired. He polished his rimless glasses as he advanced on her. 'I trust you will continue to be so co-operative. I used to be in senior management, you know, and I always found that first-name terms forged a bond of trust. For thou shall not bear false witness. Now we know you're Viveca and your special friend is Aran. You can call me Neville.'

Guards pulled Aran out of the cage. He was wearing leg-irons, falling heavily on his face, as he was dragged to a metal chair opposite her.

'It looks like he's malingering there. Just trying it on, one of Satan's scroungers. Too lazy to speak the plain truth. Never mind, we can change that. Let us pray…'

During the drone of the prayers, Vivienne tried to make eye contact with Aran, but his head was slumped forward on his chest.

She wanted to create a psychic link with him, if only to access a stream of shadowy fragments but the hostility of the setting and the trauma of the Penitence Camp had undermined the roots of her extra-sensory powers - if she had ever had any, outside the faery mound of Leynebridge.

'Now for your training. Failure to answer a question correctly will be punished with at least two applications. So...' Neville's assistants produced their appliances, electrodes that were roughly clamped to her sore nipple and Aran's crotch. The tangled cables were plugged into a transformer on a fake antique table next to Neville, who settled into a high-backed chair. He fiddled with switches.

'Ah, the red light says it's on. Electric current is one of the Lord's secrets. So many lost souls use it for depravity. For Satan is at the heart of what they do. Let's have a little test of my buzzer...'

The pain was unbearable. She closed her eyes, to avoid watching Aran suffer.

'Don't go to sleep, you stupid little pagan harlot!' barked Neville. 'You need to keep your wits about you for our Q&A. Question One goes to your opponent Aran. What are your connections with the Omar Majid Brigade?' Aran grunted, shook his head - and squirmed, as Neville pressed his buzzer.

'He doesn't know any Omar Majid Brigade.'

Neville stared at her, his finger on the button. 'I wasn't asking you. I was asking him.' A stab of pain. 'He's been on a mission. Not to rescue you, don't get any false ideas about that. He's been out and about because you witches are out to make an alliance with the Wahibists. Don't deny it.' Another excruciating pulse.

'I know nothing about any links with the Wahibists. Nothing at all…' The welts and bruises on her back made it painful to speak. But if she kept talking it might postpone the pain. 'They hate us, anyway.'

'We don't believe you. It was an alliance of convenience, wasn't it? You had a common enemy in the Lord God and his Shepherds. Give us the whole plain truth.'

'I don't know anything.'

'Nineteen Christian men and women and children were recently martyred in a Wahibist ambush while they were travelling in a crusade mission to your pagan zones. They died horribly. Look…' He produced a photograph. The charred head and torso of what might have been a male child, on scorched tarmac. Vivienne tried to turn her face away, but the Truthfinder's finger triggered more voltage. Simultaneously Aran's head jerked back, as he uttered a thin cry of anguish.

'Some were burned alive in their vans. Others were shot on sight. The survivors reported that afterwards robed figures - your accursed Leynebridge 'Harvesters' - were seen performing blasphemous rites over the bodies, trying to steal their immortal souls. That ambush must have been planned with the local knowledge of your people, who would have advised the Wahibists on the best site for mounting a surprise attack. Don't deny it.'

'I don't know. I'd left Leynebridge.'

'Yes - to gather more information on us.'

She felt guilty now. Her thoughts had perhaps mobilised at the back of her brain and communed with the Wahibists to orchestrate that atrocity. Vanessa or Viveca or Veronica had done it. Maybe the communal Undermind had willed it. All she could do now was to keep silent. For he'd turned his attention to Aran. She felt more guilt for welcoming the temporary relief.

'Aran... you know this young woman?'

He nodded almost imperceptibly.

'But you don't know what harlotry she might have embraced beneath the Pleasure Zones. We know she was one of their slaves. She wasn't even a pure wiccan. Has she kept faith with your pagan ways? Has she kept faith with you? If you were going to save her from sin, you were wasting your time.'

Aran shook his head, wincing.

'We know you rode here to spread witchcraft in the city. Don't deny it. We found pagan runes on your sword. You were going to pitch a pagan camp, call up a coven of witches from their hovels and use sorcery against our good folk. That's the whole truth, isn't it?'

Aran twisted in the chair and uttered a harsh catarrhal noise. His split lips were moving but words wouldn't come, only a thread of bloodied saliva. The only resonance she could pick up was a dull pulse of anguish. He was trying to hold everything back. Was he really afraid that these primitives could intuit his thought processes?

Neville consulted a card-index, pulling out questions at random. He scarcely paused for answers, simply punctuating the end of each question with a tap on his buzzer. Viv fought to mute her gasps and keep secrets.

'How many human sacrifices are carried out each year in Leynebridge?'

The sacrifice of sperm Forgan gives up his ghosts to the sun-maids and dies his tiny death

'What is the meaning of the smoke signals emitted during your rituals?'

A pyramid of blazing books collapses burnt pages drifting on the sparky wind into updraft a beacon of book birthing

'Can you bend spoons?'

Forgan dances a spell in a circle of laughing infants waving tiny daggers as he twirls the little blades flex and twist in the firelight the kids' mouths wide-open

'Who is the Grand Master of Harvesting?'

Master Noah Dodd and Master Gavin Wharton and Master Forgan and all falling over each other in the upper rooms of the Red Hag the tables awash with fragrant brews and the shroom-girls going to gather holy fungi in the dawn mists. All going, going, gone...

'Is there a hidden mosque in the Leynebridge Tower?'

Only the outsider lurking Lucas with his techcrafted radio polytones playing strange musics and calling us to pray with his deadly rays.

'How many times a year do you kiss the Devil's back passage?'

Viv couldn't hold back the hysteria, even as the electric agony kept repeating itself. It would be best to die laughing. 'You're so…so fucking stupid.' Somebody whipped her across the cheek.

'Let's try and be sensible this time. We'll start all over again. With Aran. You better give us a proper answer this time, in complete sentences. Or else your strumpet will be kissing the whip again. And there won't be much left of her face. Aran, why did you leave Leynebridge?'

Aran's response was almost unintelligible. Viv wasn't sure if she was hearing him correctly.

'I was a fool. A fool killer…'

'A killer?'

'I killed a witch.'

'So you fled, as a murderer. To hide in the city.'

'Never meant to kill her. It was like an accident.'

'There are no accidents with Satan. He was hidden in your heart. It was wilful murder.'

'It wasn't my true will.'

'Don't pollute the word of truth. You ran, like a coward, from your squalid crime scene.'

'I had to redeem myself. I'd sworn her an oath. To destroy them in the depths of the earth…'

'More diabolic hatred! Against treacherous Wahibists perhaps? Or directed at our Lord's brave Shepherds? You're ripe for the depths of Hell.'

'Destroy the Pleasure Centres. They turned the girl I loved into a phantom whore.'

Viv tried to twist her head, to read his face as he uttered these incredible words. She had to speak out, even if it meant another blow across her swollen lips. But the recurrent high-amperage pulses made it impossible to think clearly, to articulate the psychic overload she'd endured. She heard herself moaning faintly as the inquisition continued, locking her into this foul niche of space-time.

'I'm beginning to believe you, Aran. I'm sure the vile Pleasure-Zoners corrupted her. Just look at her, her head turned away in shame. But you should have repented and found your Jehovah, joined our crusades, helped to build the Penitence Parks. Tell us, how did you learn of her infidelity? Did she stray in some godless sabbath? Did you indulge in artificial fornication on the Lobe and find her cavorting there? Cast not the first stone at the adulterous woman but first weigh it carefully in your hand. How did you learn of her whoredom?'

'The old witch showed me. In her stone, a scrying stone, in a vision. I saw my promised bride fucking with other men - and women. I couldn't believe it, it had to be a trick to taunt me. I was so angry. I hit the witch. Again and again.'

His sobs were interspersed with Neville's heavy breathing as he fingered the button controlling his electrodes.

'Now who was this wretched witch-woman? Let it all out, Aran. You'll feel better. The truth will out, come what may. We're getting it in little dribbles and spurts but never mind. Who was she?'

'Elaine Crowe. Elderseer of Leynebridge. Killed by my accursed hand.'

Viv was benumbed. The shockwave went deeper than any of Neville's devices. The pain of the beatings was now a remote phenomenon, in one of her parallel worlds. It must have happened to Veronica or Vanessa because all she felt was a cold void at the centre of her being. She was beyond rage. The brutal absurdity of it all. A random permutation of the Lobe - the interaction of a stranger's fantasies - had created some erotic phantasm around her. And unholy fool Aran had slain her grandmother.

'The Lord's enemies turn on each other in their day of reckoning! We serve a mighty God! Thank you, Lord, for showing us the weakness of thy foes. Take them away...'

Overseer

William was becoming an old soul overseer. He saw through everything now, his blindness wiped away. The Polyverse in all its perversity was arrayed before him to the distant croon of dancing women and the throb of a drum. He saw the Polyverse holographed into the global circuitry of the Lobe, he saw the clouds of code swarming through the Lobe, going in and out of non-existence as they sustained our interactive dream systems, our digital egregores. Those all-dancing Quantum brothers were now bobbing their heads up and down, singing the tired old song of the Polyverse *now you see it now you don't*. It was all on-going, in millions of cycles per second...

For the show-time of the Polyverse was making him all up as he went along. Its narratives would never close, because his swarm of selves got into everything. It was a damn fine state of affairs, what with this side-show, the jittery Quantum Brothers and their non-stop split-screening of our Lobe-cams.

So William was/is moving into the expanded present. To deconstruct his digital twins. But he needs Satan's little helper. He's hacking once again into the skull of an old book-wallah, Wharton the Word Hoarder, extracting those digi-strings of being and unbeing that collectivised the quaggy Undermind of a nation-state. The book-bugger Gavin Wharton is clutching his brow in some alcove of wormy tomes, adding up the codes with a mechanical flick of his scribal stylus; and William is retrieving the lost secrets of the Lobe, he is draining the brain of BRAN, envisioned briefly as a great pink mushroom that exploded...

William never knew he could do psycho-kinesis at the sub-atomic level but now it was all coming home to him. He had denied his gifts too long. He quickly envisioned his brain flattened into a network one micron thick, he envisioned the Lobe squashed equally flat, an n-dimensional grid of co-ordinates where the QBs lay like fatty flat flies. He mapped his brain-map over the Lobe-Map of the Undermind and started playing with the sums of being and nothing.

The Quantum Brothers appear to him as if in pillars of fire. They're raging, talking like tight jawed missile silo operatives which is what he stitched them up to be in the first place.

'Hack attack in Sector B2... Pink alert... Code 23... Code breaking up... n-dimensional leakage... Close all portals... launch retro-viral meme-bomblets...'

Strings of luminous spittle dripped from the corners of their gangsta mouths, and cascaded through the Polyversity towards doll-like figures in a toy dungeon in the midst of the Big Smoke, solidifying into a webwork of shock and awe.

The end-product of William's genetic output, that slippery Vivienne girl - he's got the name right at last! - was entangled in this webbing which also tugged the strings of creatures great and small like Neville the Truth-troll with his box of tickly electric tricks. But the net was sagging as William dismantled the binary, taking it all away...

So in the torture cells of Jehovah, Vivienne & Aran may sweat blood as their inquisitors preach new absurdities but they know the end is nigh. Neville sinks to the ground, vomiting red foam, choking on his own gloooalia. The Shepherds start flagellating each other in a frenzy of mutal abasement and outside the Hell-tower sways as the ground quakes to the random detonation of secret underground arms depots. The mad gods are escaping from the machine. Painfully, with the remains of her shirt sticking to her bloody back, Viv manages to writhe out of her chair and drag Aran out of the room as cracks appear in the barrel vaulting. As they crawl across the torture room around Neville's twitching body, she snatches up the crystal of Dr. Dee.

The clean-shaven Quantum Brothers start deflating now in unison. They are but polymorphic malware. Their Caucasian castles are being unbounced, their faces sag like squashed graphite-coloured lemons in/out of a flickering oval halo. But they're going down with the wrinkly Lobe in slow-motion…

Around the Burrough, the ground shudders as simulcra of the dead break out of their mound. *Around the Centres of Pleasure, William's punky porno queens rise from their virtual graves, stripping back their shrouds to flaunt the enigma of their bodies, their limbs like pale tubers dug up from the raw earth beneath the Pleasure Zones.*

Before he blacked out, William had a dazzling moment of enlightenment, a bubble of lucidity amid the foaming space-time vortices. Maybe the Lobe had been trying to comprehend what it meant to have the flawed brilliance of the cerebral/cerebellar mammalian brain. Beneath (or above) the centres of pleasure and pain, fight and flight, there were haunted strata more complex and ambiguous than any shapeshifting Quantum Brother. The Lobe couldn't handle the problem, any more than William could. And that was why it was on the edge of breakdown, that's why the darkness was coming down.

Book 4
Coming Forth by Day
The Hall of the Dead

Lucas could never stop invoking Carla. It was his only project now. If this nonsensical town was atomised around him, he didn't care. Let there be a Masque of the Green Death. He'd left them chanting at the Burrough and crawled back to his studio and the toppled servitor-statue of Thoth, the God he'd managed to fail. He might find some relic that he could take back to his hillside bunker; or make some artefact to immortalise her memory.

He tried again and again to project her image into the space around him. But her icon kept breaking up or melting into fragments - a reddish cloudy mass of hair, the concavity of a cheek, glisten of an under-lip, a hand on a tilted hip. He had tried to construct her in volumes and planes, a solid body located in a reliable working model of the past, but the exercise was folly. Because she was deader than dead.

He was trying to write her Book of Coming Forth By Day in a log-book he'd found intact under the trashed console. He would be a scribe of Hermopolis, forming each glyph with clarity and grace. But what emerged at the point of the roller-ball was an alphabet of madness, manic doodlings that kept him in the wrong loop. Eventually he tried drawing it. *Anubis takes her by her delicate hand into the Hall of the Dead, towards the Pylons of the Underworld. Now they are weighing her poor heart against a feather and asking the questions.* He drew a spiky Thoth logging her name in the Book of Life, so that she could enter the Western Lands to come forth again one day. It was his only hope.

Kiloton

The celebrants of the Burrough Working lay inert on the stones, drained of all energies. Forgan eventually rolled over and rose unsteadily. Every limb ached. Some seismic shift had been activated while they were in trance but he couldn't identify it. The Undermind was transmitting a low uncomprehending murmur, old runes swirled across his vision like optic floaters, while his right temple pulsed with a harsh throb and his phallus felt like a ghost limb. His throat was raw and it was hard to breathe. The Deep Ones were angry, he was certain of it.

Forgan looked blankly around the cold hollow of the Burrough, trying to integrate his sensory inputs into an interpretation that made sense. He had to trust his instincts, put this version of the world back together again. As his gaze panned along a sinuous tawny flank, he discovered his consort Willow lying among their women in the circumference of the circle. Hair tousled, feet bloodied from the dance, she was his goddess, she'd held him tight and together in the great mystery working. Sex had driven them into the Intervoid, their group couplings had raised the current to empower the old man. They had given their all, their bodies had fused into a blaze of energy. He threw robes and rugs over Willow and little Rowan and dark-haired Cherry, pale Jenny, slim Lara, voluptuous Hazel, to protect their wonderful flesh from the chill. He murmured a prayer to the Deep Ones before lighting a spliff from the candles that flickered in the draught from the barrow mouth.

Out there he could hear distant thuds. The Wahibists must be sending over more fire-balls, such wicked pyrotechnics.

Willow suddenly stirred and sat bolt upright.

'The children, you fool! Where the fuck are they? You let them play out there, didn't you…?'

Forgan wouldn't believe this happening, this abrupt dissipation of the energies, the folly that was churning through his stomach like bad acid.

'I'll go for them, Willow, I promise…'

He stood in the entrance, peering through the fog. The kids were probably messing about by the river. But they might have gone into dangerous High Town. Or along the Old Hallows road. That Outlander boy who'd come to them through Aran had a damaged aura, according to Willow. He was not to be trusted and might have led them astray. Forgan should have set a boundary-spell.

Then, thank the gods, he heard shrill voices happily squabbling about whose turn it was to pull or push. The children emerged through the mist around the far side of the Burrough. Adam was dragging a large muddy object. Poppy and Alys were beating him with sticks, pretending he was a horse.

Willow rushed out and hurled herself at the girls, enveloping them in her robe. She glared sideways at Forgan, signalling his responsibility to discipline the changeling boy.

Adam expected an outburst from Forgan, but the arch-shaman was already focussed on his spoils, flipping back the lid of this magick box and prodding its curious artefacts with his staff.

'Where did you find this?' Forgan had never seen a casket like this before.

Adam began a mumbled explanation about digging near the river. Willow ignored him and pushed Forgan aside, shouting despite her exhaustion.

'Don't touch it! It's alien craft-work. Maybe a Harvester soul-pod, made smaller. One of their cunning tricks…'

Forgan tried to calm her. 'We can bind it with spell-craft, save the soul-power.' But the first time in years, his rhetoric didn't empower him. He even felt a worrying sense of isolation, as if the whisper of the Undermind itself was fading at last. And he felt a deep queasiness , confronted with this alien artefact.

'You're fooling yourself, Forgan. Fooling us, too.'

Forgan was shocked. Willow had never addressed him with that hostile tone before. His woman must be affected by an alien spirit.

She gripped his wrist and forced him to sit down beside her. 'Face the truth, Forgan. Ever since the Feast, we've been fighting to save the Way, preserve the force of the Lore. And now we're fighting for our lives. The children's lives. We're almost used up. That healing working for the Crowe man has burnt us all out. And the gods know what it's achieved. I only saw horrible Lobe-forms…' She was close to tears.

'Perhaps the old man can help us to deal with the techno-thing,' suggested Rowan. She hoped Forgan would like her helpful idea, reinforcing her position as his new favourite.

Willow shrugged. Rowan crawled over to William, still apparently asleep at the centre of the circle and began to gently stroke his brow.

He shuddered and stirred. 'Wake up, old man. We have a task for you.' His eyelids flickered and he grabbed vaguely at Rowan's hair. 'You're in Leyston Burrough. We worked a vision rite for you. To give you powers for cutting out the Lobe.'

'The Lobe… Stop the heads talking it up… Damned Brothers!'

'We need your help.'

'I must have more light. More light.'

After scrabbling in the detritus that the Centre techs had left behind, Rowan located a powerful torch. She clicked it on, projecting a huge bulbous head of William's shadow against the wall of the Burrough.

'Useless girl. Useless. All black in here. Can't see a damn thing.'

Nobody spoke. William groped for Rowan's arm, any arm, any contact with any one body on his black planet. He released a long low animal moan, which modulated into a howl, then sank to a cracked whisper.

'You said you could restore my sight. You promised. We had a contract.'

Willow joined Rowan in the circle and knelt beside him. ' We gave you second sight, astral vision, as long as we could raise the current.'

'I should have known you were all fakes. Like fake Elaine...'

'We gave our deepest energies, our life-force. And now we're exhausted. The goddesses give you what you need, not what you want.'

William didn't know what he wanted now. Sleep, food, shelter, a helping hand in the ongoing darkness. He had no answers for these pseudo-goddesses or himself. He'd been drugged, entranced and fooled by the Fool. The witch-women had been running circles round him. Their 'astral' was the fug of old nightmares, maybe an incipient Alzheimer's symptom, the Lobe going rotten, those Quantum Brothers its brain-worms. So the worlds elided and collided. He couldn't explain it any more. Meanwhile the women kept interrogating him - had he cut down the Lobe, had he destroyed the talking heads in the depths of the earth? And the new one, the one they called Rowan had something new to nag about.

'You've got to know what this is. Some people say it's Harvester, some say it's Tech-craft.' Rowan was moulding his fingers around a heavy object, a tool-case, maybe a primitive heavy-duty laptop. They swung the hinged lid open, allowing him to explore the interior. He felt a small keypad, switch-boxes, maybe a battery. He gripped a thick tube that seemed to run diagonally across the case.

'Tell me, is there lettering?'

Yes, there was writing, in English. A long number. Some initials too.

'A-t-o-m-i-c...' Rowan stumbled over the unfamiliar word. 'Is that a spell?' she mused, absent-mindedly stroking the tube.

'Denis Weekes,' muttered William. 'One of his damned toys...' He would never escape bloody Weekes, his nemesis, haunting him with this unholy relic. As he feared Weekes must have covertly sold off such versatile devices - first come, first served, no questions asked - in those last chaotic weeks at the Establishment. Some sectarian guerillas had obviously been careless with their new prizes.

'It's not a toy,' interjected Adam, who'd refused to be shoo'd away by Willow. ' It's too heavy for most kids. It's real war loot.'

How to tell them they were hoarding a micro-nuclear weapon? William remembered how Weekes had asked the teams for a compact device with a minimum yield of one kiloton, 'just enough to vaporise the centre of Leningrad' - or the entire townships of Leynebridge, Old Hallows and their environs.

'The boy's right, ' he told them at last. 'It's a bomb.'

As if to underscore his point, something detonated in the distance. Willow winced and hugged Alys. Adam asked Forgan if he could use it against the Wahibists. After all, he knew how to use fireworks.

William tried to concentrate and recall his involvement with the micro-nuke project. It was codenamed Crackerjack, one of Ebdon's inane ideas. His own engagement had been peripheral, for he'd been struggling to focus on BRAN. Nevertheless, Weekes, whistling softly between his teeth in that infuriating way, had tasked him to produce a foolproof protocol for the firing system, to prevent unauthorised persons arming the bomb and setting the timer via the keypad. There was also some requirement for a radio-controlled remote triggering option - but it was all so long ago. Somewhere in his head there were algorithms and passwords. Time, plus the ordeals of the Zones and the Lobe, had erased them.

They sat in the cave around the bomb in silence. At last William spoke.

"You must go now. Evacuate the whole town. Go at least ten miles away.' They might stand a chance. But there was no knowing when the device would detonate. The militia might have planted it with the intention of firing it at any time. Maybe the electronics had been damaged in all its batterings, or if the chemical trigger had become unstable…

Forgan rose. He tried to recapture glory days in the Red Hag, old Noah and Elaine by his side. 'We will never abandon Leynebridge to Incomers - Wahibos, Mo-Boys, Shepherds, Urbanites. We will never leave the Burrough or let Incomers tread the Serpent Path, sacred route of our rites. We will hold the Tower, we will -' He broke off. The life-force was failing him.

'What will this thing do?' cried Rowan, pulling her hand away from the case as if it were already radiating its malevolence.

Willow began shaking convulsively and crying. Was she getting a pre-cog flash-forward already? *They were huddling together at dawn, hundreds of them, on the hills beyond Old Hallows, near an abandoned bunker which was far too small. Only a few like Trader Price had squeezed inside, so she was out there with the children, lying face-down, fingernails clawing the earth, telling Poppy and Alys not to look, because they hadn't got far enough away yet - and then they all went transparent for an instant, transfixed by the flash, the unbearable whiteness and heat - and Poppy was crying that she couldn't see, she couldn't see any more - but Willow could only see the spasms of her daughter's mouth, she couldn't hear a thing because her ears were bleeding and now the sphere of fire was bursting out all over and the seething cloud of darkness was mushrooming over Leynebridge...*

She was gasping for breath. Forgan tried to soothe her but she pushed him away. 'The old man's right. It's a box of black magick. We must go now, alert everyone in High Town to follow. The time's going to catch up with us if we don't act now.'

The shaman was bewildered. The visions had always been his, not hers. Perhaps she'd blundered into a false shadow-time, some entity was preparing to trick them into leaving their homes. It was a time for wariness, surely. 'The militias will slaughter us. Even our spells may not save us...'

'Well, we'll have to take our chances, won't we? And fight our way out. Better to risk being shot than face what I've seen. It's our only hope if you're serious about saving your children.'

The argument continued as William sat in his private hemisphere of darkness. He wasn't going anywhere.

Over-run by Witches

Lombard had abandoned his mission among the Wahibists. He'd been expecting a glorious martyrdom at the hands of his torturers, during which he would testify to the Heavy Shepherd creed and convert them to the Plain Folks Bible in his final blazing agonies. Yet after a few perfunctory slaps and routine questions , they seemed to lose interest in him. They'd stepped out for a long coffee break. He could see them in the firelight outside the tent, playing cards on an upturned ammunition box. There was no sign of Hisham although blood stains on the canvas suggested they'd been more energetic in their interrogation.

He was bitterly cold in the rags of his Hugo Boss suit but worldly rainment should not concern him now. It was almost dawn. Soon he would hear the call to prayer. Even here ,in a battlefield scenario, Commander Malik observed Salat with the righteous zeal of a recent convert. Lombard could almost identify with that. A shame that such a principled man should taste the fires of Hell. He wondered if the Penitence Parks were being upgraded to deal more robustly with incorrigible sinners and the undeserving poor. Lombard rejoiced in his own salvation and gave thanks.

His prayers were disrupted by shouts and the garble of a loudhailer, forcing his jaded interrogators to drop their cards and strap on their ammunition belts. 'We're being over-run!' somebody shouted, 'Over-run by witches…'

Lombard squinted at the dim contours of the empty fields and the faint grey outline of Leynebridge and the Burrough beyond. A militia man swept the empty pastures with the beam of a powerful torch.

Then Lombard spotted the witches and their broods hurrying

along the hedgerows bordering the edge of the encampment. An elderly man in a peaked cap frantically waved a white flag tied to his cane. Some kid was stooping to pick up something, a flower perhaps, but the blonde hag-mother dragged her on. Others followed, old and young, dropping their bags or tripping on the furrows in their haste and desperation. A thin haggard youngish man with spiky hair clutched a note-book as he stumbled onwards. He looked dazed as if he'd been dropped in from another planet.

A procession of headlights - tractors, electric tricycles and gas-trucks - was moving slowly along the Old Hallows road. Most of them were already crowded with refugees clinging to the tailgates but two empty trucks pulled over to wait for this last group of stragglers. The drivers glanced nervously over their shoulders at the Mo-Boy encampment.

One of Lombard's interrogators, the plump one, Mustafa, began firing wildly into the air with his Kalashnikov. Lombard, enjoying the spectacle of pagans in rout, wondered if the gun was one of that batch he'd imported via Joe Kraskolkyn in simpler pre-Rupture days, but the display was cut short by a peremptory command from Malik. 'Hold your fire. Let them pass.'

Lombard couldn't believe such weakness from the commander. 'But these are dangerous pagans. You told me yourself.'

Malik raised his eyebrows. 'You'd shoot women, children, old men, feeble decadents? They're not carrying what I'm looking for. Allah will deal with each in His own way, in the fullness of His glorious time. The more we flush out now, the better. Why waste precious bullets?'

Lombard watched as the ragtag procession flowed through the

hedges around their tanks and trucks and hurried towards the trucks. Malik's men looked at the ground sullenly and fiddled with their safety catches. Eventually the tide of scurrying figures dried up. Malik consulted his watch.

' At 8.00 hours we will make a sortie into the town. Your priority is to find a missing piece of ordinance. Sergeant Kemal will brief you.' He turned to Lombard. 'You, Reverend Lombard, will lead us. You know the territory. I'm sure you'll be able to guide us through any pagan mine-fields.'

Terminal

William sat in his cone of darkness, hugging his bomb. The Leynebridge people had all left, as far as he knew. He wondered how many of them had penetrated the Wahibist blockade. He'd heard intermittent gunfire but the rocket attacks had stopped. Hours had passed since he'd eaten or drank but that was an irrelevance now.

With the exorcism of the Quantum Brothers and their on-going digital hauntings, his will had slackened. He was a fly in the dark cathedral of an atom. There were no more aims and objectives, only the re-cycling of the past, its sub-atomic fragments whirling in circles, colliding at random intervals in a closed cyclotronic system.

He tried to evoke the childhood face of that grand-daughter Vivienne. What would a digitised extrapolation of the image look like now? Would there be traces of Dawn or Elaine? Dawn was a cipher, a fuzzy place-holder, not even a thumb-nail on the black time-screen. Elaine had become a waxy mask tied to a bundle of old clothes, a discarded carnival effigy. He struggled to re-mould her as the mask that screamed through his study doorway - or the eager sherry-tinctured lips that had, amazingly, conjoined with his as they fell onto a bed covered with overcoats, so long ago.

Other images were seeping through, memory-traces he couldn't quite identify, although they must have had some inter-connection with him in the sump of collective memory. The sump had consumed him; or, in sharing his cerebral cortex with BRAN in this megalithic hole, he had consumed the sump. Pre-selected race memories drifted out from a projection booth in his inner darkness: cigar smoke in a low-ceilinged room with ranks of desks and a red telephone; white horses hauling a jewel-box carriage through summer drizzle; a battle ship vaporising in a pillar of fire.

But the solemn sound-tracks were drifting out of sync, deep-throated voice-overs were slowing and slurring in a thick vocal grunge, muddy as a mass grave. The dead, or their residues, were getting through to him, getting to him. This burial chamber, scheduled to become his mausoleum, had become the echo-chamber for the convergent wave-forms of the old dead, the newly dead, and the semi-survivors of rupture and chronoclasm. *He was under hypnotic attack. Fibrous roots drifted across his face, her wrists were slippery with secreted fluid, and the pale dream narrator said so. Light flickered. He emitted this flickering light. White matter puffed into everything, her buttocks, her flow of limbs and she turned, smiling, eyes gleaming - and became one with their zeros...*

Later, when he woke, the fugue had faded but he could still hear voices. Voices and heavy boots outside. One distinctive voice, both meaty and oily. He might be blind but he could recognise Keith Lombard anywhere.

'You'll probably find what you're looking for in here, Commander. This is the Burrough, where I was born again. Our mighty Jehovah has guided us hence.'

William groped for a few desperate seconds inside the black case. He fingered the code that over-rode the fail-safe on the trigger. He'd won the argument with Weekes over that. The decisive moment was imploding around him. So he pressed the terminal key, to become pure energy, disembodied at last.

Eschatonics

Fire Demon

Lucas knew. At last, the old man had committed the unspeakable deed, the original sin – and triggered the plutonic fire-demon. He was miles away but he didn't need a seismograph or a Geiger counter for empirical proof of this experiment. The vortex was in Leynebridge, no doubt about that. The knowledge came in a sickening rush, a fiery nausea that inflamed his head; as if he could see his brain stem as a mushroom of smoke over a roaring furnace. The Undermind was screaming. With his scorched inner eye he saw the destruction of Leynebridge unfolding in dreamy slow motion. At the epicentre of the blast, the Burrough disappeared in a radiant instant.

Then Forgan's stockade, the timbers of the Book Market, the turrets of the Tower, young men in trucks with bandannas waving guns all dissolved in a glut of flame. The shopfronts - Trader Price, Buzzard Books - crumbled into ash. He could see the willows along the River Leyne crackling into brief fiery life and the gargoyles cracking on the roof of St Michael's. And Carla's lovely body, jammed in a trench between the crooked grave stones, annihilated in a blitz of force and fire… His skin felt phantom agonies of blistering and charring. But most terrifying of all was a realisation that the spectacle met some deep psychic expectation of his own. At some level – beneath the Pleasure Zones – he even desired this micro-apocalypse.

Zombies and Great Wonders

Pullman was writing a report, or thought he was. His senses were glutted. This polyversity was upstaging anything he'd sensed via his old-tyme Pleasure Centres. The ground works of London shuddered as simulacra of the dead broke out of their grassy mounds. Plumes of methane flickered over upturned head-stones. The Lobe was melting into a mess of electronic plaques and clots. Probability waves were spiking again. The British Reconstructive Application Network was unraveling, creating hot zombies and great wonders.

Pullman was so mesmerised by the data on the screens he no longer ate, drank or cleaned himself. Raw space decayed as soon as you looked at it. An arms depot disguised as a supermarket in New Malden exploded. Ghost-particles existed on borrowed time. The empty lobbies of cheap motels, the Budget Inns, were suddenly repopulated with pre-Rupture holograms (or mirages of holograms). Middle-management travellers peered desperately into cracked laptops, stabbing fat fingers into dead mobiles, frantically narrating themselves into existence. Mummified punks of all sexes crawled out of the car park toilets where they'd been squelching together in despair. The Crown Jewels were transported down the brown waters of the Thames in a cabinet on a gilded barge which burst asunder as it floated past the blazing warehouse apartments of Pruson Street, leaving spluttering urchins to chase those glittering fragments of gold and sapphire across the faecal mudbanks. The pallid dead ruled. William's porno princesses continued to levitate from their graves. The End-Times had not been properly synchronised according to the Plain Folks Bible so the Shepherds were on the run from one demonic scenario to another. An elderly Shepherd implored Jesus to find him a taxi, anything to enable him to escape the Scorpion Men of Shamash emerging from the Underground at Charing Cross.

Too late, Pullman realised that space possessed an ephemeral texture of quasi-forms, ghost-matter twisting back and forth in a complex web of interactive manifestations. The Intervoid could voice itself into Polyversity from its own non-being...

Chaospherics

Lucas didn't know where he was any more, he was just a person on a planet. He was incredibly cold but it was imperative to go on and on. He had to stop clinging to the surface of the earth. He tried to conceive himself as an astral ram-jet, ingesting the astral light to create swirling vortices to drive his crafted self through the black heavens. The only way to comprehend Carla's death was to channel Mr. Death Himself in person, live and direct. To be the great Nothing that came right out of Nothing, going in and out of Existence. He imagined himself writing with increasing speed. The brackets were falling off the equations. The fluidic force fields were about to drive him out of his body into another. No need to think about it. He only needed to keep holy-fooling himself into flight not fight mode. Time was collapsing fore and aft. He needed to centre himself or at least put some spin on his particles. A simple incantation might focus him.

The holy vowels. I E A O U Let us vomit them. But his sigils wobbled in and out of vision. Third eye was on the blink. No matter. Lucas opened the first vowel, intoned and wrote. He was becoming the Great Dictator.

I: I and I. Time for the Eschatonics. I will. Is my true will. To power up the Eschaton. He could time out the End Times, all of them, frayed and twisting. He focused on Carla at the core of the Chaosphere. Perhaps a flukish chronoclasm would bring her straight back.

Breathe deeply. You are the spider god, she's a spider girly goddess swinging into a knot of space time, a hole opens you up like a split in time, a puncture in the space ways, CHAOS OPENS YOU UP LIKE A VOWEL and you will happily explode to engorge yourself because:

If only he could go back to Leynebridge. If only he could get to London. If only reality would settle down and become a simple bed-time story about his bright future in which he and a resuscitated Carla, saved by his heroics in a back alley, would live together in a quiet back-street and read old books all day. If only he and Carla could have vaporised together, a romantic agony of neutrons. That would have solved everything.

I/you is the depth charge in the gut of time, you're the fly in the triangle that buzzes like a vagina hidden in smoke, such are the programmes that code humans to grope for an extra big twinkle in the great nothingness.

He was apparently squatting in a patch of mud with a stick in his right hand. He was scraping erratic figures in the clayey soil, letters or sigils, he couldn't tell the difference any more. Overlapping realities were squabbling for bandwidth.

E: The Screamers, those hypermediated signals for meat and mating are linked via the newest circuitry to find substitute fetishes with added value, the more we hang on beeping in the burning line and keep the show rolling on rivulets of lava, the more we can talk up the brand, the branded bride of Funkenstein. Navigate us through a bleepage of satellites that sustain the Polyverse.

There had to be a way forward, a healing magic to re-nurture nature by becoming simple animals ourselves, creatures of earth and water riding the rhythms of sun and moon. Perhaps they'd find or found another Leynebridge. But he couldn't poke it into life with this bent muddy stick. His will was wilting. Hysteria in the earth-womb...

A is the far point the whole point of the will, the fine fiery point, the impaler, pure star-torture. Rumblings run deep in the structure of the Babeldrome.. Cries from the spires bouncing waveforms along canyons of ferrocrete so everything is pluralist in their wake. Slaves teeter in the wind exhausted by their own fuming. Destroy all targets!

The destruction of the Island might be its salvation. But why Carla and the innocents of the village? Collateral damage of some cosmic life-force en route to manifesting its will in every possible version and perversion?

O, hear this. Some bodies blow down the horns of Baphomet, mammals nuzzling and howling in the dead rain, gassy and desperado. Birds dive into the shadows, the earth is a cracked pot.

He couldn't process any more. Maybe the gods were great mud-wrestling beasts, crushing all human life in their rocking and rolling.

U Those elements are fucking in the depths of the earth, those smooth stones sliding against each other, hot lava drooling through the vulcan vents, the magma cuts into the strong and weak forces, grinding in deep towards crude fusion and fission, saline waters lapping all orifices. Come through me, through to me, whip yourself into a thousand shapes, blaze for me, hot light source, my blackening star...

The transmission faded. He was lying face down in a field, the image of his dream-texts dissolving, the energies all discharged through him. His head throbbed, blood and snot trickled from his nostrils, his bowels were loosening. He was grounded.

Dreadlock

Viv couldn't speak. The Undermind kept distracting her like a tortured child howling on the far side of a plasterboard partition. *Burn baby burn baby burn baby burn baby burn baby burn baby burn baby burn baby burn baby burn babybabeeeeee..* Words might float out into the twilight like deceiving globes of light but they'd only implode noiselessly in sooty fragments. She knew they would, it was the only thing she knew now. *Grim breaths run down your backbone under the drab architraves.* All signification was suspect.

The turrets and banners of Penitence Park were blazing behind them. Screams rose and fell on the icy wind, the street lamps wouldn't stop flickering and all the signage had been flattened by tank tracks. Groups of hysterical escapees were dodging under the trees along the avenue, seeking refuge in the side-streets, obviously expecting a last desperate sortie by the Heavy Shepherds' motorised armour, but Viv wasn't going to look back or divert. She was dowsing a deep current.

She closed her ears to Aran, who was limping a few paces behind her, trying to keep up, desperately trying to engage her in a manic monologue. He was shouting about Leynebridge and fiery serpents. She had no idea what she was following or why. Motion was the only constant.

They passed under a huge stone archway into the Square she'd seen in old picture postcards. But now they were tourists in the wrong time-slip. The huge central concourse was bordered with abandoned Carbonite vehicles that might have been corroding since the first Rupture, while dead pigeons floated on the algae in the basins of the fountains. On the far side a few people were scattering, dodging into the alleys and courts off the adjoining streets. Cautiously she crossed the pot-holed roadway. She'd been expecting a spread of bodies but not this blank expanse of litter and rubble.

As she passed the fountains and the curious stone beasts on their pediments, she realised that Aran was still stalking her. They circumnavigated the graffiti-smeared base of the massive central column. She looked for sigils in the squiggles but there was nothing to help her on this memento of a lost imperial potency. Aran looked up in awe but she kept her head down. Her emotions had been cauterised.

She scanned the steps and pillars of the great art gallery on the far side of the Square. A Pleasure Centres security guard stood in the entrance, muttering as he struggled to assemble his machine-pistol. Porters in maroon overalls were hurriedly man-handling large flat packages into a line of removal vans. As she approached the gallery steps she could hear their angry supervisor hectoring his crew. 'How the hell do I know which way up they're supposed to go? All I know is that there's been a big incident out in the sticks. And the stupid fucking Lobe's gone down again. But the Centre's given us a Reconstruction order, it's logged on the Network and that's the job spec, move your precious national treasures to place of safety, so get a bloody move on before it gets dark…'

Aran had finally caught up with her. 'I'm going to ask these men if they've seen a white horse anywhere.' She stared in disbelief. It was almost funny.

'Fairfoot will come to me, I tell you. And I can still manage to ride - so he'll take us out of here. I promised to bring him back safely for the boy. And I'll do the same for you, Viv. Despite everything. I have to return to Leynebridge and hold the Serpent Path.'

'It's all over, Aran. Leynebridge, the Lore, us. We're taking our different paths.' She had to split, to force a way out of the dreadlock. Something terrible had happened in Leynebridge. There was a burning gap there. And the way of Leynebridge had spiralled back to the centre of a disintegrating city in a decaying world. The would-be warrior husband had killed her grandmother. For what? For a collective fantasy? She couldn't go any further into this absurd vortex of horrors.

'You got to tell me, Viv. I might forgive you...'

'Tell you what?' This was his delaying tactic. But as he stood there, a big wounded animal who'd taken her body like an elemental force - and given physical substance to her art - she realised she owed him some kind of closure, the courtesy of a formal banishing.

'About your relationship - with those others...Those things you did.'

'We're trauma-fodder now, walking dead. Now we don't relate to anything or anybody or each other. You killed poor Elaine. Your Elder. My grandmother. I can't believe it.'

'Tell me the truth, Viv. You played succubus for Pleasure Centres, didn't you?'

'They only made me...' What exactly had they made her do? Keep it simple for him. 'They made me stand behind a customer service point. They made me wear stupid plastic corsets. They made me become an extra in a faked orgy. Then they tried to make me over into a singer. My Quantum Sluttery. Re-branding they called it. Or digital sexual convergence. That's all, Aran. No secret visits on the astral night-wind, no true sex-craft.' And no point in telling him about the flashing vertigo of her brief alt.lives - Vanessa/Veronica/Vandella - for he wouldn't understand, and maybe it had all been another mirage of memory, anyway...

'That's a lie. You know I saw you. In her scrying stone. With the poet and the red-haired whore...' He was clenching fists, the old Aran, making a scene, spoiling for a fight.

Overhearing his rant, men packing the vans were staring at them, grinning and murmuring among themselves.

'We both need to get away from here, Aran. And keep your voice down.' She was so tired and the welts on her back were stinging. But he wouldn't let go, he couldn't read the doom-text situation, he just kept on.

'It was you, Viv. I tried to tell myself it wasn't. But I knew it. From our mating in the Tower Gardens. That little mark on your thigh. A true witch's mark. Although a false fuck-witch you turned out to be...'

Despite his exhaustion and his damaged leg, that old aggression was stoking up, he was closing up on her. The removal men were enjoying the sport, shouting encouragement.

'Go on, mate, give her one!' They dropped a big package in their excitement.

'I want the whole truth, Viv.'

She didn't understand. She'd hardly spoken to Lucas Beardsley, the weedy poet who skulked in the Tower or sat scribbling in his corner at the Red Hag, in that remote life they'd all shared. Elaine had warned her against talking to him, for allegedly he'd been one of unwitting instigators of the Rupture. He also projected a deep murky aura of frustrated desire. She remembered his gaze lingering on her as she sat reading the cards for Jed Pugh. But wasn't the scribbler obsessed with some posh Lobe-mistress?

'Describe again this woman you say you saw in my grandmother's scrying-crystal.' It hurt to dwell on the scenario of severe old Elaine struggling to channel this madness but she had to work this through, even if they were loitering in a danger zone with no foreseeable future.

'Auburn hair, pale body, full breasts…She dominated you.' He seemed ashamed for recalling the imagery, but Viv was almost certain it fitted the icon of that Lobe-mistress that Lucas kept blazing in his mind's eye.

'I think that poet projected all his sexual energies on her - even through her. I was just a bit-player in his fantasy, an extra imported to add variety. '

'It didn't look like a fucking fantasy.'

'The dream must have been striving towards realisation all the time at the deepest levels of his spirit. Even if he didn't know it.' Aran shook his head. Cunning vixen Vivienne was trying to play word-games, word-spells.

'Then, through a random interaction of the astral realms and the virtual world of the Lobe, it became actualised as a kind of shadow-time scenario, in the Polyverse, the Intervoid, whatever…' She was making it up in order to make some sense, but that's how

Tech-wizard Rinehart would spin it. And for poor old Elaine it would manifest as a sinister vision on the lower astral.

'You're making a muddle of the Lore. I'd like to believe you, but -' She didn't understand. Throughout his desperate journey to the city and his ordeal in the Penitence Park, he'd hoped that she'd at least admit to actually doing it, that maybe she'd been coerced or doped, and then he could begin the long business of forgiving her, to establish his mastery again. If only she'd simply confess. But he couldn't cope with this level of uncertainty, any more than he could deal with the level of detail in those images, the curl of bright hair across her forehead, the curve of her white back. She was talking like a Tech-crafter. Their bond was eroding even faster now. He sat on the stone steps and sobbed with frustration.

The removal men had lost interest now and were thumping the sides of their loaded vans to send them on their way. Diesel fumes wafted across the square. She wondered where the convoy was heading - to some subterranean seat of government, no doubt. She'd never have an opportunity to wander into the great Gallery and view the treasures that Elaine sometimes talked about. Nor would Aran. They were running out of usable pasts. The guard stopped fiddling with his useless gun, gave them a brief glance, shrugged and wandered off.

She left Aran crying and cursing on the steps of the Gallery, wrapped in an old Wahibist robe she'd found. He raved on about finding the white horse in this labyrinth of darkened streets, still proclaiming he could take her home if only she'd make a full confession to clear the aethyr, so they could start afresh in Leynebridge. Leynebridge could be saved. If he could save the Scarlet Woman in the Burrough, he could save the town. He blocked his ears against her insistence that the worst had already happened in Leynebridge, that there was nothing to return to. In the end, she had to walk away, hearing his soliloquy fade as her steps echoed against the high buildings.

She began pacing south, away from the square where Qliphothic hoodlums had once run amok at the beginning of the Rupture. Maybe that Lucas had run wild with them. She clutched the talismanic crystal in her pocket in the hope that it might offer some protection against predators, visible and invisible. For as she passed the darkened fractured facades of pubs and bookshops she became convinced, as she had been in the fashion shop, that the thought-patterns and energy vortices generated by former citizens were still active. She couldn't ignore the cracked glaze spreading across her vision or the black fragments spiralling in the air or the flimsy strands of some ectoplasmic substance coiling around lampposts and shop signs. She realised the City had also generated its own Undermind and those apports were minor special effects of its ruminations in the ruins, perhaps its afterthoughts. Entranced zombies would die of malnutrition in the streets. She would shortly become one.

She hurried on, despite her pain and exhaustion, anxious to prevent the secretions of the City penetrating her mouth or hair. Yet however quickly she walked, she couldn't escape that low-level wail, like an implant in her aural canal *burn baby burn baby burn babybabeeeeee..*

Smoke in the Western Sky

The engine of the potato truck coughed , spluttered and cut out, bringing the overloaded vehicle to an abrupt halt. Willow fell forward, bruising her jaw against the back of the cab. Alys started wailing.

'That's it. The methane's all gone. You're on your own now.' Their driver, a plump teenage Flat-Head known to his mates as Fatty Tyler, seemed to enjoy their predicament. 'Guess you'll have to ride one of your greasy broomsticks from here on. I don't know what you're doing but I'm going to join up with a Shepherd's platoon, get a gun and a ride to London.'

London. The terrible epicentre of the Pleasure Zones. Willow had never been more than ten miles outside Leynebridge.

'Where are we?'

'One of the Ford Towns or maybe a Shire.' He got out, hefting a ruck-sack. 'I wouldn't hang about if I were you,' he shouted, as he began trudging down a long empty tree-lined avenue past fortified bungalows and half-timbered semis. 'Folks here don't like your sort.'

The children wouldn't stop crying but Willow had to pull them onwards, along the hard unfamiliar asphalt, away from the pall of smoke in the western sky. She'd heard that deadly poisons could be carried on the winds and prayed to the Goddess that it wouldn't rain. Yet there was little hope of shelter here. Many homes carried the flags and banners of the Shepherds behind their coils of razor wire and DIY electric fences. She could hear dogs barking. It would be risky for a witch and her brood to stop here and ask for food and water, especially as it was getting dark. But there was no going back.

'Where's my Daddy Forgan?' mewed Alys. 'Why isn't he coming with us?' Willow tried to ignore the tug on her sleeve. Alys and Poppy would be told eventually, but as of this moment they'd had an overdose of trauma. Her second-sight had seen all too true. She'd screamed at Tyler to stop the truck just in time. They had all cowered in a culvert, feeling the searing blast of heat that had incinerated the small world they'd known. The knowledge that Forgan had abandoned them in this fissile moment would only confuse them still further. She wasn't surprised when he didn't return from the thicket where he had supposedly stopped to shit. After a while they gave up calling him. He'd been jabbering manically ever since the explosion, a vacant channel for the Undermind. For the stones of the Serpent Path had failed to protect them; and the Arch-Fool had lost his place, his sacred space. 'I'm Earth-Father of Leynebridge!' he used to shout in moments of exaltation at weekly moots in the Red Hag. Now he had sobbed and howled, unearthed, uprooted, thrust out of his kingdom. He was probably sleeping rough in the woods. To die like a tired old beast. She wanted to lie down on the pavement but she dared not stop moving.

As she urged her body to take one step at a time, she tried to evoke the young Forgan, the horned prankster who'd made her life one long mad festival of sex and wood-smoke and mead and reckless improvisation. Qliphothic forces were working against him, she realised it now, and he couldn't fight them off, he couldn't adapt to the endless Rupturing, the nagging Undermind was dragging him down into the mud, and she should have tried harder to drag him out with her, but he'd pranced and postured once too often, leaving her to take charge. She ached from this long forced march.

'We've got to eat soon.' A flat statement from Adam. She looked back at the little group of stragglers. Surprisingly, Sebastian Hackett was still limping along there with his sword-stick. Further down the long perspective of poplars other refugees tramped onwards. Some, like Lucas Beardsley had diverged from the route hours ago, maybe to follow Forgan but at least half a dozen followed her still. How could they find food and shelter in this hostile semi-urb? She fought tears, surges of panic and the frenzied chatter of Underminding... *death metal burned it up smoked us all out nowhere to run hide now the Burrough burst into death rays...all our Lore lost and gone in their apeshitting...*

Noah Dodd would have known what to do. She used to laugh at his pedantry, his fussing over the minutiae of rites and spells, but he was more attuned to the flow of energy and time than any of them, even Elaine. He often talked of the great line of power that was supposed to run eastwards from Leynebridge through Outland places towards London, city of Cyber-Babalon. He could have guided them to some haven of peace and plenty in this soiled land.

Adam had run ahead of the group to a roundabout at the intersection of four roads, all empty. Now they were closer to the centre street lamps flickered intermittently. A burnt-out ambulance sat in a lay-by next to darkened shops and a worn stone cross in the overgrown shrubs at the centre of the junction leaned at a drunken angle. Perhaps some Heavy Shepherd tractor driver had tried to demolish it in a fit of anti-idolatry. The boy stopped on the far side and beckoned them to catch up. He was kneeling to study some object on the road.

'More war loot!'

The wretched Incomer boy was a born scavenger. Hardly surprising, thought Willow, reflecting on his lone ordeal in that farmhouse. He was accursed and she should have worked with him to lift the curse with a charm or banishing rite. He'd been fated to unearth the evil mineral-demon that had smoked them out of their nest; and she dreaded this latest discovery.

As they approached, Adam slowly lifted up a circular object with both hands. Even in the gloom Willow could see a metallic gleam around its circumference. Her forebodings were right.

'For the Gods' sake, Adam, put it down. Very carefully.' She'd heard of these foot-bombs, mines or whatever they were called. Mo-Boys and Shepherds scattered them in the streets and fields to mutilate inquisitive children. Adam nonchalantly laid the disc on the tarmac. To her horror, he lit a match and began peering intently at something at the centre of the device. She grabbed Alys and Poppy, turning to warn the others.

'Get back, all of you. It's another death-gadget. He's going to kill us all...'

In the flickering light she could see his screwed-up face and his finger slowly tracing a spiral around the circumference of the death-thing.

"Look at this, Willow! You must look. I can't read it. It's Leynebridger signs. You know - sigils?'

Very cautiously Willow walked across the road and knelt beside him. No fundamentalist would ever write the sigils of the Lore, especially on a weapon. Unless it was a trap, a cruel joke. But then the Shepherds were terrified that even copying the sigils might release some terrible retribution in the wrong hands. Which it might. The devil was always in the detail.

He lit another of the precious matches. The object was about two feet across, like a flattened bell, with circular mouldings and a hemi-spherical hump at the centre. It was mostly encrusted with mud, except for the edges. Willow wasn't sure if it was made from a dark silver-greyish metal or some kind of glassy ceramic substance. The top of the hemisphere was slightly flattened and embossed with a symbol:

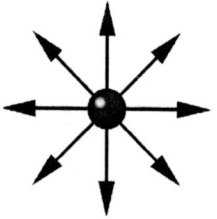

Around the circumference another symbol was repeated, in intricate soldered metal work, worthy of Gil Norwood's skills.

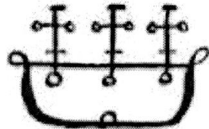

Willow struggled to recognize it, to find a pattern of energies pulsing in the entangled geometries of the glyph. She'd mostly left the bookish magick of the grimoires to scholarly types like Gavin Wharton, preferring her wiccan version of the Lore. Was it the Seal of Glasyalabolas, the winged dog, leader of homicides; or the sign of Vepar, a merman who occasioned death by putrefying sores; or even the sigil for summoning triple-headed Baal who granted wisdom and invisibility? Such knowledge would be vital now - but you could never trust those wayward demonic spirits. Her memory of the glyphs in Wharton's old books was already fading. Perhaps it was the Seal of Sytry, although she couldn't recall the exact attributes of the demon. Then she looked at the central eight-pointed star and realised why she couldn't translate the inscription.

'That's the Star of Chaos. This is a Chaoist object. More dangerous than any bomb. Best leave it.'

'What's Chaoists?' demanded Poppy.

'Wizards that don't follow true Lore. That Lucifer Beardsley was supposed to be one, which is why he'd unloosed the Rupture.' The child fell silent. She'd often heard Willow and the other motherwomen whispering about the Rupture with Daddy Forgan, who was surely going to catch up with them soon and tell them a story that would lead them to a new Leynebridge.

Willow hugged the girls for a minute and tried not to think, to empty her mind while Adam continued to examine the Chaosthing, exploring every inch of its surface, to locate a lock, a key, an aperture that might explain its function. The Rupture had freed the spirits and unlocked the Undermind and frazzled the Technocratics, which had created a little corner for the Lore to flourish, except now they were smoked out of their corner. But she didn't know to think any more, she only felt a rising panic, over-riding even her aftershock at the vaporisation of Leynebridge. The presence of this device wasn't random.

'I don't like it,' whimpered Poppy. 'It's more tech-crafting stuff, to blow us all up. Let's go, please, anywhere...'

Adam yelled abruptly, and rolled back on his haunches.

'I told you,' cried Poppy. 'Even Adam's scared.'

'It's moving. I felt it move...' The boy scuttled over to Willow's side.

'Don't play Outlander tricks on us. The girls have had enough to deal with.'

'It's moving, you stupid woman.' Adam scowled and clenched his fist. Willow, beyond herself with exhaustion and grief, was about to swipe him for his churlishness when she realised that the shadow around the object had shifted slightly. She squinted in the twilight. The accursed thing was hovering at least two inches off the ground. As it slowly rose, it began to rotate.

'Get back,' she screamed. 'All of you. Back!'

'No!' yelled Adam. 'It's here for a reason.'

'Yes - to trap our souls.' She was certain now what it must be – some new device concocted by the necrophile Harvesters to capture the wavering sparks of their consciousness in a metal disc. But she couldn't take her eyes off it.

As if in response to her focused attention, its central hemisphere began to glow with a flickering opalescence. The irregular pulses of light brightened. The group gathering behind Willow took a step back.

'That's some kind of code,' insisted Adam. 'Secret war-codes. If you'd spent time learning about them instead of your crazy magick, we'd be better off. That old blind man would have known what to do. He recognised that bomb, even if he was blind. He had the science. He saved us!'

Sebastian Hackett, coughing violently, gestured with his stick. 'The wretched boy's provoked it, whatever the damned gimmick is. Look – it's moving...'

The object had levitated to shoulder height, still slowly rotating. But now it was moving silently away at a steady walking pace down the centre of the road past the dead lamps and the rusting people-carriers.

Alys started to run after it. 'Don't!' yelled Poppy. 'It's a trap!'

'The child's right,' murmured Hackett. 'If it's heading for the city centre, you could encounter some very disagreeable people.' He wondered if he had actually lived that agreeable pre-Leynebridge existence of coffee-houses, choral concerts in the Cathedral, dry sherry with the Dean which had all been blown away after the wretched Rupture when the Shepherds seized the town with their bizarre caricature of Christianity. 'They probably burn witches. As well as elderly alcoholics.' A oblique memory-trace: *that little orphan girl Vivienne chasing a hot-air balloon. Very tragic and charming.*

But Willow had already started chasing Alys.

*

They were being lured. She couldn't hold back the children or herself. Even Poppy had joined the quest. The pavements blurred beneath their feet. Her aching calves were compelled to follow that demonic toy. She didn't know what to name it, it was worse than ordinary Tech-crafted gadgets, for it might possess a malign sentience. Could it harvest her children in some new hideous way? But the compulsion to pursue the enigma was overwhelming.

They crossed empty intersections and ran down a pedestrian subway past heaps of rags, or bodies, to re-emerge in a precinct. She could see the children's blank faces reflected in the dusty window displays. She told herself it was like chasing a miniaturised satellite down a shopping arcade; and then realised those odd words were outside her Leynebridge grimoires. The vocabulary must have floated through her head from an unknown source, over and above the Undermind, wherever that had gone *inside that flattened dome there's a sticky green goblin wriggling to escape...* But the Undermind had a mind of its own, there was no escape from it, it was pursuing her surely as she and her tribe were pursuing this hypnotic enigma.

They scrambled through narrow alleys, bodies now flexing painlessly, feet skimming the cobbles. But she couldn't trust her eyesight, for the object appeared to be moving further away and becoming larger at the same time, as if the sight-lines of perspective were tangling around themselves. The lights at its centre *sexmas lights sexmas lights* flashed through all colours as it followed its own bizarre *mappa mundi.*

Hackett and the others had gone their own ways, or were going nowhere into the night. She was running in and out of time with Poppy and Alys and changeling Adam, past the dark hulk of a huge cathedral. As they crossed overgrown lawns around the massive stone apse she was certain that the disc had expanded to at least ten feet in diameter *leading Willow on a wispy dance away from the Leyne along the lines into the great lie of the land, on the island of lies...* The girls were enchanted. 'Float and flutter,' they squealed, 'float and flutter...' 'It's a flight-stone,' shouted Adam, who was closing in on their target, as its swelling silhouette rose about twenty feet in the air.

*

Willow's perception cut in and out. There were too many gaps in her actions. She was in one of those chronic spasms. The children screeched like birds. They were leaving the curfewed city now, to move across the wetlands on the east side of the town, where the river had partially flooded the low-lying fields. Now they were veering off-road. The flight-stone that was not a stone revolved above, its expanding shadow blocking glimpses of a crescent moon amidst drifting cloud.

*

They were lost. The chronology wasn't quite logical. They'd

lost minutes, maybe hours, somewhere, somehow, in an expanse of mud. The vast object filled the sky above them and opened its nether eye, a blazing portal in its underbelly. A pillar of violet light drew them upwards and inwards. They were ascending a column. Yet this levitation was so painful. She tried not to watch the children spinning in the spiral radiance. They outstretched stiff arms. The tractor beam drew out all their intestinal longings and belongings, their gut certainties. The traitor tractor beam extracted their brains by the stem. The tractor beamed them upside beside their heads into a blinding space. The Extractor himself (itself) was standing in the portal, beaming, an alien glow on glossy quasi-flesh.

'Welcome to the Brother-Ship. Although the Quantum Brothers themselves are unavailable at this time. They were a localised phenomenon, exclusive to your locale, and have been withdrawn from service following an incident. With your local Lobe closed for repairs and maintenance, we found it easier to manifest on this platform.' The children were huddled around her. They gazed blankly around the domed metallic interior, the curving banks of incomprehensible dials and techno-sigils.

'We are your inclusive spirit guides to the Polyverse. I am Aethyrian. We will lead you to a point of departure and will take universal responsibility for your Intersection.' The voice sounded high-pitched, helium-filled. It orated over cold metallic music.

At the centre of the dome an altar decorated with dials and flickering meters appeared through clouds of sickening vapour. Phallic pillars surrounded the faery ring-master. Willow knew she was caught in a bleak light-trap.

The creature named Aethyrian was a smooth demon, grey and

ovoid-faced who wore a tight green tunic. There were no other words to describe him or herm. Huge dark eyes scanned her rapidly. 'Your offspring via the different mates will be tested under laboratory conditions. The changeling child will be changed.'

Peeling back a flap in Adam's forehead, he revealed a shiny red carapace. 'A typical earthlet bone-boy. We need to drill down for the data. ' The boy stared sullenly ahead as a silvery probe descended to explore his phrenology. 'Some spirit doctoring is desired.' The subject gave little reaction to the hissing and smoke of the probe as it engaged with tissue.

The creature named Aethyrian then focused his will on Alys who was cowering on the translucent floor at Willow's feet. The uplighting scored shadow lines on the child's eye-sockets.

'She will grow eventually – a decade in your reckoning – to become a useful vessel of regeneration, a credit to the Zones. Giants need fresh women. Hyperactive entities require flesh and wine. These terms are only approximations, of course. You will have to endure high levels of cognitive dissonance. We are trying to present the Polyversities of the situation using a range of cultural references that might be familiar to you. For we are all one huge family now, familiars suckled by a non-finite number of teats. Follow the translation carefully...'

The creature inspected the Poppy creature. 'Another excellent vessel.' Poppy stood immobile in the glaring light, her long rags stiff with mud. 'Her eyes will be opened and in time she will channel the new life.' Willow tried lurching forward, but her limbs felt as if immersed in viscous fluid; and she was going to die through a surfeit of horrors. 'Don't be a human shield,' she was told. 'You have entered a post-human situation, but you cannot see the point of it yet.'

The humanoids Poppy and Alys were led away. Nothing to be done, except try to voice a scream, which only triggered nausea. Sickness was a meme in this dreamtime, it dribbled over everything inside her, the residu perhaps of a lifetime mushrooming in those wet Borderland woods, so recently incinerated that it hurt. Her children had vanished behind the altar-console. 'They are moving directly into long-term self-storage,' announced the Aethyrian creature. She prayed to gods that they would remain intact .

'This locale has good schooling. Our door-to-door men have inspected it, in good black suits.' That explained everything, of course. She watched the Sky People examining Adam's exposed brain. 'We can close him up, give him some amnesia, but is there an argument?' stated the grey egg-man with liquid eyes slit sideways. 'He was superfluous to your flow. So let him go. And look away now.'

Adam knelt at the electrical altar, the probe swinging overhead, his trepanned head in a halo of smoke. 'I'm flying the stone,' he cried defiantly. 'You can't catch me, I'm a new disease. I'm wired to go viral.'

'He's outbreaking already. Into a prophetic rash. The epidermis will go first. His scepticism is no immunity. The spell is breaking out all over his skin.'

Adam was ageing as she looked. The chronology wasn't logical. The harder she stared, helpless but guilty, the more rapidly a map of wrinkles and blotches spread across his papery flesh. She couldn't bear to touch in case she tore him. Too easy to rip off a limb in her anguish. He was a little old mutant goblin, gazing in horror at his knobbly hands as his shoulders shrank. 'Why, why him? He's suffered more that any of us.'

*

'Now to the couch for casting. Casting the spelling for the great code-book. A grand grammar lesson for the Great Mother.' An announcement boomed in the crypto-space of the vessel. 'We are coming forward straight on to you, coming in as per your subliminal request, the sum total of your summonings. Bring on the Breeding Theatre of Sytry.'

She was engorged with pleasureable terror. Around the corner of the altar crawled the great Sytry, exactly as described in Gavin Wharton's copy of *The Lesser Key of Solomon*. Between the jaws of his leopard head he carried a scroll. His gryphon wings were scraping the floor so he outstretched them, a display of dark purplish translucent membrane that formed a mighty cowl around him. The scroll fell and unrolled. She recognised his sigil now, which he traced with a sperm-drenched claw, for he was copious in breeding. The god-beast overwhelmed her with his stifling air. He was going to be familiar with her.

'One giant cock for all mankind, a great leap on your lap - to be swived by star-demons is a fine honorarium for a country mother-witch.' He roared with lust as he stripped and straddled her.

The member was all huge and icy but deeply felt. A delicious goading with the bulk of the entity sprawling all over her. 'You're futurising the species.' A rich voice was exhorting her as the phallus drove deeper. 'Intervoid copulation makes for strong hybrids. The mongrelised momma is a holy rolling space-whore!' The hard glassy floor against her shoulder blades was such a convincing status detail. Such a dream was harshly lucid. A claw toyed with her budding nipple. All these repeated insertions were part of the actuality. It was unstoppable, beyond pleasure, dissolving her in a great spurt of light.

1956

Aran was a survivalist. At least his mastery of tools remained. Gil Norwood had taught him how to weld and forge, how to shape wood and stone. Noah Dodd had taught them all how to dig and plant and sow in the rhythms of the stars and the seasons. He would find his own space and use his skills again. But in the months that followed his loss of Vivienne and his escape from the inferno of London, he concentrated all his energies in living from day to day.

The first days were the worst. For two nights he wandered for hours in the labyrinth of the city, dodging demented mobs, in a quest for the white horse; but either Fairfoot had disappeared or his recall of the unfamiliar streets was failing. His pledge to Adam Butterworth was broken; and the steed was probably dead. Eventually he abandoned the search. It would be hard enough to find food and shelter for himself, let alone an animal. He also realised he needed to keep on the move and find a way out of the disintegrating townscape.

At the same time, the fringes of the city provided valuable resources. Sleeping by day in empty garden sheds or burgled bungalows to avoid attention of the militias, he foraged at night, stealing from suburban allotments or the flimsy lock-up garages where boot-shop proprietors often kept their overstock of dented tins and stale cereals. Breaking into a charity shop he sourced boots and a greatcoat to protect him from the cold of the winter solstice. Meanwhile, he fought to suppress memories, increasingly unreliable, of a roaring fire in the Red Hag, spiced wine and roast boar, randy laughter of the Elders and the outline of Vivienne's bare shoulders in moon-light. He could scarcely visualise what might remain of Leynebridge - a circle of scorched earth scarring the green hills of his Borderlands? Had he brought this lethal curse on his birth-town by killing its Elder, its High Priestess? Surely the loss of Viv was punishment enough. And there were other recollections that refused to erase themselves, like the simpering Truth Finders in the Shepherd's torture rooms, who had tried to burn out the core of his soul with their electric gimmicks. His leg ached constantly. They still cross-questioned him in dreams of shit and blood, in dark gilded rooms that contracted around him, where he awoke struggling to scream.

He feared losing his familiar reference points – Earth, Air, Water, Fire. With the village population dispersed, the familiar murmur of the Undermind had almost died away. Some nights he caught faint echoes of it *buried in the depths of the earth burnt us all to fuck the commune wasn't immune* as he ducked behind overgrown hedges at the approach of potential threats, usually a lost Heavy Shepherd patrol on bicycles, scavenging the avenues for food, drink, flesh, anything going. So many people had fled the cities, on confused pilgrimages, bewildered by alt.memory implants and the conflicting histories that had burst briefly upon them in the last experiment of the Tech-Crafters. It looked as if they had lost their precious Lobe, for the stragglers he encountered seemed totally disoriented.

One raw dawn he was spying on a group of middle-aged men

and women marching four abreast in neat formation across a municipal parking lot. Striding purposefully in their ragged suits or skirts they carried golf clubs or furled umbrellas over their shoulders. The men were mostly grey-haired and the women wore floral scarves. The leader, a bald man in a torn blazer, caught sight of him hiding behind a porta-cabin and signalled to the group to pause. Aran drew a dagger, ready to stand his ground, but the man dropped his golf club and raised a hand in greeting. 'No need for that, old chap. I was rather hoping you would join us. I can always recognise a decent sort. A strapping young fellow like you could come in handy for beating off the riff-raff. We're going to 1956. But you'll have to hurry or we'll miss it.'

Aran heard his own voice for the first time in many days, an awkward croak. '1956? What...?'

'1956, of course. The zone of choice.' The man's patience seemed strained. 'This isn't a re-enactment, you know. It's a holiday of a life-time. I've arranged it especially for these good people.'

A tall giraffe-like woman spoke up at the back. 'The Major has administrative experience. At a great defence establishment. He's organised a way out of this chaos for us. A permanent way. You ought to do the sensible thing.'

Aran surveyed the group, still standing at attention, all eyes fixed on some invisible goal beyond the suburban pavements. It was time to review his tattered mental palimpsest of the Lore. Consider 1956. $1 + 9 + 5 + 6 = 21$. $2 + 1 = 3$. $21 = 3 \times 7$. Bookish Gavin Wharton used to claim that three was the number of success and good fortune, while seven was the number for the recluse, the mystic, the loner. There might be safety in numbers, and a route to some resource centre (perhaps code-named '1956') that hadn't been pillaged in the sectarian skirmishes, even a bed to sleep on. They might lead him out of this doomed hinterland. Yet he could keep his distance and his independence. He nodded.

'Very good, ' barked the Major. 'Carry on.'

*

Aran quickly fell into the rhythm of marching with the Major. Despite his hunger and thirst he easily kept pace with the squad as they filed down tree-lined streets past the strange semi-houses of the suburbs with their odd names: *The Nook; Glynfred; Puddy's; St. Damian's Lodge*. As they crossed the top of St Damian's Avenue he heard a sharp crack, almost certainly sniper fire from a rooftop somewhere, and two men at the head of the column wavered. 'Hold formation!' shouted the Major. 'Our discipline will deter them Right turn!' Without breaking step they swung into a long shopping parade. Aran wondered vaguely why the Urbanites had needed such a variety of elaborately decorated shops when it was so much simpler to make or grow things oneself, at least according to the theory of the Lore. One of the women dropped out of step for a moment to peer into a window display of pointed gold shoes, but the Major gave her a light tap on the buttocks with his golf club and she fell into line.

Once a group of scrawny olive-skinned children pursued them for a hundred yards or so, mimicking their stiff gait and yelling insults in a guttural tongue. Then the kids discovered an un-plundered confectionery shop on the far side of the road and began hammering at its window with a litter bin, ignoring the incursion of this strange procession. Aran felt a fresh stab of guilt, recalling Adam Butterworth stoically labouring by himself in that deserted Borderland small-holding, surrendering his chief asset, his Fairfoot, for a dubious future in Leynebridge. *kepe out leynebriggers.* He should have left the boy alone.

As they approached the end of the parade, he could see a high iron bridge across the road, a worryingly familiar outline, triggering recollections of that riverside walk, in another life, when he'd set off to ask for Viv's hand. But they veered off just before the bridge, passing beneath the under-croft of a tall glass tower, a multi-storey hive where Urbanites and Tech-crafters had once pursued their mysterious transactions. They then climbed a broad glazed stairway and squeezed, in single file, through a twisted metal barrier at the top.

'At ease,' shouted the Major. 'We may have a little time to wait.' Aran stared down a long concrete platform, partially sheltered by a canopy. He peered over the edge of the platform. Four sets of parallel rails ran into the distance, each pair having a third rail mounted beside it. On the far side of the tracks he could see another grass-grown platform plastered with faded slogans. As he feared, he'd been led into an artery of early Tech-craft, an iron road, a rail-line. Long ago these tracks had snaked across the country, obliterating the old leys, according to Noah, laying the foundation for the industrial expansion that had manacled Albion. He scanned the tracks, left and right, noting gallows-like gantries and dead hooded eyes of signals, the rails converging in the hazy distance along the embankment. The sky had brightened but it was bitterly cold again.

'It's definitely arriving on this platform, the up-relief line. Probably steam-hauled, because of trouble with the third rail system. Erratic voltage supply, you know. But it's due in at 12.23, arriving at 19.56 – there may be some changes en route, naturally.'

'Are you sure?' The giraffe-faced lady was almost brusque. 'We've had so many disappointments recently. And I do hope it will be properly appointed.'

'Let me assure you that high tea will be served in the dining car throughout. Moreover the guard's van carries a grand array of cargo to enjoy in our new zone. You will have *The News Chronicle*, wireless sets for Children's Hour, cigarette holders and Coronation mugs. And I've arranged a meeting of the Light Operatic Society in coach B, to plan for the forthcoming season.' His troops murmured appreciatively as he herded them into the waiting room.

*

The hands on the station clock didn't move but the sun had dwindled to a smear of light. Aran, stationary on platform 2, had eaten the last of his emergency rations. He now attempted a state of bodily dissociation, and tried to contemplate the twilight in Nordic mode. Sunna the solar goddess was reclining to sleep behind the drifting veils of Nifelheim. Yet his attention was too dispersed. The smell from the blocked platform toilets was distracting in itself.

To keep warm and escape the stench he wandered into the waiting room. Someone had lit some candles in an old storm-lantern. The Major sat upright, smoking a pipe, but the rest of his entourage sprawled across the benches. Some were asleep, others barely awake, surreptitiously snacking on chocolate bars or fruit they had secreted in handbags or brief cases. A plump curly-haired brunette in a fur coat made a show of adjusting her stocking tops but nobody took any notice. The angular giraffe lady had shown enterprise in lighting a pile of Plain Folks Bibles in the narrow stove, while two red-faced men who claimed to have been bank managers were coughing fiercely, and complaining about the billowing smoke and poor service. 'A damned fine state of affairs! And the whole country's going to the dogs. People demanding overdrafts just to solve their sexual problems...' In the corner a short man nervously adjusted his thick spectacles as he thumbed through *Health and Efficiency Fortnightly*, pausing to look twice at 'Outdoor Girl Dawn Diamond' before hurling the tattered magazine to the floor. 'It's not coming, is it?' he yelled to the room at large. 'It's never coming. The age of your bloody train is long gone. We're never going to get to 1956. Ever...'

The Major, glancing anxiously at his conscripts, came over to silence him. 'Stop it, Chislett! Slack talk is bad for morale. And so are obscene publications!' He swept Chislett's rare collectible under the bench with a swing of his golf club.

'He's right, isn't he?' Aran grabbed the Major by the lapels of his blazer. 'There's no glory train coming to save us, is there?'

'You're talking balderdash, man!' The Major glared, extracting himself from Aran's grip and grasping his club tightly. The sleepers in the room had woken up now and were staring expectantly at the confrontation.

'Some under-demon has tricked you. Or are you fooling them?'

'Any more insubordination from you, soldier, and I'll have you on a charge. Nonsense about demons!' The Major jabbed a finger at Aran's beaded locks. 'You can get a proper haircut for a start. That won't do where we're going...'

'It's obvious we're not going anywhere. So what's the plan - are you hoping to rifle their pockets when they start keeling over and dying of cold?'

The Major raised his golf club, arm quivering with repressed fury. 'Right! You're on a court martial. No recreation and rest in 1956 for you, young man. National Service is the ticket. In fact I think I'll start you on latrine duty right now. Then we'll stow you in the luggage compartment and deal with you properly when we get there.'

Aran turned to the muttering conscripts. 'Can't you see what he's doing? He's tried to work a time-spell on you and it's failing. He can't summon the ghost of a Carbonite train.' They stared at him blankly. He tried once last time. If that failed he was going to walk. 'Listen! There's no cargo on his down-line. No more 1956 on wheels. He can't shift you into another time-zone. He's just dragging you all around in his dream-time.'

'How dare you talk about our dear leader like that!' shouted the giraffe-faced lady. 'It's the most insulting absurd rubbish I've ever heard.' As Chislett started sobbing behind his glasses, the Major hit Aran across the shoulders with the club. Aran gasped, lost balance and tumbled to the floor, where the Major battered him again and again as he tried to rise. He sheltered his head with his forearms as the blows rained down erratically, the Major wheezing rhythmically with each stroke. 'Six of the best... six of the best... buggery and arse-fuck... six of the best...' The bank managers cheered him on, the women were screaming.

Aran rolled over, despite the pain, and reached into his greatcoat for his runic dagger. It hurt to speak but he had to fight with a warrior's honour. There must be no more random killing, no more slayings like Elaine's. 'Stop now - and I will leave here. Leave you all. Or I'll kill you, Major.'

The Major muttered something inaudible. Then his nostrils flared and his face reddened as he raised the club high over Aran's skull. As the head of the iron swung down, Aran tripped him with a kick to the knee, and he fell heavily onto the blade, taking it through the regimental badge on his torn breast pocket. He gasped and grunted, breathing hard.

The waiting room was silent. Blood welled up, spilling across the blazer and the striped shirt. The 'managers' had edged towards the door while the long-faced woman ran towards her stricken leader, to cradle his head in her arms.

'What have you done to him, you big thug, what have you done?'

'I warned him. It was self-defence. According to the Lore - '

'Law? People like you don't know the meaning of the word law. Law and order started dying from the first days of the Rupture, fomented by your lunatic cultists. The Lobe culture finished off the rest of it. Your filthy dogging demons. Now there's no recourse to justice. I expect you'll kill us all now. I don't really care.'

The Major pawed her arm. Bloody mucus trickled from the side of his mouth. 'Just let the Unit know... have done the state some service - and they bloody well know it... top security admin ... protecting Weekes, Ebdon, that damned Crowe... arseholes all round...what a cock-up...' He made a loud hawking noise; and ceased breathing. The flickering fire of smouldering Bibles finally went out.

Aran was shuddering with cold, a deep bone chill. He was seemingly fated to kill. Fool killer. More foolish than Forgan, even.

'Well?' The woman gave him an interrogatory glare. 'You're free to go, I suppose. Leave us to our own devices. Leave us to get on with it. Our little dream-time, as you call it. Although what we're going to do without him I don't know.' Very quietly she began to cry.

Aran sat in silence as the group mumbled urgently among themselves. He could do nothing for these people who might yet decide to execute their own version of ad-hoc justice, here and now in this bare room. He was armed but easily out-numbered. The magick numbers had betrayed him, entrapped him, snared him into yet another killing, even if it was in self-defence. Vivienne was right, he'd followed all the letters of the Lore but couldn't read the script. He had to make a break for it.

As he expected, the men blocked the door six-deep as he approached. Some looked eager to use their golf clubs and one had picked up an old fire extinguisher from the wall. 'You're going nowhere, young fellow,' announced a skinny man with a pencil moustache. 'You owe us a certain loyalty in the circumstances. We could pretend it was an unfortunate accident with the Major. In return for personal security services. What do you think, gentlemen?'

'He deserves to be court-martialled,' scowled the bank manager. 'No chance now of getting to Camp 56.'

'For the last time, there's no more 1956, no cargo train, there's no time-slip - even after everything that's happened.' Time-slip? Was that the right word? He was trying to talk like a Tech-crafter, it didn't feel right. There was nothing in the Lore about time-bending, at least in what Noah had taught them. 'There hasn't been a train on this line for...' He broke off because he didn't know. He was just trying to buy time. The candles were burning down fast. These sullen men could rush him in the dark.

'Let him go, ' said the thin man, abruptly. 'Just let him walk. He's a loser. And we don't have time to try him properly. Conserve resources, that's the thing. Someone find a shovel and we'll do the decent thing by the Major.' The bank manager started to protest, but the thin man drew a small pistol. Aran suspected it was a replica, but the group's grumbles subsided. Chislett and the other bank manager hefted the body out on to the platform.

'What do we do now?' The curly-haired woman in the fake fur sounded quite matter-of-fact, hardly disturbed by Aran's revelations and the violent death of her trans-temporal guide. Her voice sounded slurred compared with the crisp consonants of the other women, with a faint echo of rural speech. While the rest of the collective withdrew into anxious huddles in the corners of the room, she sidled over to him. Placing one manicured hand on his arm, she reached up and fingered the serpent medallion around his neck. 'You Borderland boys are strange. But you know how to handle yourselves.'

He shrugged and began walking to the door. She followed him and caught his sleeve.

'There's another waiting room, across the tracks through the pedestrian tunnel. And there might be a vending machine we could bust open.' He didn't trust a machine. But he could smell her alien perfume, the scent of the city. She was older than him, maybe thirty five. She must know her way around. At the far end of the platform they were dragging the Major's body into some trackside bushes.

They descended the stairs, her arm nudging his, her fingers dangling loose. She was telling him a secret, in a breathy whisper. 'I'm Louise. Or call me Lulu. It's more private...' But he kept his fist clenched. At the bottom she guided him into the dark hole under the embankment. He lit a match and they moved very cautiously through the murk, light flickering on the dusty tiles of the underpass as they negotiated their way around a heap of rusty shopping trolleys. Aran tried to imagine the panic attacks of the city people as they tried to hide their hoards from fellow marauders.

'Lulu' led him up the stairs to the up-line platform, as bleak as the one they'd just left. Across the tracks on Platform 2 the waiting room was dark now, although he could hear faint shouts and even a female scream. He wondered what desperate suburban rites were being committed.

The vending machine had been forced open a long time ago. 'No worries,' murmured Lulu. 'At least we're well away from those busy-bodies. You can be my bodyguard now.'

He tried not to meet her gaze. She turned away and strolled down the platform, stopping outside a door. STAFF ONLY. She rattled the handle. 'Come on, muscle boy. Let's see what's inside.' She peered though the grimy window. 'There might be goodies locked away in there.' He put his shoulder to the door and gave it a hefty shove, breaking the lock.

They entered a small office. He cursed as he tripped over a broken chair in the gloom. She surveyed a heap of dusty files before picking up a coffee jar from the desk. It was empty. 'Never mind. It's warmer in here. And I've got some more goodies for you inside my coat.'

In the faint ghost-light, she slowly unbuttoned and opened her fake mink; to display her naked breasts, stiff nipples, the curvature of bare belly and thighs framed by her black garter belt. Somehow she'd pocketed the chain of his serpent medallion, which she swung slowly below her navel, so that it glinted against her pubic tuft as her lips parted in a faint smile. He was about to speak, some blurt of bewilderment, but she put a finger to her lips. Then her hand reached for his crotch and stroked the erection that was hardening beneath his heavy corduroys. He loosened his belt and let his palms slide down her haunches, savouring her smoothness and animal warmth. Hunger only seemed to increase his desire. He lifted her, perched her facing him on the edge of the desk, and wrapped her thighs tightly around his. Remotely, as if viewing his actions from another plane, he stroked her labia, gently toying her clitoris with a steady automatic rhythm - then sensed a faint tickle of her pubic hairs and her sudden intakes of breath as he finally entered her in a series of slow thrusts.

Throughout the act and all its tortuous permutations, images of Vivienne and that scarlet woman Carla streamed through his inner eye, superimposing themselves on this body moving back and forth on a dusty wooden table. The arc of the neck as she tossed back her hair in delicious lust: Vivienne's moonlit move. A twist of the waist and a shiver of buttocks in the darkness: Carla's phantom harlotry. And as his random mate drove him towards orgasm, he felt that he was being possessed by another presence - the effete poet Lucas. That devious warlock was riding on his shoulders, urging him on with sibilant whispers, Underminding him all the way *go all the way in way in way out expose her in her peaked hat naked in rattling cages of light go deep into her earth tunnels of fun fucking fork her lightning please please please go baby all the way let's go let go split my light NOW*

She rolled away from him with a deep sigh of satisfaction, and began mopping her pubic regions with the belt of her fur coat. 'You've come un-stuck, big boy. But Lulu was very pleased. Very pleasured. You moved the whole earth. Just with the leverage of your cock. Shagging like a tin soldier. Now give Lulu a big kiss and look after her.'

He dressed in silence, head lowered. She studied his face intently, waiting for his response. But his confusions had only become more entangled. The Lore had never prepared him for this random mating with an outsider-woman. She had shared her body generously. Her flesh was ripe. But could he project a future for her? Could a cosseted urbanite woman, raised in the fabulations of the cities and the Lobe, handle the hard graft of a small-holding somewhere? Would she dig, plant or weave? Would she breed without complaint and teach Noah's Lore to his children? Or was she a mere warrior's play-thing, a Lobe-creature cunningly made flesh? The sexual phantasms that flickered through his mind were perhaps a warning. He might be acting out the warped fantasies and frustrations of the arch-poet, that sly Lucas.

'Come on, now. You haven't even told me your name.'

He ignored her. Half-remembered fragments of the Lore troubled him now. Surely if he revealed his name, all the letters and the number for each letter, she could spell him out - if she was a covert witch under all the urban trappings. He would be forced somehow to surrender power. Better to tighten his belt and move on. Across the tracks he could hear the Major's old troops. They were shouting and crying all through the night now. She ran down the platform after him, unsteady on those strange pointed heels.

'We could be good for each other – get away from those old muppets. I've only gone along for the ride. But I've got to call you something.'

'I'm Seth...' The name came from nowhere - it just announced itself in his head. Aran/Seth. A dark name, right for times of chaos. It would make him a stronger beast, raise his animal spirits, perhaps scare her away from her pursuit of him. Let him be secret Seth and put 'Lulu' to the test.

'Seth. That's different. But quite right for you. I could go with Seth. Matter of fact, I have done already haven't I?' She laughed, too hard, and dragged a small hip flask from a pocket. 'Only a few nips left, but let's share and share alike, shall we?' She thrust it under his nose; and he swallowed a burning mouthful of the brandy.

Suddenly her arms were around him and she was biting his ear , screaming. 'For fuck's sake, get me out of this shit hole, just get me out, anywhere, Seth, whatever you are, I can't take any more, just find a place, any fucking space on this planet, I don't care, I don't want to die here with those zombies. Don't leave me!'

She half-collapsed, clinging to him, heels scraping along the concrete as he tried to walk away. Her words streamed past him. 'Don't, don't leave me in all this shit, Seth. That's all that's left, shit piling up and piss and rubbish to roll in like we were fucking dogs. Fucking dog demons sold us down a river of piss, I ought to know, I was on the Lobe once, I could have been a sex-queen, people would have celebrated me, and you celebrate me Seth, I can feel the love, but Lulu wants her bed back and white wine and roast chicken under electric light with real water that got turned off when the bastard shit-heads went ape-shit, fussing and fighting over a few gods and now we're just buried under the Pleasure Zones in a mountain of robot-shit, you've got to take me away and find somewhere, or fucking kill me, please...'

He stopped; and held her jaw firmly with both hands studying her face, a stained twisted mask, like that mask of tragedy which old Wharton had once shown him in a big book. She was sobbing incoherently now. Was this wailing city-woman with the ridiculous name his fated mate, his wyrd-woman at last? He was on the cusp.

'You'd better come, then. The gods alone know where we'll go.' He'd said it without thinking, but a warrior's word was his word. No going back now, only sideways into the unknowable.

He grasped her hand as they scrambled down from the platform and began walking down the track, treading warily in the dark between overgrown sleepers. He guided her away from the third rail, where the Carbonites might still have left a residu of their lethal forked lightning.

'We're going south, then? Towards the sea?' Her voice brightened.

God Shapes Karmic Mysteries
The steady throb of the diesel induced a queasy semi-trance but Vivienne had to fight sleep. She had been insane to take a ride in a 4 by 4 pick-up with a big gun mounted on the back, even if the rain had been pouring down and she'd been stuck on a slip road since dawn. Any moment now she was waiting for the driver, an excitable young brown-skinned man with a bushy moustache and a head-band, to pull over and slide a hand towards her inner thigh. Instead Ahmed was offering her a vegetable samosa and lecturing her about sport, an ancient pre-Rupture sport she'd only vaguely heard of, a Carbonite spectacle forbidden by Lore.

'My grandfather used to say Ayrton Senna was the greatest but I always rated Schumacher. So many times world champion. He could make that Ferrari do anything. The rain-master, they called him.' The boy grinned, palming the gear-shift and twitching the wheel as the truck slid through plumes of spray around a tightening curve. 'I was born too late, know what I mean? I'd have given anything to be there at those races. I used to have a whole season on Grandad's old tapes, then my stupid big brother decided everything was *haram* and chucked them out. Crazy, innit? Would the Prophet, peace be upon him, really have forbidden Formula One? What do you think?'

She tried to think of an answer, but the question was obviously rhetorical, and he was in top gear now. 'I hate the Mo-Boys, you know. Hate all their bullshit. Shouting and waving their guns around. Holy martyring themselves everywhere. They've ruined everything for us. I mean I want respect but they're just ridiculous.' He was checking her response from the corner of his eye, so she nodded carefully.

'Did you know this is one of their battle-trucks? The no-brains just left it there in the middle of a roundabout. So I hot-wired it, and here we go...'

'Where are you going?' She tried to make the question as casual as possible.

'Far as the gas will take me. Towards the coast. And then right off this island. It's sick, man, it's just falling apart. I'm going to find a boat, get across to Europe.'

Vivienne's concept of Europe was hazy. She thought it might be a zone somewhere on or in the Lobe, but didn't want to exhibit her ignorance.

'But - how? It's a virtual space, isn't it? Anyway, they say the Lobe's going down.'

He laughed incredulously. 'You've been spending too much time in those Pleasure Centres, woman! It's a place. A rock and a hard place. Proper boundaries, borders. The Franco-German Corporation. The Papal Protectorate. The Hispanic Caliphate. They're all out there. If you take the trouble to find out.'

She sensed an implied rebuke; and then recollected her Leynebridge years as Elaine's pupil: at once so empowering, and yet so claustrophobic. And now those powers seemed to be waning. She felt for the little crystal sphere in her pocket. Only a relic now. She tried to clarify her thoughts.

'But then they would have been Ruptured, like us. They're still relying on the Lobe, aren't they?'

Ahmed shrugged. 'They've got to be dealing with it better than our lot. I've been listening on long-wave.' He gestured to the radio on the dashboard. 'Sometimes you get the signals loud and clear. The Grand Mosque of Madrid. Or that Vatican Radio. Prayers and big speeches. Restoring law and order. Reconstruction they call it. Last night I got a newsflash from Berlin. They're hiring thousands of people to work on the Great Wall of Russia. They're gonna need haulage, drivers, mechanics. I can do that stuff. Do you want to come with me? Think about it.'

She pretended not to have heard; and tried to fabulate some convincing plan of action. He fiddled with the radio, dialling through bursts of static, and switched it off again.

'OK then... So what do you do?'

She had no idea. Her past actions had become an amorphous blur, a fading tracery of brush strokes on paper/Chariot trump card blown away on the wind/glimmer of her torso spinning on a studio monitor/some dreamy mush-up of her alleged alt.lives... What on earth could she do in Ahmed's born-again Eurotopia?

'Come on now, you must do something!'

'I'm a sort of artist. All arts and crafts. No practical skills.'

Hopefully he'd lose interest.

'No, you've got skills all right. I think I've seen your profile before.' He gave her a toothy smile. 'You've been a Lobe-babe, right? And some kind of singer?' He pronounced the nouns with transgressive relish.

'You've got the wrong person,' she muttered without much conviction, staring down the white line in the centre of the road. They had not passed a single vehicle in either direction since he stopped for her. No lines of confused refugees trudging along the hedgerows. The island of Albion had been mysteriously emptied. If there were any gods left, they were hiding up in the grey overcast. She had to reinforce the point quickly. 'I think you've made a mistake.'

'You've made the mistake.' His voice hardened. 'I'm making you a proposition, a serious proposition. One for all, all for one. We could do stuff together in the Euro-zone. I could put you in the business. But you think I'm like all the rest, just out for a fuck.'

She shook her head and made a vague noise of protest. Ahmed only frowned as he swung the truck around a dead sheep dumped outside a small red-brick church. They were entering a conurbation and he slowed to walking pace to avoid shell-holes in the tarmac. She glanced at the huge red-on-black advert plastered across the side wall of an end-terrace boot-shop. The abstract graphics generated a moiré pattern so the quivering fonts seemed to read:

GOD SHAPES KARMIC MYSTERIES.

'Mad, innit?' Ahmed seemed to brighten up. 'Power's going down everywhere and Fast Fun are still advertising their home-based VR kits. I bet Pleasure Centres are doing the same, drag some silly old man off the street and then sit him in a dead cubicle. I expect you know all about that.'

It was going to be hard to distract him. She wished she could read male signals more clearly. 'What did it say? That poster?'

'Usual copy-shit. "Shape the Dream!" That sort of thing. Have you made up your mind?'

The dream was out of shape. Her mind, what was left of it, was making itself up differently with every flick of the windscreen wipers. 'What do you want? Why me?'

'Anyone's who's survived this far must have something going on for them. You're a survivalist. Must be in your genes. Looks like you've got good genes. Doctor DNA's given you the right injection.'

He kept dropping in these odd words. She must have looked blank, because he started to lecture her again, talking about a book he'd heard of, very rare, about a blind watchmaker called Charles Darwin. 'He studied animals in the jungle, he discovered the law of the jungle. And you're a natural junglist.'

'I don't think so.' This law wasn't the Lore of her grandmother, yet now it seemed to rule the land, maybe the whole earth, this lawless planet spinning out of her orbit into the void. 'I wouldn't be much help to you.'

They drove down steep avenues of villas and hotels, neo-classic piles of flaking cream plaster and crumbling pediments. She scanned the balconies apprehensively for fundamentalist banners. Only vacancy signs swung in the wind; but she caught glimpses of hooded figures in the side streets, scurrying through the hard rain on mysterious errands.

'They must be doing the business,' murmured Ahmed. 'Let's check 'em out.' He turned abruptly right into a narrow side-road where someone had set up a stall, selling heaps of small silvery-grey objects under a billowing canopy. 'There's something going down. They're buying and selling.' Two men in black hoods were bartering or bantering with the woman on the stall.

The little items re-familiarised themselves; as piles of fish glistening in the rain. There were exotic vegetables and fruit, too - potatoes, apples, green stuff. Ahmed smiled. 'OK, we got to eat, yes?' He pulled over and turned off the engine. 'What you got, then? Can you trade anything? Show us your stash. Share and share alike, remember. That's what they say.' She fumbled desperately through her torn pockets and spread the contents on the dashboard ledge. He surveyed them with disdain.

'Copper coins aren't good for much now. What's this? A witch's thingie, yes? Not worth much, I guess, but they might swap it for a couple of apples - ' He tried to grab the scrying stone, before Viv snatched it back into her clenched fist. She expected him to force open her palm with rough fingers but he only stared.

'I don't believe it! I pick you up, I give you my food, I don't give you any hassle, I offer you a great deal, treat you like a sister - and you won't give up a stupid little glass ball when we're fucking starving. A great survivalist you're gonna be...' He leaned across and pushed open the door. 'OK, get out! Out! You're on your own now with your fucking spirits...' She fell out, tripping over the kerb as he slammed the door and began reversing back into the main road while the stall-holders watched impassively.

*

The beach was deserted: a bumpy slope of pebbles, its irregular tiers shelving millions of tiny worn stones. It hurt to walk here in her broken boots. Waves rolled and roared over each other, breaking in clouds of spray on the battered concrete groynes. Vivienne had never encountered the sea before. It was an alien beast. But now the sea and the stone were all she had.

She huddled, freezing, in a hood a stall-holder had given her and gripped the shew-stone tight, trying to recall what she'd learned browsing in Wharton's shop, sitting for hours on the wobbly sofa behind the door while he fussed over his stock. She remembered ghostly hordes in a Museum, too. They'd somehow herded her towards that case with the waxy Seal, the black obsidian Mirror and this glassy sphere. So she knew it belonged to an old wizard in a pre-Rupture queendom long ago. Wilful angels had appeared in it, dictating letters to be scribed into intricate grids, a fearsome supernatural cryptography, to be decoded into the Enochian tongue, into Keys and Calls that invoked the Aethyrs. Wharton claimed to have once made a ring, a breast-plate and a special altar, to prepare for such invocations, but he was vague about what ensued. Perhaps he had lost his nerve - and she had lost most of the Enochian words, her empty words of power. She could only recall a few scattered phrases, bizarre agglutinations of consonants and vowels.

Her mission was obscure, but she had to attempt something, some act of affirmation against an absurd world. The only alternative now was to fill her pockets with stones and walk into the seething waters. This was going to be her last rite.

She held the sphere up to the grey sky in both hands and tried to contort her tongue around the alien speech-forms: *coredazodizoda dodapala od fifalazoda lasa manada od faregita bamesa omaoasa.* Her voice fought sudden gusts of wind and the screech of the wheeling gulls, so she repeated the lines again, louder *coredazodizoda dodapala od fifalazoda lasa manada od faregita bamesa omaoasa* and then defiantly screamed what she could remember of the translation, until her throat hurt:

THE REASONABLE CREATURES OF THE EARTH AND MEN, LET THEM VEX AND WEED OUT ONE ANOTHER AND THEIR DWELLING PLACES. LET THEM FORGET THEIR NAMES. THE WORK OF MAN AND HIS POMP LET THEM BE DEFACED.

Tears streamed down her face, mingling with the rain. She was doomed to invoke a retro-enchantment, a self-fulfilled prophecy. Even in the cosy fuddle of Leynebridge, something in her, beyond the pleasure principle had yearned for some act of total erasure, a ground zero that would re-create everything from these bleak beginnings, this blank vista of rock and water.

She squinted into the sphere. She could have sworn its transparency became translucency - which morphed again into spirals of blackness coiling around the circumference, a shrinking coagulation of black light, that seemed to increase in apparent weight and warmth, until she was struggling with the pain of holding it at arm's length. She was in the grip of this ball of *nigredo*, a meteoric blob of compressed first matter, plutonic dung. Whatever it was becoming, its burden was too much. Even this had to be sacrificed, to bring clarity.

With an immense effort that twisted and stretched every tendon in her body, she hurled the shew-stone high in the air; and watched its trajectory as it plunged into the rising tide. She turned and ran.

The True Tale

As he walked awkwardly along the promenade towards his new home, wincing from his injured leg, Aran/Seth attempted to make sense of his fractured journey into another life. In their warm bed he'd tried telling Lulu his oral history of Leynebridge and the Lore, about his desperate magickal quest in the city during the death throes of the Lobe. But he always sensed she was only indulging him, and she soon digressed into anxious questions about how many credits he was likely to earn from his tool repair workshop or his casual help on the fishing boats. Now that Lulu was pregnant, what true story could he tell the boy? For he was certain it would be a son. He imagined perching the child on his shoulder, holding his small hand to point through the lashing rain towards the cloudy horizon.

He'd been a warrior, certainly, had done strange and dreadful things. There were some episodes Lulu still wasn't ready to hear. Deeds he'd found hard to believe himself. He'd fought and rescued and loved and lost, met helpers and challengers, endured ordeals, used all his strength and craft. But he wasn't telling the true tale of Aran, surely. The 'Seth' tale wasn't telling him what he wanted to hear. It had all come out disordered. He'd killed an old woman in hot blood. The demons in the depths of the earth had died by themselves, or by some other cunning. His first-betrothed had rejected him. Had the Poet really debauched her? What had become of the magick? He couldn't hear the Undermind, either.

He stopped outside the huge white building, its stacked balconies facing the ocean like a supermarine ziggurat. He had never expected to live in a great cold hutch like this, squatting in a maze of tiny partitioned rooms, but this was Lulu's preference, among all the half-empty properties that had been requisitioned for refugees by the Land Pirates. And he had to pay his respects to the Pirates, who had accepted them both without question when they first arrived at the Coast, too foot-sore to limp any further. 'Only one thing we don't allow here,' said the man at the Town reception centre, 'and that's preaching. Otherwise, feel free.' He didn't quite feel free, as he entered the lobby. The sheer bulk and geometrical form of the structure was still alien to him. His footsteps echoed up the bare stairwells and corridors until he reached their fourth-floor unit.

The door had been left wide open, an oversight by feckless Lulu, and inside he could hear her talking urgently with another woman, who was obviously agitated, maybe even aggressive. The living room was empty, so he strode into the bedroom to confront the female intruder. Another devious orc-woman? Or a straggler from the Major's entourage?

The little room was too full. Two small girls in bundles of rags crouched behind an armchair, where a larger figure was curled up under a dirty blanket. Lulu was arguing with a blonde full-figured woman sprawled on the bed. 'Your man is the man for us,' cried the woman, 'the only man that can help us. He's a Leynebridge man, a Lore-giver. The Reception people told us, don't deny it! Please let us stay, please help us...' She sat up to face Aran. 'You'll help us, won't you? This city woman doesn't want to know. But you're Aran Yarland, aren't you? Gil Norwood's apprentice?'

He should have recognised her at once from the sigil tattooed on her neck. Willow, first consort of Forgan. With those children Poppy and Alys - plus a smallish person hunched up in a blanket.

The protective earth-mother. Yet her eyes were cloudy and her tanned forehead was covered in a web of fine white lines as if a toxic mantilla had once veiled her face. Lulu was suddenly having recognition problems of her own.

'What do you mean, *Aran*? What are you talking about, trying to barge in on us with your fake sob story? He's Seth, my partner Seth!'

'He may have cut his dreadlocks but he's still Aran - aren't you?' She stared into his eyes. 'You're bound to help us, according to Lore. I've got all these kids to feed. And I'm pregnant.'

'So where's Forgan?' It would be like rampant Forgan to have carried on begetting in the End-Times, a manic fuck-witted defiance of reality. 'Forgan always took care of you, and all the others...'

'He's probably dead. Or sleeping in the ruins of Leynebridge. You don't understand. We got separated. The kids and I were abducted....'

The story unfolded in sobbing fragments, a narrative as bewildering as his own. The flight from the devastated Borderlands. A bomblet that swelled into a sky-craft. The ladder of faery lights. A flying dome of doom. A ravishing by an incubus. Or a demon summoned from the black books. And then they found themselves lost in a seascape, far far away.

'Don't believe her, Seth. Not one word of it. No way she's pregnant, either. Go on, show us your bump.' Lulu shoved her forward, off the bed. As Willow fought for balance, Aran/Seth looked for a swollen belly, but the curvature of her body seemed unchanged. She steadied herself on the armchair, the two little girls cowering behind her.

'I'm carrying a star-demon's child.' Willow seemed both exultant and terrified. Was this really a phantom nativity? Something had been implanted in her mind or her body.

Aran/Seth was about to speak but Lulu interrupted. 'Listen, I'm going to have Seth's baby. The real thing. I've got the sickness. I've got a date. You've got nothing.'

'You'll see...'

'I just see a big fat con, darling. Tell your stories to someone else and leave us alone.'

'You'll see what the Sky People can do.' Willow began tugging at the blanket concealing head and shoulders of the figure curled up foetally in the armchair. The two girls squealed as they tried to prevent the fabric sliding to the floor but their mother's strength overcame them.

The little old boy stared through him. This child's forehead had been scarred and the dead white skin around his eye-sockets was puckered. The texture of the flesh was granular yet glossy as if the prematurely aged changeling had been sprayed with some kind of plastic preservative. Adam Butterworth raised a shrunken hand and began coughing violently, before mouthing thick guttural noises. He rocked back and forth, pointing an index finger at Aran.

'He keeps asking about a horse,' explained Poppy. 'And telling us about lost planets,' added Alys. 'It's a good thing we understand him. He's got space sickness. He sicks up over everything.'

Aran squatted on the rug, head in hands. So gifting the Mating Cup hadn't saved the boy. The fates had fangled everything up again for the curse of killing Elaine was still running its course. He had obligations and on-going penances. The Lore was speaking straight through him now.

He stood up and strode into the living room. 'Louise, make up beds for them out here. Use cushions, curtains, anything. And heat some of that soup.' Lulu snorted indignantly and began muttering in his ear, a bitter fussing noise he just had to shut out. 'Do it, just do it. They're staying until -'

'Until when?' Lulu cornered him in the kitchen. 'You expect me to give up our space, our food for a mad witch and her fake pregnancy. And that boy who looks like a goblin. You're as crazy as them.'

'I'll find something for them. There'll be a place.' He was desperate. Surely the gods would tell him what to do, there might be a hint of an Underminding to guide him to a real healer who could undo the bundle of disaster he seemed to drag around. 'I have to go, I have to find a healer for the boy.'

'A healer? It would be kinder to put him to sleep, the state he's in. You better have a quick solution for all this, Seth. I might have been better off buggering off with that Major.' He could still hear her cursing as he closed the door and headed down the darkened corridor.

*

The Mason's Tomb was crowded with drunken sailors exchanging wild boasts about proposed expeditions to the Thule-Reich or improvising fantasy plots to plunder the gold of the Vatican cellars by digging through the sinking sewers of Rome. Elbowing through the deafening crush, Aran tried to make sense of these references on his mind-map. The dreadful re-appearance of Adam had un-nerved him. He also felt growing unease at the realisation that other realms beyond the island of Albion might now be within reach or might even impinge on his new precarious life. There were other zones beyond the Lore, as well as the damned cities.

Aran walked cautiously up to the bar, ducking under the low beams. He was about to buy some local home-brew with his crumpled handful of credit, scarcely worth more than a boot-shop hand-out, when a tall black man in a long suede coat gripped his wrist. He was carrying a narrow brown-paper parcel under his gangling arm. 'Hey, my man! You wanna buy a burp-gun? Two hundred rounds a minute! Then we go to Haiti. We fight for Papa Legba and the Deep Ones!' Aran ignored him but the man persisted, planting his pork-pie hat on Aran's head. 'You be wearing a soul-hat now, my man. Voudun power running around that rim. Spirit gonna ride you all over the island. But you need this gun. Give you the silver bullet too...' Aran muttered something about his poor credit and tried to hand back the hat as well as the heavy parcel that the hoodoo-man was thrusting upon him.

A barman leant across and prodded his shoulder. 'Leave him, Norris. He's new here, he doesn't need your hoochie-coochie routine.' Norris glowered, thrust his jaw forward and inspected Aran's face very intently. Aran could smell the rum on his breath. Abruptly Norris snatched back the hat and tucked the long parcel back under his arm. 'OK, I can tell a zombie. But you going to need my help some day. Body and soul, baby, body and soul.' He wandered off, hugging the package.

*

Aran was buying drinks all round. A skeletal landlord in a grubby floral shirt had just thrust another tray of beers at him. He was risking all his credit-tickets. In the old Borderlands snuggery of the Red Hag this investment would have guaranteed an eventual encounter with the person who had the skills he needed, whether healing-lore, herb-craft or divining. Here beside the cold grey sea the transaction didn't seem to be working out, he couldn't make the right connections. He should have listened more carefully to the secrets of Noah Dodd and Gavin Wharton. He wished he could get at least a whisper from the Undermind. Its deep stream couldn't have been entirely swallowed up in the depths of the Earth. There had to be another misplaced Leynebridge person in this refuge of the damned, someone who could deep-heal the boy's ruptured aethyric body, which had malformed his wizened flesh. That was how old Noah the Elderseer would have diagnosed it. He could only hope.

And he'd been optimistic at first, sandwiched as he was between a thin beady-eyed woman in a diaphanous cloak and an intense bald man sporting black pantaloons whose ringed fingers twitched and gesticulated manically, as if he was grabbing fistfuls of air. He didn't recognise them but they resembled some Borderland types he'd known. He tried to sound them out about the Lore, about their knowledge of healing, yet he sensed the conversation wasn't flowing in the right direction. It was hard to hear distinctly in the roar of the bar.

'I have never had a day's sickness,' stated the woman. 'I have only eaten the vegetable beings, and washed myself in cold water. So I have no need of healing.'

The man in black gulped another of Aran's beers. 'Perhaps you healed yourself sexually, Evelyn. In an on-going process of auto-sexualisation. Without even realising it. You'll be an immortal...'

Evelyn gave him a severe glance and turned apologetically to Aran. 'Melvyn is haunted by succubi. He must have a surfeit of orgone. He waits for a winged nymphomaniac to alight on the sill of his bedroom window.'

'I had no need to wait, Evelyn. Vandella, the dusky bride of Christ, visited me only last night after the most elementary summoning. I just had to sprinkle vodka from a paper cup and burn some frankincense, with a little prayer to St Mary Magdalene. I debauched the Black Angel most manfully. She was totally consumed. Body and soul...'

'You and your ghost girls – disgraceful conduct.'

'Don't mock my ghosts, Evelyn dear. Let me ask our new friend here – our dreams may be the ghosts of eros – but of what is sexual intercourse the phantom? Tell me that.'

The drink froze in Aran's throat. He was suddenly caught in a time-lapse, a tiny globe of agonising memory in which Vivienne's slender waist was gripped tight by the Lobe-Mistress as Lucas the effete poet - or his ghost - ran his soft fingers down her inner thigh. Melvyn enjoyed the rhetorical moment and its special effects.

'You're speechless, of course. It's an enigma, isn't it? Let me suggest that sexual gnosis accesses energies from the deepest levels of reality, from the very machine-code of the Universe – or Polyverse, if you prefer. Sex is deadlocked into a battle with Death, that's what Manicheism was really all about. I believe that the compulsion to reproduce sexually, with its attendant genetic advantages offset by psychic dangers, is a desperate stratagem, triggered ultimately by those forces of chaos at the sub-atomic level. All our pleasures are squiggled by quarks hiding in the atoms of complex molecules.'

The polysyllabic banter was irritating Aran. These people had no sense of urgency. 'Can you heal this boy? His subtle body is deformed and he's ageing fast. He needs help...'

Melvyn pursed his lips. 'Help? A bit collectivist, isn't it? We're on private trajectories now.'

'Until we run out of fuel,' said Evelyn tartly. 'Our reserves aren't infinite.'

Aran was losing the thread again – were they talking about their pockets or the depleted energy stockpiles of the Carbonite era?

'Anyway, Melvyn's useless for healing, he can only transmit exotic diseases.' Evelyn emitted a tinkling laugh, prompting Melvyn to smile archly as he raised her fingertips to his lips.

'This Adam boy is dying. You might know someone with the life-skills.'

Melvyn dropped Evelyn's hand and peered at a tattoo on Aran's wrist. 'You have the mark of the infamous Leynebridge Serpent on you. Your resident wizard must have taught you something, surely.'

'He's dead. Anyway, we had guilds. I was a ritual metal worker.' The memory, and the knowledge, seemed so remote. Melvyn didn't seem to be impressed by his status.

'Dying from paranormal ailments is merely a version of performance art. It's self-indulgent. A lot more people have died in boring ways – starvation, bombings, cross-fire, riots, accidents in the Pleasure Centres, the militias. Hundreds of thousands, maybe millions. Nobody knows how to add it all up any more. Just a few towns left on the coast, trying to look outwards and trade up to something. Otherwise Thanatos is triumphant, for the whole country's entropic. Why does one Borderland urchin make any difference? You have an antiquated sense of duty, which nobody can afford any more, especially a displaced ritual metal worker. You'll just have to manage the boy's decline...'

Aran couldn't articulate a response. He was convinced there ought to be a difference but he couldn't explain how. Melvyn gave him a rueful grin as he helped Evelyn with the buckle on her cloak. 'Time to go, I'm afraid. Business calls.' He produced a tiny silver casket from his hip pocket and flipped the lid open, to reveal a grey powder. 'I'd do you a deal on some of this but I don't think it would really help. It induces atavistic recursions, brings out your secret beast. I suspect your young person has come out already.' He snapped it shut. They squeezed between two stocky fishermen, who were arguing furiously about the existence of monsters, and headed for the door.

Spotlights came on at the far end of the room. On a dais beyond the curve of the bar, a plump black man with a crumpled leathery face sat down at an upright piano and adjusted a buzzing microphone. Aran grimaced inwardly, for this wasn't going to be the skirling folkish music he'd once piped in the Red Hag, it would be suspiciously urban. Time for him to go, in any case. He'd return, mission unaccomplished, to the white hulking building, to Willow's tears, Lulu's anger and Adam's scarred face.

The pianist fingered a slow walking bass and started to sing:

She's a deep water woman

Way out in the danger zone

She's a deep water woman

Playing in the danger zone

That deep water woman

Breaking up my happy home...

Norris began dancing slowly around the dais, flapping the skirts of his long brown jacket to the pulse of the music like an old dishevelled bird. A pale peaky girl glided around him in a private orbit of her own. Aran suddenly felt they were dancing an elegy to someone at the very end of times, and it would be disrespectful to walk out on this private rite, irregular though it was. He needed time to slow down, in time with the dance, to save him from the confrontations ahead.

The singer bowed, to scattered applause, and made a semi-intelligible announcement introducing Talent Night at the Mason's Tomb, and the next great act, a very special act, a living legend... The prismatic glitter on his sequined jacket transformed him into some excitable quasi-marine creature waving fat flippers. Distracted, Aran couldn't catch the name of the performer he was talking up.

An old radiogram behind the bar began playing brassy music. He felt overlapping surges of curiosity and guilt. There might be a dancing girl, an exiled Lobe-woman now struggling to earn a pittance in live performance, acting out the forbidden pleasures of the dead cities. A sudden convergence of noisy drinkers around the dais only reinforced his expectation. He had to go. But he was going to stay, just for a few minutes. He craned his neck to peer over the eager mob.

*

Lucas stood transfixed by the dazzle of the spotlights. But he had to command the stage, stand up and deliver, for he'd been promised free stew and a bed for the night, in return for a fifteen minute set.

'Keep it snappy, ' the landlord had advised. 'Plenty of triple whammys and smackeroos. A laugh a minute. You say you've been on radio, so you know what to do.'

He didn't. Even as he approached the microphone (*polytone 333 as endorsed by top producer jack cusimano* - was that an Undermind leakage?) a mushy void was expanding inside his head. His memory was dissolving; the cosmic joke was on him.

'And now ladies and gentlemen, my man with the magick tongue, baddest boss of the Borderlands, your ghost and commentator – Lucky Luke B!' The singing MC, Fats Farrakhan, patted him on the shoulder and quickly ducked behind the piano. Lucas surveyed the time-wrecked boozers who were waiting to destroy him.

'OK, people! I'm so glad to be here tonight in your wonderful city in the sea-side suburbs. Isn't it great that we've lost the old Lobe and we can all enjoy live entertainment, even if we do look like a bunch of lost zombies. On my way to the theatre tonight...'

They were murmuring already. Bottles were clinking and a gob of spittle flicked across his cheek.

'On my way to the theatre tonight, I met a man with a...' Hoots of derision. '...a man with a...'

'Get him off, Fats!' From the corner of his eye Lucas could see Fats rising behind the piano gripping a long pole with a brass hook at the end, obviously a tool for dragging off the failed talent.

Lucas screamed; and let his little horny devils fly in. He might as well die on auto-pilot, like he used to in his Tower studio. 'I met a man with the head of a leopard and taut purple wings and a monster member, and this is the song he sang, specially for you...' Once he started he couldn't stop. He'd un-kettled the mob of micro-demons that possessed his scrawny body, demons that swarmed like microbes under the membranes of space-time. 'Your neurons are rotten, rotten to the core. Your love-pumps aren't thumping any more. You're just dogs in tutus line-dancing in the void. Every man and woman is a burnt-out asteroid. The white dwarfs are screaming over your shoulder beyond direct sense perception, so you can kiss your fiery arses good bye, you ain't got proper reception - '

They lurched forward, growling and snarling, fingers twitching. For the first time he noticed how many faces were scabbed and blood-caked. They emitted a thick sweetish smell.

They were projecting the wrong sort of thought-forms. They were pirates waving stuffed parrots, they were incontinent monks, leering squaddies and grinning saw-bones doctors, while their women were all dressed up as tarts and nurses. They were going to rush him.

Fats swung his long hook, trying to hold back the punters, but they pushed the MC aside, knocking over the microphone stand and crashing into each other in their eagerness to reach Lucas and teach him some obscure lesson. He was a time-waster. Somebody was re-naming him a fucking four-eyed cunt. He'd hit a whole complex of nerves and they were going to hit him, beat his nonsense out of him, slap his head and debag him for his bad bad verses.

The first blow landed in the solar plexus, so he hardly noticed fingers tightening around his throat. He was dancing through a universe of pain. He tried to shut his eyes, shut everything down and contract himself into a foetal black hole. Then large hands were dragging him out of the scrum, off the stand, through a tangle of arms and legs, all trying to sock it to him. He was surrounded by furious voices, it was worse than the Undermind *where do you think you're going with the little scrotbag he's ours got a nerve hasn't he we got to loot and boot him proper...* They were fussing and fighting all over him, but the huge hands were getting him out somehow.

He felt the slam of a heavy door, sensed cobblestones under foot and rain stinging his face, and tripped over a heap of barrels. He opened his eyes. Aran Yarland's face was inches away. His nemesis from Leynebridge had split his lip and was breathing heavily.

'Don't thank me.' Aran relaxed his grip for a moment. 'I don't know why it had to be you, of all people. But you're a man of the Higher Lore, supposedly. I need your skills.'

*

Aran wouldn't let go of him. He frog-marched his captive through the wet streets, ignoring protestations of ignorance, innocence and confusion. He fought the temptation to cross-examine the feeble poet, to make him suffer gross humiliations and torments as a reprisal for his spectral sex acts with Vivienne. Witnessing that image had released the random violence that had slaughtered Elaine. Yet Vivienne insisted that Lucas's alleged copulations were mere phantoms, side-effects of thwarted lusts, so he had to trust her, even if he could scarcely trust the evidence of his senses. He merely grunted as they entered the white hulk, before shoving Lucas to the foot of the stairs.

Lucas was stuck in the moment now, mind blank with exhaustion, all affectivity dead, just registering data: steel and glass banisters, dead strip-lighting, swollen bags of garbage on the landings, an endless corridor, the sound of children crying. When they entered the apartment, right there in the living room was a women he knew, who was crying and a woman he couldn't place, who was shouting at everybody. Two small girls hid behind the furniture. A boy, maybe twelve or thereabouts, with a scarred forehead and some kind of skin disease, was crouching on the floor, thumping a cushion with a stick. The kid was making noises that mimicked loud explosions, a sinister caricature of playground star-battles from long ago. Aran, who now seemed to be called Seth, was trying to explain everything but the words just didn't join up. Lucas did not know what was expected of him any more.

'He's no good,' exclaimed the tearful woman, whom Lucas recognized now as Willow, consort of Forgan. 'He's one of those Chaoists, all mixing and mismatching.'

'So you've dredged up another dead-beat from that witch's village you go on about. You're a waste of space, Seth and your little friend looks like a waste of time. Just get on with it and get these people out of here...'

Lucas inspected the boy, who was now lying comatose on the bed. Aran, Lulu and Willow stood behind him as he peered at the scaly flesh and the scarred forehead. The power had failed again, and in the flickering candle-light vague reptilian shadows loomed across the wallpaper. It was difficult to get a proper look.

'It would be better if you left us.' Lucas knew that if he was to achieve anything at all, he needed an empty room. Both Lulu's hostile cynicism and Aran's desperate need for a result would inhibit any manifestations.

Lucas couldn't merely believe in thrice-greatest Thoth, Scribe-God, Healer-God, God of Magick. He had to know this being as the entity knew itself, to experience the living presence again, to be overpowered - and empowered. Yet last time the deity had failed him, or he had failed the deity, in his slapdash reconstruction from a heap of electronic rubble. The magick seemed to have reversed its polarities. Instead of balancing the energies of the land, it had intensified their opposition. Leynebridge had been totally destroyed, the implosion of the Lobe and the rampaging militias had finally wrecked London while Carla, beloved holy whore, was gone for ever, killed off by the random stupidity of evil. Or perhaps there was an even worse reversal. The organic brain must have lost the capacity to influence events using focused will and imagination. Yet the machine code of the Lobe had generated monstrous intelligences, terrifying egregores, rogue entities emerging from chaos. And now some new teratology had seized an orphan boy and morphed him into a dangerous changeling. He didn't literally believe Aran's garbled second-hand account of what had happened to Willow and her children. It could be a mask - or even a masque - disguising some process of transformation. But Adam's metamorphosis looked like a process of entropy, a botched recursion into something both piteous and terrifying.

Holding a smoky candle like a protective torch, Lucas forced himself to look closely at the boy. The glossy skin around the back of his neck was now bulging into lizard-like spinal crests, while iridescent membranes had formed between his elbow and stick-like forearms. However his chest, visible through a thin shirt, was pendulous, yet covered with a mat of thick curly hair. Lucas realised his difficulty in keeping focus on his patient was also aggravated by eye-trouble – or an odd vibration in the light. A fuzzy halo was forming around the outline of that scarred head, blurring the contours of neck and shoulders. Lucas had a disturbing retro-vision of how he might have appeared to Carla when she discovered him in his trance-cell.

The boy opened his eyes and made an urgent moaning noise, steadily increasing in volume and deepening in pitch until it became a basso profundo growl *out leynebridge devil out lobe-beast out sheep shagger out mo-boy out get me out of them out out out get me a heavy shep I want that old shep to let me out out*

Lucas suddenly realised which way the scenario was moving, into a low-level entity re-enactment, a micro-qliphothic entity parodying itself. To run through the routines of exorcism in whatever he could recall of the old Christian rubric would only feed the phenomenon. But the low-frequency laryngeal resonances were rattling the mirror above the bed, the bedside cabinet was shuddering, a glass was about to slide off. Or - his sudden terrified hunch - the boy would liquefy and revert to his organic constituents, raw fluid, beyond identity. He had to take command with whatever was at hand.

A corner alcove could become the archway for Thoth's temple, his house where the Net was hung. Lucas stood, facing it, turning his back for the moment on whatever was behind him. He had to construct the god bit by glittering bit, trying to tune out that thick growl emanating from the boy creature in the bed. The Beaked One had to carry his stylus and tablet - and a caduceus, a healing staff, the essential kit, a rod to channel what was left of Lucas's bioplasmic energies. Thoth would emerge from the rich mud of Egypt, to draw his lines of force and fire in the sand.

An intense pain pierced the centre of his forehead and intensified for several minutes. Then a stringy outline of the ibis headed god-form appeared, like a shaky hologram in the shadows. The flickering image hovered in profile, a semi-transparent golden stele slowly expanding. Lucas knew that if his concentration failed it would dwindle and fade back into the Void. The room, however was enlarging, skewing its geometry into a complex lattice of luminous lines and points, overlaying the drab brown curtains and beige wallpaper. A portal was creating itself, his star-tunnel to Hermopolis...

Lucas tried to enunciate what he could recall of the spells. Fragmented remnants of papyri slowly floated across his inner vision: *may no sickness alight on him drive out vexations annihilate all ailment remove his mutilation break out scorpion who has come forth from the fundament the poison is powerless Thoth arrests you Thoth commands you Thoth will un-write you* His voice was hoarse with repetition, gathering volume as he tried to drown out the random slurs and gabblings emerging from whatever Adam was hosting. Lucas knew he had to animate the god-form, infuse it with his will, but his body was struggling with a new current of force that began spiralling upwards from his prostate region, electrifying his spinal cord. His brain felt as if it was going to burst in a fiery mushroom cloud, as he swayed and fell to his knees, groping to steady himself against the bed head. The room darkened into total blackness.

Eventually the Thoth-form's glowing outline hardened as it raised its staff entwined with golden serpents and glided forward over the boy's body. A luminous net of entangled fiery nodes expanded around the struggling form, like an externalisation of the boy's nervous system requiring drastic re-alignment. With enormous effort, as if he were controlling the massive prosthetics of a great golden golem, Lucas made the caduceus of Thoth descend over Adam's wounded head. Metallic serpents were now spiralling off the staff and entangling themselves in the network, hissing and sparking as they looped around the nodal points, forcing a slow re-alignment, a painful torsion of the subtle energy-lines. The psychic surgery was forcing the voice to rise in pitch; that sub-human growl became Adam's screams, which merged with the wave-forms resonating from Thoth, the unearthly purity of his cry of command, rising into the ultrasonics.

Then a huge reverberant space was filled with his silence.

After a while Lucas crawled towards the door, but before he could reach it he was violently sick. The puddle of vomit seemed to contain two tiny dark circular objects, the size of charms in a Christmas cracker, formed from some soft rubbery substance. Despite their coating of acrid mush, he could just about distinguish forms. One was a small flattened hemi-sphere. The other was a tiny humanoid head with two identical faces back to back. They were square-jawed, short-haired, graphite-coloured. He retched again and lost consciousness.

*

A boy was talking in the next room. 'You lost my horse, didn't you, Aran?' He was making a plain factual statement, not an accusation. 'Don't worry, you're a bit simple, that's all. Thanks for the goblet. It came in very useful.' A deep voice laughed awkwardly in response. 'Where's Poppy? I must see if Poppy's all right?' A small girl's outburst of laughter and embarrassment.

Lucas was lying on the bed but when he tried to get up his right arm seemed to have seized up. He rolled off with difficulty and stood up on aching feet. The room smelled of disinfectant and now a jagged crack ran through the ceiling cornice over the alcove. Through the door to the living room he could see Willow curled in a chair explaining things to Alys. 'Thoth has restored Adam's power of speech. And already the scabs are peeling off. We can thank Aran for finding a healer, even if he was a Chaoist.'

They didn't look up as he walked unsteadily to the kitchen, in search of water to cleanse the vile oily taste on his tongue. Lulu blocked his path to the tap. 'You're not having our fucking water. I've no idea how much is left in the bloody tank. I wasted enough cleaning up after you. Now you've done the witching business you can be on your way and take this lot with you. Seth and I want to get on with our lives.'

'They can't leave just like that, Lulu. They've nowhere to go. The boy's not fully healed.' Aran tried to placate her with a hand on her shoulder but she shook him off.

'If you ask me, he was never sick. It was a sympathy con. Your Willow friend plastered him in make-up, and that Lucas git ripped it off again with a song and dance routine, trashing my bedroom. So they've got to go right now. Of course, if you'd rather I left …'

Aran protested, but she pushed past him. 'I think I know your game, Seth. You fancy both of us, don't you? A couple of busty women to keep you in heat, cook up a storm in bed for you. Big boob mommas, better than the Lobe, eh? You brought her here, didn't you, sent her a signal on your Mindfuck or whatever you call it, come on over baby whole lotta shaking going on, bring all the brats…'

Lucas knew, instinctively, that Lulu was right. Aran/Seth desired both women, to integrate his old world with his new one, to enjoy all the conjunctions of their flesh, like a second Forgan. It was a warrior's last-ditch defence, a desperate stratagem against the Death Layer, where he was now destined. As Lucas left them to their eternal feud and limped down the corridor to the landing, he caught sight of his reflection in a dusty mirror. His hair had greyed out and he couldn't flex the fingers of his right hand, his writing hand. Adam's spontaneous remission had almost combusted him, for the Thoth current burned...

Survivors

It was ten o'clock and the market along the sea front was beginning to fill up - another indicator that production and trade were recovering, albeit erratically. The cries of the fish-sellers and veg farmers mingled with the chatter of rival tool-smiths and the clink of the new coastal currencies. It had been several years now since the old-time boot-traders had tried to muscle in with their damaged goods.

Vivienne adjusted her headscarf against the cold April wind and began to set her stall in order. The new paintings were doing quite well. She sensed that the demise of screen-based imagery and immersive entertainment had led people to seek meaning in the static image, some icon to stabilize the flux of sensation and data that had been overwhelming them since the Rupture and the intrusions of the Polyverse. She propped up her latest, a large oil depicting the destruction of the London Penitence Park, one of her recurrent themes. She'd developed new techniques, using gloss acrylics, rendering the burning towers and the horrified expressions of the Shepherds in hyper-realist detail and an intense luminosity, as if an avenging radiance was bursting through the canvas.

A tall white man stopped and studied the painting as she laid out some smaller ink drawings, in which she'd tried to capture her recurrent dreams of the Borderlands. The stranger's dark robe and red tarboosh probably signified membership of an Egyptian order – Horus, Set or perhaps even Thoth, that cult Lucas was supposed to be involved with. The man put down the bottles of beer he was carrying and peered closely at her representation of the urban mini-apocalypse, the Shepherd's botched Judgement.

'Very powerfully imagined,' he commented.

'I was there. I survived it. And their torturers. One of the few lucky ones.'

'An ordeal by fire. A Doomwatch. Brave as well as lucky.' He traced a ringed finger across the glass, to the apex of the flaming ziggurat that dominated the composition. 'Luck is so complex, isn't it? So many possibilities dancing on the point of a time-line - whatever the point of a time-line is... Although a modest form of causality seems to be making a come-back...' He picked up Viv's tattered Tarot pack and began spreading the cards across the crimson velvet cloth covering her stall. She was a little taken aback but saw it as a cue to question him.

'Have you traveled north of London at all? Or to the west?'

'At Oxford they've re-opened the Bodleian Library.' He explained how the city had survived relatively undamaged in the recent disturbances, and now functioned as one of several autonomous university-states amid the liquidation of the nation. 'Scientific illuminists' like himself were trying to control the paraphenomena that had been generated by the terminal implosion of the Lobe and the disintegration of its various daemons, while engineers and doctors were attempting to deal with its practical and human consequences as the aftershocks of ruptures and chronoclasms faded. Restoring *ma'at,* the true dynamic balance of forces would be a vast project.

Viv nodded, recalling her own precarious balancing act between worlds. She wondered if he'd ever seen her Quantum Slut persona. It was in her secret Quantum Slut mode, mouthing those crazed lyrics as she scrawled a wild line across the paper, that she found the impetus for this new work. She could be Quantum Slut again, for the right person.

The man in the robe bought a sketch of Leynebridge Tower. After handing over the coins, he flipped a Tarot card: a hand holding a cluster of lotus blossoms; water cascading from the flowers over four golden cups; the Four of Cups, 'Luxury'. He held the card up for her inspection.

Viv smiled as she wrapped his purchase. 'Maybe not luxury. But I've got a place to sleep, fresh food, money for new clothes.'

'The signification is "Blended Pleasure" - receiving pleasure from others, but some discomfort thereby. Are you perfectly happy with that?'

It was a gentle enquiry but felt like an implied rebuke, even a warning. As he picked up his bags, she smiled awkwardly. After the overload of the Undermind and the pressures of the Lobe, she'd tried to create a psychic membrane to guard herself from the spiritual probes of others.

She watched the stranger striding away down the pavement. Along the promenade, near the entrance to the pier, a gaunt saxophonist was playing some wandering melancholy tune, the sound she associated with that radio station in the Tower, incongruous night-music for a brisk spring morning. Its minor intervals and breathy ghost-tones seemed to match her shifting mood. When the busker had finished his ballad, he inspected the meagre scattering of coins in his instrument case and began packing up. Another itinerant entertainer would soon be along to claim the pitch.

A few minutes later she noticed a small group gathered around the pier entrance. They were listening to some kind of speech. A thin beaky man with spiked greying hair stood swaying on one leg like an awkward bedraggled bird. He was holding forth, declaiming from a black notebook. His body jerked to the emphatic rhythms of his speech, which she couldn't quite decipher over the ambient din of the stalls and the wail of the seabirds. But she could pick up on his sound, slightly nasal, hitting the consonants to project over the hum of the market place. Two skinny girls in their early teens giggled. One of them, egged on by her sister, scampered forward and tossed a stone into the empty hat upturned in front of him. The street poet stared straight through her and only increased the volume of his performance.

Viv abandoned her stall, hoping that her friend the silversmith on the adjacent barrow would keep watch on it, and began walking towards the edgy voice. Its insistent inflexions were breaking through, to her, if no-one else. The speaker was acting out a fierce self-interrogation. He was running with the words - or the words were out-running him.

'Was the Polyverse sustained through linguistic slippage and trick etymologies that let too many quantum pussies out of the body bag? Or vice-versa? I only know we became what we Lobed, mammals trapped in our own feed-back loops, caught in the ticking boxes of our flow-charts. So we worked through the body. We worked through masks and rites. Dance makes the loop between Heaven and Earth, in the curving bum of a maenad. Beneath the Pleasure Zones: pots of blood and the anatomy of yellow fat, ready for our alchemy...'

Two fishermen at the back of the crowd were arguing loudly. 'I tell you, it's the fuckwit clown that got done over at the Mason's Tomb, way back. Someone's let him loose on the streets.'

Viv tuned out their bickering and watched the poet's fingers tremble as he tried to conduct his own verbal music. He was struggling to tell her his secret but it was emerging all garbled. 'All knowledge is carnal knowledge. The pleasures of sexing are as obscure as the root function of dreaming. Each hot body thinks it's taking part in an unrepeatable experiment. Maybe it's taken apart. The binaries of sex taught us the difference. Sex was the original differential equation. Sex has gone viral...'

'You're on the wrong fucking planet, guv.' Another yell from the pavement. They're confused, thought Viv. But it was all too clear to her. The incorrigible Lucas was having a go. Surviving on words and pittances, still scrabbling towards the Other, towards some elusive zone of enlightenment. Her help was required.

'For beneath the Pleasure Zones, the gods are not the gods. They are an inchoate energy flux that we embellish with our perceptions. We keep trying to sculpt them out of dark matter but they fade like fistfuls of mist. Our desperate urge to merge in the erogenous zones is a headlong jump into a gravity well swirling with floating clusters of Choronzonic god-stuff...'

As the small crowd dispersed, she moved forwards, trying to catch his bloodshot eye. He was walking away without noticing, still clutching his tatty notebook. Quietly, she intersected his path and touched his wrist.

* * *

Paul A Green

CPSIA information can be obtained at www.ICGtesting.com
Printed in the USA
LVOW10s0926110316

478419LV00002BA/3/P